THE CHRISTMAS STAR

SYLVIE KURTZ

All rights reserved.

No part of this publication may be sold, copied, distributed, reproduced or transmitted in any form or by any means, mechanical or digital, including photocopying and recording or by any information storage and retrieval system without the prior written permission of both the publisher, Oliver Heber Books and the author, Sylvie Kurtz, except in the case of brief quotations embodied in critical articles and reviews.

PUBLISHER'S NOTE: This is a work of fiction. Names, characters, places, and incidents either are the product of the author's imagination or are used fictitiously. Any resemblance to actual persons, living or dead, business establishments, events, or locales is entirely coincidental.

The Christmas Star Copyright 2024 © Sylvie Kurtz

Cover art by Dar Albert at Wicked Smart Designs

Published by Oliver-Heber Books

0 9 8 7 6 5 4 3 2 1

For anyone who has ever gone through a crisis of confidence.

"The ache for home lives in all of us, the safe place where we can go as we are and not be questioned."

— MAYA ANGELOU

1

"Confidence (n):
1. The ability to believe in yourself even when you have insecurities, are vulnerable, or feel like total sh*t.
2. A tool that can be strengthened, developed, or—when necessary—faked."

— FROM RADICAL CONFIDENCE BY LISA BILYEU

"Are you sure you have the right person?" I asked the woman whose name I'd already forgotten. I continued to pack my suitcase for my next destination—a friend's couch in Chicago. A suitcase that had seen much too much action over the past three months. Not in a having-fun way. Good thing I'd pared down my belongings to fit into just a couple of bags.

"You are Allegra Livingstone, are you not?" Her prim and proper voice grated on my nerves, reminding me much too much of my mother in reprimand mode. "You own Elegant Events, correct?"

Owned. Past tense.

After that last disastrous event in June—the one that was supposed to cement my reputation as a top event planner in the D.C. area and instead shattered it—I'd booked exactly zero events. Hence, the multiple moves and the fast-dwindling savings. But some people had a long reach and, when they were in destruction mode, a little thing like allowing you to pay rent or eat meant nothing.

And there was no way I'd ask either of my parents for help. They'd made it abundantly clear that they didn't approve of the way I'd wasted my education and my potential, not to mention all the opportunities they'd given me.

I dropped onto the motel bed, making my suitcase rollercoaster on the too-soft mattress. My well-read copy of *The Confident Woman* toppled to the floor with a splat, an echo of my frittering self-assurance. If only I could be more like the woman who wrote this book, then I wouldn't have to keep reinventing myself. *Grow a spine, Allegra.*

I sat up straighter, hoping the confidence would follow. "Look, I don't know who you are, or what you want, but don't you think that it's time to move on to smearing someone else's name?"

"I beg your pardon?" The woman sounded insulted.

I sighed, tired, so tired of fighting this unfair fight. "This isn't the first time I've had a job offer disguised as an interview for a tabloid."

Everyone wanted the inside scoop on Senator Becker's disastrous event. What they didn't realize is that all they'd find was my mistakes.

Instead of an answer, my phone dinged with the arrival of several texts.

"Go ahead," the woman said, sounding as if she was giving an order rather than a suggestion. "Take a look. Then call me back."

I had every intention of turning my phone off and going back to my packing. But curiosity got the better of me, and I looked at the texts, each with a link.

The first one led to the Brighton Village, New Hampshire page, showing off a place that looked as if it belonged inside a snow globe. Apparently, each new month brought an excuse to put on a festival.

I frowned at something niggling my memory.

Brighton, New Hampshire.

I sucked in a breath, reached for the long chain around my neck, fingering the charm it held, and dropped back to another suitcase in another time...

I GLANCED AROUND MY BEDROOM—A bedroom decorated in my mother's magazine-photo-shoot-ready taste rather than mine—tossing the last few things into a suitcase. Today was move-in day for freshmen at Wheaton College, and I couldn't wait to get there. Of course, Wheaton College wasn't my parents' first choice for me, and I'd heard my father say, "It's the best I could do for her, Eliza. Deal with it."

But I didn't care what they thought, Wheaton was *my* first choice. I liked that it was small and away from both my parents' houses in Beacon Hill. The prospect of finally getting a chance to express my own voice in my own way, in spite of my father choosing a business major for me I cared nothing about, bubbled through my veins. Would I get along with my roommate? Would I make friends? Would I finally get to act my age?

A knock at the door interrupted my thoughts. My mother stood there, looking uncharacteristically unsure in her Diane von Furstenberg wrap dress and Givenchy sling-backs, which made me freeze in place. Eliza Campbell Livingstone, with her perfect posture and excellent taste, was always certain, always decisive.

"Is everything okay?" I asked, frowning.

She nodded and glided over to my bed where she sat on the edge near the foot and urged me to do the same with a pat of her manicured hand on the mattress. She toyed with the long gold chain at her neck, the one that held a tarnished pointy dodecagram charm she hid in her bra. A charm that in no way matched the sophisticated look she cultivated. "There's something I need to talk to you about."

"That's okay. Maggie gave me the birds-and-bees talk a long time ago." Maggie being the house manager who, for all intents, had raised me.

"It's more serious than that," my mother said with uncharacteristic tentativeness.

I raised an eyebrow, curious as to what could derail my mother's singular drive to appear in total control at all times. "Okay."

She licked her lips as if spilling the words was the hardest thing she'd ever done. And seeing her like that made her more human, less Stepford wife.

She pulled the chain over her head and slipped it over mine.

"Uh, Mom, not my style." I made a move to take it off, but she put her hands over mine.

"It's a reminder," she said, insistent.

"Of what?"

She sighed long and hard and her gaze sought the window. "My grandmother believed in curses."

I made an inner eye roll. I didn't believe in curses, or omens, or luck of any kind. I'd learned the hard way that I was responsible for myself, even if that led to more failures than success.

"You'll be on your own now, making your own decisions."

I'd been on my own forever with my parents too busy

fighting each other and making good impressions on strangers to care what was happening in their daughter's life.

"Mom, really?" I plucked the brown-and-white stuffed puppy off my pillow and placed it in the suitcase. "*A dog is too much trouble, Allegra.*" According to Mom, anyway. So Maggie had given me this poor substitute. That I'd loved it so much told a story right there.

My mother gave me a small smile. "I believe in making your own luck, but I also believe in not inviting bad luck, especially when it's so easy to avoid."

"So," I said, exasperation filling my voice, "what do I need to avoid?"

"A small town called Brighton in New Hampshire."

I'd expected a warning about people who would want to take advantage of me because of my father's name. Not a warning about a small town I would never see. "I doubt that'll ever come up."

"If it does, you must find an excuse not to go."

"Why?"

She closed her eyes and stilled. Then she opened her eyes again and speared me with a look so intense that my pulse raced for a moment. "The curse is real, Allegra."

"Sure," I said, and looked around the room for anything else I might have forgotten to pack.

My mother reached for my hand and squeezed it, hard. "Promise me!"

"Ouch!" I extricated my hand from her iron grip. "What?"

"Promise me you will never step foot in that town."

I growled, shaking the circulation back into my hand. "I promise!"

"Thank you." She stood up, spine rod-straight and headed toward the door.

"And what happens if I do go there?" I asked, zipping the suitcase closed.

She stopped in her tracks as if blasted by ice. Her voice came at me as if from another dimension. "You'll die."

I shook my head and stuffed the charm back into my blouse, then opened the second text.

The link went to a job listing for a Town Administrator position for Brighton Village. Although I had no idea what a Town Administrator did, the description listed on Brighton site sounded an awful lot like event planning on steroids.

I clicked on the woman's phone number and, when she answered, I didn't bother with hello. "Why me?"

The woman hesitated. "Your presence was requested by Harold Spencer, the Earl of Candlewick."

It sounded so hoity-toity—something my mother would swoon over—that I wrinkled my nose. "Since when do we have earls in the US?"

"Since his family immigrated to American in the 1800s. The title is one of respect."

"Why is he interested in me?"

"Apparently, he's taken with the events you've engineered in the past and wants you to apply for the Town Administrator position." I detected a note of disdain in her voice. She didn't agree with this earl. And that, more than her commanding tone, made me think this offer could be real.

I stared out the window at the flat, yellowed landscape that was Dallas in late August. An acquaintance had offered me a job that magically disappeared while I'd traveled there from North Carolina, where another job had also disappeared while I'd traveled there from Virginia, like some sort of event-planning *Groundhog Day*. Would this Town Administrator position poof away, too?

"Has he heard about my last event?" I asked, a weight that was becoming way too familiar settling in my chest.

"Yes." Simple. No explanation.

I turned my attention back to the room, doing a dummy check to make sure I hadn't forgotten anything. "We're back to why."

"I have made my position clear that Brighton needs someone with more experience, someone without a tainted reputation. But the earl insists that everyone deserves a second chance. Including you."

I sucked in a breath, my mind working like a search engine for why a complete stranger would want to offer someone they didn't know a second chance. I wanted to say no. To just move on to the next lead, the next job, the next reinvention.

But the idea of a second chance to do something I loved brought tears to my eyes. Could I go through another rejection?

Before I could answer, the woman said, "Your interview is September third. One p.m. sharp. I will forward you all the information you need." The line filled with a haughty sniff. "I suggest that you make the most of this opportunity."

She made it sound as if I blew this chance, I wouldn't get another.

She expected me to fail.

She expected my failure to justify her judgment.

I picked up *The Confident Woman* from the floor, smoothing out the ruffled pages.

What she didn't realize was that I was raised on disapproval and rejection. Not counting my last event's disaster, the one thing I could do really well was put myself in someone else's skin and bring their dream event to life as if it took no effort.

I ran my thumb along the fore edge of *The Confident Woman*, flipping the pages, willing their advice to act boldly, to take risks, to try new things to fill me with the title's promised confidence.

This job would be something new. Something that would make me feel uncomfortable. Something at which I could very well fail.

But it was also the second chance I needed to prove that making people happy mattered, that joy mattered.

New Hampshire might just be small enough and far enough for Senator Travis Becker to leave me alone. And Brighton's supposed curse couldn't be any worse than what I was living right now.

"I'll be there."

2

"Nobody is born with confidence: it is a gift you give yourself."

— *FROM "HOW TO BE A CONFIDENT WOMAN" BY VANESSA VAN EDWARDS*

I woke up with a smile on my lips, already mentally reviewing my to-do list for the day, looking forward to ticking boxes. I did a quick check of my email to see if any fires needed putting out. Then I moved on to my project management software that kept track of everything I needed to do to juggle Brighton's next three festivals. Satisfied with my day's plan, I got up.

After getting the Town Administrator job last September—with a six-month probation period—I'd hit the ground running. One apple festival, one dog adoption festival and one harvest festival later, I hadn't stopped moving. I was loving the job, the town and the people. If I could just last another three months, this job would be mine and I could make a home here.

And maybe being a true Brightonian would give me a little

more leeway to try a few new things and not just the same old, same old.

With Thanksgiving coming late this year, not only did I have to finish preparing for all the varied activities at the annual Pop-Up Christmas Village at Candlewick Park, but also for the Festival of Lights Gala at the Candlewick Estate on the twenty-first, and the tree lighting on the town square on Christmas Eve. Which, according to local lore, was the most important day of the year. Then the Ice Festival followed right after, starting with New Year's Eve fireworks and a January 1st ice carving competition. Quickly followed by the Chocolate Festival in February.

I raced through my morning routine, getting the coffee going, dressing in layers against the cold, and reviewing the task list on my phone. One of the priorities for today was taking the Christmas Star to the Three Jeweled Angels jewelry store to have it spiffed up in time for Christmas Eve. Apparently, the job was delicate and took a long time. Not just anyone could do the task. I dug Lucy's—the woman whose job I'd taken over—binder out of my messenger bag on the kitchen chair.

At the counter in my tiny kitchen in the apartment over the Charmed Card and Paper Shop, I took another sip of my mushroom-cocoa coffee—something that was supposed to give me energy—and frowned. Nowhere in Lucy's notes did she mention where this Christmas Star was stored. On my phone's to-do list for today, I added: *ask Lucy where the Star is*.

As I finished the note, my phone rang, and the caller avatar showed my mother in all her plastic-surgeried glory. I groaned. I hadn't heard from her in over six months. And I didn't have time for her this morning. I thought about ignoring her, sighed and answered.

"Hey, Mom." I wanted to add, "I'm still alive," but didn't.

"Is that any way to greet your mother?"

I put on my most haughty voice. "Hello, mother dear, what did you want?"

"Can't a mother inquire as to her daughter's welfare?"

I reached for my messenger bag on a kitchen chair, placed it on the counter and packed what I'd need to get through the day, including some snack-size packets of nuts in case lunch never materialized. "Most normal mothers do so on a regular basis."

"The phone works both ways, daughter dear."

"You are absolutely right." It indeed did, except that every time I called, she never had time to talk because something more important was worthy of her attention. "Unless you have something urgent, I have to go. I'm late for work."

"Oh, you found a job?"

"You sound surprised." Her lack of confidence in me had surely contributed to my need to depend on my copy of *The Confident Woman* to shore up my low self-esteem.

"Well, after, you know."

"Yes, mother dear, thank you for inquiring how I was after that disaster and offering support." *You're only six months late.*

"I wasn't in the country when it happened. I had no idea."

The story of my life. "As I said, I have to go."

"And you're good?" she asked, and I had to chastise myself for wondering what she really wanted but didn't dare ask.

"Of course," I said, filling a travel mug with the rest of the coffee-mushroom-cocoa sludge. "I always land on my feet."

"Good, good."

I snapped the travel mug's cover in place. That spider sense in my chest tingled. Something was off. "Mom?"

"Where is this job?"

I hesitated, not wanting another lecture on curses and not listening. "Brighton."

She sucked in a long breath. "New Hampshire?"

I checked the time on my phone. I had exactly two minutes

to get to Regina's office where I had no doubt she was already waiting to go over the day's duties and the list of notes from yesterday. "Still alive, Mom."

"Allegra—"

"Mom, I really don't have time for this, okay. I have a list ten miles long to get through today. Despite the curse, I'm still alive. I'm well. Thriving, even. Now, please go back to your regularly scheduled life. You've done your motherly duty. Bye, talk to you later."

With that, I hung up on her. A touch of guilt shook through my nervous system. But she hadn't reached out after my life fell apart when I really could have used someone, anyone, in my corner.

She never calls unless she needs something, I reminded myself.

Mad running through my veins, I jerked on the messenger bag's handle and knocked over my breakfast mug. It rolled, hesitated at the counter's lip, then crashed to the floor, spilling a mess of ceramic, coffee, cream and mushroom hot chocolate on the tile floor.

I crouched to pick up the pottery shards and mop up the mess, then mentally added replacing the mug to my to-do list.

I really hoped this wasn't an omen as to how my day would go.

THE MORNING MEETING in Regina's office started with a warning about punctuality, followed by praise for my efforts at the Harvest Festival. I hated disappointing her when she was taking so much time to show me the ropes.

My day went downhill from there. I'd spent the morning wading in a sea of paperwork—board meeting agenda, report for the board meeting, processing accounts payable for the week. That didn't count the personnel fires I'd had to squash and a chat with the bank about one of the town accounts. Not my favorite part of the job.

In between all that, I'd tried to call Lucy, the previous Town Administrator, but she hadn't answered her phone. Now that I had a few minutes to breathe, I decided to take a walk to her home and ask her about the Star in person.

Although the walk through town with its cheerful red ribbons, wreaths and lights did me good after sitting all morning, Lucy lived farther than I expected. By the time I reached her duplex north of town, my cheeks hurt from the cold, my fingers were frozen in spite of my gloves, and my toes begged for warmer socks.

The reason for Lucy not answering her phone became evident as soon as I climbed the three bricked stairs to the door. The baby was crying. I really hoped she hadn't been crying all morning. Poor Lucy.

I used the dragonfly doorknocker in the middle of the crooked wreath. When Lucy answered, her face sported as many tears as Baby Autumn's. I dropped my messenger bag to the floor in the entryway, closed the door behind me and reached for the baby. "Here, let me hold her for a minute while you take a breather."

Lucy handed over her daughter. "She cries." Lucy hiccupped, holding herself tight. "All. The. Time."

"What did the doctor say?" Lucy had mentioned taking Autumn for a check-up during one of our daily talks.

"That she's perfectly healthy. How can this be healthy? It's driving me mad." She pulled at her hair that looked as if it hadn't seen a wash in a while. "She's fed. She's dry. She's warm. I don't know what to do anymore."

I rocked the crying baby from side to side. "Why don't you go take a shower? We'll be fine here for fifteen minutes."

Lucy glanced toward the upper floor with longing, then back at the baby. "I haven't showered in five days."

"Go."

"She's crying."

"We'll be fine."

Fresh tears pouring down Lucy's face, she dragged her tired body up the stairs, toward the bathroom.

In the living room, I spotted a rocking chair, sat down and rocked, baby crying as if her three-month old heart was breaking. "What is up with all that noise?"

Autumn scrunched her eyes harder and cried louder, feet kicking, arms flaying.

"That is some pair of lungs you have."

I cooed at her, concentrating on keeping my breath even and my pulse calm. Eventually, the noise lessened, and Autumn fell asleep. She was surprisingly heavy for someone so small.

On the coffee table, next to the pile of pacifiers, bibs, and plastic baby toys, lay a crooked stack of *Yankee* magazines. Something familiar caught my attention. With the toe of my boot, I tapped against the top edition to nudge it aside, so I could see the one below. Instead, the whole heap toppled to the carpet.

Trying not to wake the baby, I craned over at the mishmashed covers. "Come Discover New England's Artisan Craft Trail!" the sidebar urged. The cover showed a magnificent witch ball in shades of red, orange and yellow, like living fire. It hung at the end of a glassblowing pipe. The artist's hand, so familiar, reached over to the ball with an instrument, whether to shape it or to cut it, I didn't know. But that hand brought back a memory that knotted my chest, a memory I'd squashed for the past eight years. A memory I needed to keep locked away.

I leaned back in the rocker and scrunched my eyes closed, willing the image back into its box. The hardest decision I'd ever made still hurt my heart as if it had happened yesterday. I squeezed my eyes tighter. Better for him.

But instead of fading, the pain bled through.

I stared at the cover. At the man in his element. I'd made the right decision.

He'd done it. He'd made his dream come true.

Good for you, Fynn.

Lucy came back down the stairs, wearing fresh leggings and an oversize sweatshirt, and looking much more relaxed. "How did you do that?"

I glanced down at the sleeping baby, her weight warm on my chest, her breath a milky puff against my neck. "She just exhausted herself."

Toweling her hair dry, Lucy sank onto the couch. "I expected something different. All this crying...it does a number on your confidence, you know."

"I'm told it gets better."

Forehead furrowed, Lucy stared at her sleeping baby. "I sure hope so, or one of us won't survive."

"Any time you need a break, call me."

Tears pooled in Lucy's eyes.

"I mean it, Lucy."

She nodded. "I know how much time this job takes. You can't afford to come here and babysit."

"There's always a way to carve out an hour." Even if I had to face the wrath of the Dragon Lady boss. People were more important than schedules. It's too bad more people didn't realize that.

"Thank you." As if Lucy finally realized that me being in her home wasn't usual, she gasped. "You came here for a reason. How can I help you?"

"The Christmas Star." This was supposed to have been an easy box to check off the to-do list. Pick up the thing. Bring it to the jeweler's. Move on to the next item. "I'm supposed to take it to Three Jeweled Angels, but I have no idea where it's stored. I couldn't find its location in your notes."

She frowned. "That's strange. I'm sure I noted it. You'll find it in the Town Hall basement in the vault."

I'd been in the basement several times over the past few months, searching for various festival props, but had never seen a vault. "There's a vault?"

She combed her hair with her fingers. "Once you get down the stairs, it's way back in the left corner. There's a false shelf unit that hides it. You'll have to push hard where it says Caution and it'll spring open. The key is in the locked drawer of my desk. You have the key for that. The Star is in a red metal box. You'll need help carrying it, so make sure Gus is available."

Gus being Town Hall's custodian. "Thanks. The last thing I want is to let Regina down."

"You're doing fine. I think Regina's a bit hard on you because she wants you to succeed." Lucy gazed outside the window toward town.

I hadn't had anyone on my side for so long that it would take time to accept Regina's faith in me.

"I miss working, you know," Lucy said, folding the wet towel on her lap. "Not so much dealing with all the people, who can be so annoying, but I love me a good spreadsheet and a neat report."

I laughed, and the baby stirred in my arms. "Tell you what, if you want paperwork, I can bring you a stack."

She bit her bottom lip. "I love Autumn. I really do. But it feels as if my brain is turning to mush."

I leaned forward and whispered, "I really hate all the paperwork, but I really love dealing with people."

I handed her the baby. She took the weight and sighed. "I'd better try to nap while she is."

"Call if you need me. In the meantime, I have a Star to get dusted."

3

"We don't see things as they are, we see them as we are."

— ANAIS NIN

Stark light flooded the well-organized basement. The dank smell of earth and old things had me wrinkling my nose. I was glad I'd kept my coat on because in spite of the monster oil furnace churning against the back wall, the concrete walls and dirt floor didn't hang on to any heat. I wasn't sure why the town felt the need to use the ruse of a false bookcase, or why it chose Town Hall to house something it deemed so precious. But my job wasn't to figure out their logic, only to get the thing to the jeweler's.

Hundreds of old binders that went back to 1914 filled a row of bookcases along the left wall. The age of the Town Hall? The town itself, according to Regina, was incorporated in the early 1800s.

As Lucy instructed, I tapped on the Caution sign smack dab in the middle of the bookcases. Nothing happened. I pushed harder and a rusty click rewarded me. The bookcase took some muscle to move, leaving tracks in the dirt that made it easy to figure out the secret. The open bookcase revealed an old-fashioned vault. I chuckled, thinking it looked as if it had come from a movie prop shop to represent a bygone era.

The old-fashioned key with its grooved blade, multi-bitings, and star-shaped tip, resisted turning the lock. On the workbench, I found some WD-40, which helped. *I should start lifting weights*, I thought, straining to pull on the heavy metal door. The door opened with a sucking sound.

Inside, the vault was pitch black, except for a panel that showed the temperature and humidity. The vault was climate-controlled? I took out my phone and swept the flashlight around the surprisingly large room. It held a tarnished golden eagle, a broken copper bell, and rows of various things you'd find in an antique shop.

And there, along the back wall, all on its own on a sturdy wooden table, the red metal box. A huge thing that, Lucy was right, would need more than my muscle to move.

My arms barely reached around its sides. Definitely too heavy to move on my own. With the phone on its phone-case stand aimed at the box, I reached for the lid, the metal seemingly growing warm under my palms.

I lifted the cover and inside found a cushioned form in the shape of a many-pointed star, but instead of the glass Star I expected, a watermelon-size rock that approximated, I assumed, its weight sat on the cushion.

My pulse jumped. "Okay," I told myself, placing the cover back on the box as if that could hide the evidence. "No need to panic yet. It has to be somewhere."

My mind echoed with Regina's disapproving cluck. *I told the earl hiring you was a mistake.* The Star was the one thing I absolutely, positively couldn't do wrong. Not if I wanted a chance to stay in Brighton.

I thought of making discreet inquiries at the jeweler's in

case Regina had already seen to the task, considering how she was always "helping" me get my job done. But if she had, the box would have stayed with the Star, wouldn't it?

I couldn't get the image of the rock out of my head. The rock suggested intent. Someone had deliberately taken the Star and left that rock behind.

I put everything back as I'd found it, then went about my day, mind whirling. Who had taken the Star? Why? How on earth would I find it?

By the end of the day, my nerves twanged and wouldn't settle. Once home, I paced the area between the kitchen and the sofa, wearing a hole on the already thin rug. This wasn't good. No matter how much Regina wanted me to succeed, she would fire me over this. I'd have to start looking for another job. I growled at the walls. "Fudge, fudge, fudge!"

Then I slumped onto the couch, elbows on knees, head in hands. I finally had to admit that Brighton's most precious possession—the Christmas Star—was missing.

No, stolen.

On my watch.

It felt like Senator Becker's announcement party all over again.

"Okay," I said, forcing myself to act normal. I went to the kitchen, grabbed a can of soup, poured it into a large mug and microwaved it. "That the Star is missing isn't the end of the world."

Although, it certainly felt like it. I'd grown to love this job, this town, these people, since I'd arrived. I'd grown used to Regina and her gruff exactness. She cared about this town, and everything she did was for its betterment. Something I admired.

Brighton had a culture of cooperation rather than competition. All these festivals brought not only the whole town, but the whole area together. That belonging, that sense of community was something I'd searched for in a place to settle down since college graduation eight years ago.

The microwave beeped. Standing at the counter, I blew on the hot soup, letting the chicken noodle steam soothe me.

I wanted to stay in Brighton.

I needed to stay.

I hadn't had this feeling of home since college when I'd spent all my holidays with Aunt Poppy instead of enduring the I-don't-want-you-here-but-will-tolerate-you attitude both my parents emitted.

Since Fynn.

But I wasn't going to think of Fynn.

"Right," I said to no one. "Don't think of a purple elephant."

Having lost my appetite, I gave up on the soup and placed the mug in the sink.

I pulled the tarnished chain from inside my sweater and fingered the dodecagram charm. Cursed, my mother had said. Maybe she was right.

The Christmas Star wasn't exactly something that anyone could sell without it getting recognized. So, what was the point of stealing it? I'd heard that some collectors had precious items stolen, then hid them in their own personal collections. A star with a reputation for magic would certainly hold some cachet.

It could be anywhere.

I stuffed the charm back down my sweater, settled on the couch with my laptop and searched for images of the famous Christmas Star. Every single photo showed it in the town square, either on the giant tree, or being hoisted onto the treetop. Only one photo, in the Historical Society's archive, showed the Star in all its magnificence.

According to the description, it had one hundred and ten

points. "The Star," the blurb went on to say, "is a symbol of the hope of Advent. It reminds us that light shines out of darkness, that darkness cannot overcome light."

The glass had a texture I'd never seen before that made it seem to shimmer from inside even though it wasn't lit. I couldn't describe the color, except as an opaline aura.

Apparently, an angel gave it to the first earl as a gift in 1914 as he lay dying in the Church of St. Maurice. He then shared it with Brighton as his promise to redeem himself from his sins. Legend had it that as long as the Star shone on Christmas Eve, Brighton would thrive.

I wrinkled my nose. More curse nonsense. I'd come to Brighton. Three months later, I was still alive. So, great-grandma's curse wasn't real. I closed the laptop's cover and sighed. None of that helped me figure out who had taken the Star, or where it was located.

Just tell Regina about the missing Star.

Her warning during my interview last September reverberated in my mind. *"You'll notice there's a clause giving us the right to terminate your employment for any cause."*

And that brought back the usual parade of disappointments that had provided the backbeat of my childhood.

Mom's stern face, looking down at me. *"You're embarrassing me, Allegra."*

Dad dismissing me with the back of his hand. *"I expected nothing more from you."*

Everyone expected me to fail.

I sighed. More exaggeration. For one, Aunt Poppy had wanted me to succeed, had done her best to give me tools to build my confidence.

For another, Regina was going out of her way to help me succeed at my job. I didn't want to disappoint her.

I had too much on the line to not try everything I could to find the Star first.

I couldn't let one Christmas ornament, as treasured as it was, cost me the job I loved.

I wanted to stay.

I wanted to create a full life.

I wanted to participate fully in that life.

If I wanted that to happen, I had no choice.

Brighton needed a Star for its town tree lighting ceremony.

One way or another, I had to produce that Star by Christmas Eve.

4

"Regardless of how you feel inside, always try to look like a winner. Even if you are behind, a sustained look of control and confidence can give you a mental edge that results in victory."

— *DIANE ARBUS*

Somewhere in the middle of the night, my brain had come up with a Plan B. Getting Plan B in motion, while continuing my search for the original Star, had sounded plausible in those dark hours. This morning, though, as I woke up from fractured sleep, the jitters set in.

Huddled beneath the flannel sheets, I closed my eyes again, and went through the ritual Aunt Poppy had taught me to set myself up for a great day. "Today, I *choose* to be happy. I am grateful for these flannel sheets because they keep me warm and comfy on these cold nights. I am grateful for hot mushroom-cocoa coffee because it kickstarts my day and gives me energy. I am grateful for this job because I enjoy doing something that makes people happy."

I took in a long breath and let it out slowly, then flung the sheets off and hurried to the bathroom.

This plan wasn't something I could do by email or over the phone. This was something that required a personal visit. A personal visit where I had no idea how I would be received.

I headed toward the kitchen, got the coffee going and scooped three tablespoons of mushroom-cocoa into a travel mug. While the coffee brewed, I went back to the bedroom to dress.

My three a.m. Google skills had found Fynn at a small college about an hour away over the border in Vermont. After his apprenticeships all over Europe with well-known glass artists, that seemed an odd place for him to land. With his talent, I'd expected to find him at the Corning Museum in New York (his dream job), or Seattle—the center of glass arts—or Zimmerman's in Indiana. Or running his own glass studio. Although teaching was always part of his plan, so maybe not so odd after all.

Knowing he'd as soon slam the door in my face than let me in, I had to prepare for this visit carefully. Maybe if I made it sound like a challenge. Fynn had always been up for a dare.

I smiled at the memory of daring him to sneak onto the roof of the Mars Center in the middle of winter when it was technically closed. He'd pulled me along with him. Among the telescopes, stored safely in their domes, the only constellation we could identify in the sky was Orion's Belt. Daring him to take a dip in frigid Peacock Pond before Thanksgiving break. He'd turned his swim into a fundraiser. Daring him to crash one of the college president's many fancy gatherings dressed as he was in jeans and a sweatshirt. He'd come out with a plate of appetizers and a flute of champagne.

I shook my head. I had to present myself not as Allie from college but Allegra, businesswoman. That meant squeezing into a suit—the blue one that always made me feel good—even though it was Saturday, and I could have spent the day enjoying the Christmas Village. It meant preparing my case like an attorney, complete with argument and evidence.

It also might mean eating a whole lot of crow.

I pulled the suit off the hanger and paired it with a cream V-neck angora sweater for warmth and softness. I'd need both. I looked at myself in the mirror above the dresser in the bedroom. Fear filled my eyes rather than confidence. "You *can* do this, Allegra."

I tucked my copy of *The Confident Woman* in my messenger bag for courage, poured coffee over the mushroom-cocoa powder in my travel mug, then headed down to collect Beeyoncée, my sweet yellow mini-Cooper, parked in the municipal lot.

James, the British voice on my GPS app, led me out of Brighton, over the Connecticut River and into Vermont. All the way, I practiced what I would say. Should I start with an apology? "Fynn, I'm sorry..."

That sounded so lame.

Should I pretend our last fight never happened? "Hi, there Fynn. Long time no see."

I groaned.

"Fynn, I have a project you won't be able to resist."

The closer I got to Foster College, the more I feared Fynn's response.

Why would he agree to do anything for me after the way I'd left?

Except that he was my only chance to make plan B work, so I had to convince him.

Foster College had that New England feel with its stone walls, snow-covered green spaces, ancient oaks, old-fashioned redbrick buildings, and more modern dorms. I passed through the entrance arch and drove through campus to the far end of the property where a barn-like building stood. The campus map I'd printed assured me that was the Glass Studio and that it was open until three this afternoon.

In the nearby parking lot, I rested my forehead on the steering wheel. What if he wasn't there? I didn't have another address for him. "Then you'll leave him a note."

Which he'd probably feed to the furnace.

"Right, then," I said. "Let's get this over with."

I strapped my messenger bag over my shoulder and patted its side for courage. "You *can* do this, Allegra!"

I squared my shoulders, marched up the curved pathway, boots clipping on the asphalt, and reached for the metal handle on the barn door. It glided on well-oiled hinges. The first thing to hit me was the heat. They didn't call it a hot shop for nothing.

Although the exterior of the building had a rustic feel with its aged barn wood, the interior screamed "industrial" with all its metal. A wall of tools, metal shelves with tubes filled with colored glass rods and bars, bins with glass chips, and steel boxes filled with broken glass. Stainless steel worktables. Weirdly shaped metal benches. Blow torches. A kiln. An annealer. A furnace. Three square glory holes—two closed, one open, burning a bright yellow. A fan churned air and the furnace hissed while it pumped out hell-like heat.

Fynn—I would recognize him anywhere—stood at the mouth of the right-side glory hole, twirling a long blow pipe. He wore safety glasses, a T-shirt and shorts. Even though it was in the teens outside, his skin glistened with sweat. I swallowed hard against the visceral memory of that salty skin.

I stood, mesmerized by the constant motion of his toned body as he twirled the pipe, shaping the glass at the end on some sort of apparatus, so completely focused on his work that a bomb could go off and he wouldn't notice. He wasn't a skinny teen anymore. I swallowed hard, my body yearning, remembering the feel of his arms, his lips...

He was definitely a man now with all that lean muscle.

I couldn't help wondering if his heart had grown as hard as his body. *Your fault if it has.*

I hoped not, because Fynn was the nicest person I'd ever met.

I'd loved to watch him work back in college, spent hours as his helper as he experimented, talking, laughing with him. I'd missed that. There'd been a softness to Fynn then, a softness I'd needed. Still did.

Off to my left, a *woof!* caught me by surprise. I turned in its direction only to have a black-brown-and-white blur gallop at me and plant two paws firmly on my upper chest, knocking me backward, making me backpedal and crash into the door. For a second, I couldn't find my breath.

"Chill!" Fynn yelled. "Off!"

A tongue swiped at my cheeks, lifting the makeup I'd so carefully applied this morning.

"Sorry," Fynn said and yanked off the beast by the collar. "He's still in training. Here—"

He stopped, his scarred and callused hand, holding a red bandana, poised halfway to where I stood pressed awkwardly against the door. "Allie?"

For a second, I thought I saw a spark of joy in his eyes, then his gaze shuttered like blinds tumbling down over a window.

I crouched and scratched the hairy beast's bearded chin. He danced in place, and I had to play keep away from his tongue and his fishy breath. "Who's this?"

Fynn stuffed the bandana back in his cargo shorts pocket. "His name is Chill, short for Chihuly."

That made sense. Fynn had admired Dale Chihuly's work. "What kind of dog is he?"

"Bernedoodle." His voice was clipped and short. "A rescue, hence, the bad manners."

"He's new to you?"

"A couple of months. The cute puppy turned into a giant of a dog, so he was abandoned. I've got the time and the room."

That was so Fynn. "Poor puppy."

Chill flipped onto his back, four paws up, begging for a belly scratch.

"You didn't come all this way, from wherever you are now, to talk about my dog."

As Nora Roberts once said, *"If you don't ask, the answer is always no."*

"No, you're right."

He stared at Chill and pointed to the puffy plaid cushion in the corner. "Bed!"

Chill rolled back to his feet, wagged his bushy tail and licked my hand.

"Don't make me take you there!"

If a dog could roll his eyes, Chill did and took his time padding to his bed where he flopped.

Fynn took an empty white five-gallon bucket, upended it and patted it for me to sit. He turned over a second bucket and sat. "What brings you to Foster?"

"I..."

"Need a favor. I already figured that out."

"It's a long story." This was a mistake. I shouldn't have come. There was still too much rawness between us.

"I've got all afternoon," he said, but it sounded like "Hurry up."

"After college, I moved around a lot." Looking for a place to call home. But nothing ever felt right. "I eventually landed in Virginia, just outside of D.C."

"Doing events?"

I slipped my messenger bag onto my lap, holding on to it tight, and nodded, hoping the movement didn't look bobble-headed. Planning events had all started with a friend's birthday party in high school. Word got around about how well it had gone, and girls would hit me up for ideas. Then my mother asked me to plan a dinner party for her. And my father asked me to plan a cocktail party for a business affair. And it snowballed from there.

"Making other people happy became my way to fit in.

"I landed a gig to plan a black-tie outdoor affair for Senator Becker's presidential run announcement."

"Sounds like an opportunity." He slid off his safety glasses. They'd left tracks on his nose and cheeks that I wanted to smooth out.

"It was. A big one. But then he insisted I let his niece shadow me so she could learn the business. It rained the night before as we were setting up in the outdoor tent." So hard that I'd urged the senator to postpone the event, but he'd refused because the press was already scheduled.

"I was doing my last run-through before heading home for the night, when I noticed some electrical chords coming off the stage in a high traffic area. Someone could easily trip over that, so I told Hailey to stand there and watch out in case anyone walked by. I went to my car to get some duct tape from my emergency kit to tape the wires down. She wasn't listening, of course. That girl was welded to her phone. While I was gone—and it was less than five minutes—the tent started to fail. A falling speaker truss knocked Hailey over and she broke her wrist. The spoiled brat ran right to her uncle, who fired me on the spot.

"Meanwhile, the tent failure caused an electrical short that ruined the production company's audio and video equipment. They blamed the tent people, who blamed the venue for not telling them they were in a flood area, who then blamed me for not being present during the failure. A lawsuit followed..."

Fynn didn't say anything. His unflinching stare made me itch to squirm.

"And a fellow planner, who I thought was a friend, swooped

in and offered her services to 'save' his event." I tightened my grip on the messenger bag. "Something that had happened several times over the past year. Mysteriously canceled catering order, venue, flowers. After that big mess, some of my trusted vendors turned on me. And the rest, as they say, is history."

"The rain wasn't—actually none of what happened was your fault."

Except that I should have anticipated all the possible scenarios. Especially when the radar showed the rain was only going to get worse. I should have insisted on postponing the event. I shouldn't have agreed to have someone shadow me for such a major event. I'd failed big time on so many fronts. I should have known better. But I got caught up in the possibility of a big win and made rookie mistakes.

I hiked a shoulder, let it drop. "I was the face of the event. I was responsible no matter what happened. And I should have known better than to leave that spoiled girl alone for one minute."

Fynn's mouth was a straight, hard line. Something I found unnerving, because I remembered how his smiles lit up his whole face, making cute little fans at the corner of his eyes. "Where do I come in on all this?"

I patted the side of my messenger bag, hoping *The Confident Woman's* calmness would seep into me. "The senator made sure I couldn't book any more events. Any time I managed to get a nibble, by the time I got there for the initial consult, the job had magically disappeared. I couldn't find any work for three months, and my savings were down to just about nothing."

"Still don't see where I come in."

Yep, this had been a mistake, but I was here, so I might as well see it to the end. "I'm getting there. I took a job as Town Administrator for the Village of Brighton over the river in New Hampshire."

"Yeah, I know where that is."

"I'm basically in charge of making sure all goes smoothly for their monthly festivals."

"Okay."

The shop's heat had sweat dripping down my back, making me wish I'd taken off my coat. "Have you heard of their Christmas Star?"

He nodded.

I took a photo of the Star from the messenger bag and handed it to him.

He whistled. "Beautiful work."

I rolled my lips in, then blew them out along with the words I hoped wouldn't stick in my throat. "It's missing. And I need you to make me a replacement."

He frowned. "When do you need it by?"

"Yesterday."

He handed me the photo. "Sorry."

I nodded. Asking Fynn had been a long shot anyway. Chill padded between us, placing his snout on my lap.

"Do you know how much work goes into something like that?" Fynn asked, his flinty gaze boring into me. "How many points does the star have?"

"One hundred and ten." Chill tapped at my knee with a bear-size paw until I petted the top of his curly head. The curls reminded me of Fynn's and how I used to love running my fingers through them.

"Each point has four sides," he said, in a voice so cold I shivered in spite of the tropical heat in the shop. "That's four-hundred-and-forty pieces of glass that have to be cut precisely by hand. It doesn't count the core or the collar. Then those pieces have to be welded together to form the points. That's hundreds of hours of work, and not really my area of expertise."

He flicked a finger at the Star photo still in my hand, shaking the paper. "Then there's the aura glass. That opal color is called angel aura spirit glass. I'm not sure I could even get my hands on any, that's how rare it is."

"Okay," I said, moving Chill's nose out of the way so I could get up. "Thanks."

I headed toward the door.

Fynn's voice stopped me. "Why did you leave, Allie? Why wouldn't you return my calls?"

He didn't mean now; he meant then. Letting him go had taken all my courage and broken my heart.

"Because," I said, working to keep my voice neutral. "You were ready to give up going to Spain and you needed to go to Spain. Eventually, you would have resented me if you hadn't gone."

"That was my decision to make, not yours." The words came out as a growl.

I slowly turned, looking around the glass studio. "Looks like the right decision, though. You made your dreams come true."

Before he could say anything more, I hurried away back to the safety of Bee-yoncée's interior.

For a few minutes, I couldn't move, rehashing our conversation. Seeing Fynn again had opened a part of me I'd closed, a part I needed to find a way to bury again.

Plan B was a bust. I turned over Bee's engine and cranked up the heat. The hour drive would give me time to hatch Plan C.

I turned on the GPS app and said, "Home, James."

James' kind voice instructed me to drive to the motorway.

When I glanced at the rearview mirror, Fynn and Chill stood there, watching me disappear.

My heart broke all over again.

5

"I am not afraid of storms for I am learning how to sail my ship."

— *LOUISA MAY ALCOTT*

By the time I got back to my apartment, I had a list of action steps. According to my latest evening book binge, *Be Seen*, rejection always had a lesson. I'd spent the car trip home going through the five-step plan to get unstuck.

First, diagnose the situation. I'd asked something unreasonable from Fynn. Creating a one-of-a-kind star like that wasn't something anyone could whip up in an hour. And he was a glass blower, not a glass welder.

Step 2, deal with the feelings. Except that my feelings were a jumble right now. I hadn't expected that seeing Fynn would bring back so many emotions. Or the soul-deep ache I'd felt when I'd let him go. I missed him. I missed the fun we'd had. I missed the feeling of home in his arms. I'd promised myself I wouldn't make a man the center of my existence the way my mother did. I wanted Fynn, but I didn't need him. Best to stuff all those feelings back down in its box and lock it tight. Going backward was never a good idea.

Step 3, discover the hidden Yes. I was grateful for the opportunity to see Fynn successful. I'd wondered over the years but refused to look him up—my penance for hurting him. I was grateful he'd explained just how special the Star was and how difficult it would be to make a copy. I was grateful I'd gone out of my comfort zone and taken a risk. Still didn't feel good about killing Plan B, though.

Which took me to step 4, develop a plan. I had to keep looking for the Star. Finding it was still my best bet. I would have to find a way to get people to talk and somehow keep its disappearance a secret. Someone had to know something. My first stop would be the Historical Society to learn all its history, not just the online teaser meant to get you to visit.

And most important of all, step 5, do something. Doing brought momentum and momentum got things done. And I really, really needed to have a star for the lighting ceremony in eighteen days.

After all the noise, color and activity of the hot shop, my cold and dark and awfully beige apartment didn't feel inviting.

"Whose fault is that?" I asked as I stripped off my hat, scarf and coat. Just because I could lose this job in a few weeks didn't mean I couldn't make it homey in the meantime.

Two birds, I thought. I'd change, go to the Christmas Village, ask questions, and shop for a few things to make this space feel more like home. Act as if, right? If I made this home, it would become home.

The thought cheered me as I changed into black fleeced-lined tights, a base layer and a thick red Christmas sweater featuring white galloping reindeers around the neckline. Then I headed toward the Village, blaring Christmas songs on Bee's radio. The late afternoon was cold but clear, and the place looked like, well, a festival.

The naked tree branches, twined with colored lights, looked like dancers swaying in the soft breeze. The air brimmed with the scents of Christmas—pine, cinnamon and snow. Everywhere I turned, Christmas wreaths or boughs or ornaments met my gaze. Christmas music filled the air. People milled around from booth to booth, looking happy. Just what I needed to shift my mood. Answers didn't come when stressed, but rather with a relaxed brain.

"Allegra! Hi!" Dalia from the Charmed Card and Paper Shop below my apartment waved at me as she walked by. I'd helped her with a permit problem last week.

The three Harper sisters, marching as one, reminding me I still needed to get a Star to their jewelry store soon. Cher from the chocolate shop, who kept me stocked in mushroom-cocoa powder. Page from the bookstore, who shone as brightly as any Christmas tree. Piper from the flower shop, who dropped an arrangement for the Town Hall foyer every week. Angeline from The Farmhouse, where I discovered new homemade goodies every week. They all waved and smiled. Walking around, feeling seen and known felt good.

Of course, that feeling of belonging clouded when I thought of ruining everyone's Christmas Eve without the Star.

As I admired a pile of handmade quilts, someone put a hand on my shoulder. I startled and spun to find a man dressed in a black overcoat, a black fedora, camel-colored cashmere scarf and black leather gloves, way too formal for an outdoor festival.

"Allegra." His smile looked Photoshopped. "Just the person I'd hoped to run into."

"Hi, Royce." Royce Tanner was Regina's counterpart in Stoneley. They'd served for about the same amount of time, which made them notables in their respective towns. And fierce competitors, according to Lucy. I chuckled silently. He was probably one of the people Lucy hated dealing with. He *always* had a problem. "What can I do for you today?"

"I've left several messages about coordinating for the Chocolate Festival."

"Christmas is a busy time around here." The Chocolate Festival was still two months away, so most everything about it was two layers down on the to-do lists.

"Yes, but we must put all our ducks in a row."

I left the quilt booth, making a note to come back later for a lap-size quilt that would make the sofa homier. "Meredith Mills Carpenter, the tri-town coordinator, is who you really need to talk to."

"Very well." He nodded, but his jaw screwed tight.

I stopped at the Brightside Bakery booth and ordered a hot chocolate with whipped cream and candy cane sprinkles. "Would you like one?"

He shook his head as if I'd offered him a cup of poison.

"Have you gone to the Christmas Eve tree lighting before?" I asked, stepping aside to wait for my treat. Asking a few questions couldn't hurt.

"Of course, everyone in the area has," Royce said.

"Tell me your best memories of the Star."

"Oh, well, let me think." His gloved hand fiddled with the fringe of his scarf. "It's a magnificent piece of art."

"What do you think of its history?"

He scoffed. "A fabrication to lure in unsuspecting tourists."

"Allegra!" the teen from the bakery booth called.

I turned to accept my hot chocolate and took a sip. "Oh, wow! This is the best hot chocolate I've ever had."

"We use real milk and the best chocolate." Her smile reflected pride before she turned to the next customer.

I joined the mob of people ambling down the center aisle of booths, and Royce stuck to me like a barnacle on a boat.

"You don't think the legend's real?" I asked, when he insisted on strolling with me. "The angel, the earl, the redemption?"

He furrowed his face as if the thought smelled like garbage. "Of course not. Although, I wish we'd thought to use the legend first." He glanced at the crowd, and I could almost see dollar-sign envy in his eyes.

"Brighton shares its wealth," I said, enjoying another sip of hot chocolate. Way better than mushroom coffee. Regina had come up with the idea of joining the three area towns together for the benefit of all. We included Stoneley and Granite Falls in some way in all our festivals. "Stoneley is part of the Cookie Tour and—"

"Ah, yes, crumbs." He flicked away those metaphorical crumbs with the back of his hand.

Okay, so a little resentment there. Enough to steal the Star? If he didn't believe in the Star or its legend, would he engineer its theft from Brighton to tarnish its reputation? Or maybe play into their superstition of bad luck if it didn't shine? It wasn't as if Stoneley could take over all the Christmas festivities. Whether the Star's legend was real or fiction, people associated the Christmas Village with Brighton and would still flock to these fairgrounds.

I would need to look into Royce Tanner more closely.

"If you'll excuse me," I said, spotting Lucy and her husband Ryan in the crowd. "I see someone I need to speak to."

"Of course," he said, but his brows sank low over his eyes as if I'd insulted him. His pointed gaze made the spot between my shoulder blades burn. I scrunched my shoulders and hurried to catch up with Lucy. Yep, he was definitely going on my suspect list.

"Lucy!"

She turned, smiled and waved.

Lucy's puffy red coat snuggled around Baby Autumn. All that peeked through was her closed eyes.

"What did Royce want?" she asked as I neared.

"Hi, Ryan!" I enclosed all three in a loose hug. "Thanks for saving me."

"Allegra," Ryan said, chuckling, then kissed Lucy and tipped his head toward the lake. "I'm going to go reserve a fire pit."

"Oh, yes! Get a s'mores kit, too!" Lucy bounced the baby gently. "So, Royce..."

"Wanted to nitpick about the Chocolate Festival."

"Of course he did."

I pinched my lips tight, trying to decide if I should reveal my Star quandary to Lucy or not. The problem was that I wasn't a local, and I really needed an insider to help me sort through who could or couldn't have stolen the Star. "If I tell you something, do you promise on your baby's head not to tell Regina?"

She hesitated, wrapping her arms tighter around her sleeping baby. "I need a little more before I make a promise like that."

"I just don't want to lose my job, but I need a little more information."

"O-kay."

I swallowed hard, leaned in closer, and whispered my secret on a long exhale. "The Star wasn't in the vault. The box was there, but instead of the Star, I found a rock." I remembered the heat of the box against my palms in the frigid basement. "I think someone stole it."

"Oh, wow," Lucy said, fear warbling through her hushed voice. "You have to find it! Without it, all the good luck we've had in the past century will disappear."

"Do you really think the Star has that much power?"

"It does," she insisted, her gaze flitting about to make sure no one had heard our conversation. "If you'd ever gone to the lighting of the Star, you'd know it. It's the one event no one, and

I mean no one, in town misses. Rain, snow, sleet, baby, elderly, everyone still shows up."

More like the power of superstition, I thought. "If it's that important, why do they store it in a basement?"

"Because it's not the first time someone's tried to steal the Star. Only a few people know about the vault and fewer still know the Star spends the off-season there."

"The vault doesn't seem that hard to crack."

"The key is one-of-a-kind, and it's kept locked."

"Still. Why not keep the Star at the estate?"

Lucy blew a raspberry. "That's where it used to be, but someone tried to steal it there. The earl doesn't like people around and, as old as he is, he can't handle a thief on his own."

"He doesn't have an alarm system?"

"He does but it would still take the police time to get out there. Time enough for someone to hurt the earl and take the Star. That would be two tragedies. The police station is right around the corner from Town Hall. They could be there in less than a minute."

"It's not like someone has eyes on the Star every day, though." I groaned. "Someone had to know all the procedures, because the Star *isn't* in the box."

"Allegra, I can't stress how bad this is."

"I know." Superstition or not, the Star was important to Brighton, and it had gone missing on my watch. Never mind that I'd never seen it, or that I hadn't stored it after its appearance last Christmas.

"I really think you should tell Regina," Lucy said.

"I will. I just need a little more time to exhaust all the possibilities." The old-fashioned carousel music in the background sounded like a warning. I didn't want to let Regina down. I couldn't fail this time.

I needed to prove I deserved the job. That I was capable.

6

"We gain strength, and courage, and confidence by each experience in which we really stop to look fear in the face...we must do that which we think we cannot."

— *ELEANOR ROOSEVELT*

"Okay," I said, puffing out a breath. The laughter wafting around us, the chocolate, peppermint and pine scents and all the twinkling lights provided a stark contrast to the dread roiling through my chest. "Let's figure this out," I said to Lucy. "First, who knows about the vault?"

"The earl, I should say the original earl, had the vault built. Regina's predecessor supervised its build, but he's long dead. Gus and his stepson Lon know it's there because they help us take it out every year, but they don't otherwise have access to the vault."

"There's a basement full of tools. Could they have broken into it?"

"First, the lock on the vault is supposed to be impenetrable without the key. Second, it's not in Gus' character to do something like that. He takes pride in what he does."

"The stepson then. If there's something going on in his life that nobody knows about, someone else could have used that pain point to get to him."

"He's got a bad boy vibe, but it's an act. He's actually quite dependable."

I added both their names to Royce Tanner's on my mental list of suspects anyway. "Who else?"

"Regina. But we can rule her out."

"I agree." The woman might not think I was the best person for the job, but the last thing she'd do is ruin Brighton's Christmas.

"Me," Lucy said, all but baring her teeth at me. "I'm the keeper of the key. But I've been kinda busy these past three months. I've barely had time for a shower let alone to organize the theft of the Star."

"I wouldn't be talking to you if I thought you'd done it." Although, who knew when it had gone missing. Someone could have gotten the key out of her desk while her brain swirled with happy baby hormones those last few months before I arrived. The Star could have disappeared last Christmas after its yearly show on the square. Or any time during the year. The situation was looking worse by the minute. "Who else?"

As if the guilty party would suddenly appear, she glanced around at the people milling around us.

"As far as I know, that's it," she said. "Other than the Harper sisters from the jewelry store. Well, they know about the Star, take care of the Star, but I don't think they know where the vault is."

Audrey, Alice and Adele Harper, three sisters who looked eerily similar, like a triptych of adult Wednesday Adamses. I added them to my list, which still left it skimpy.

"What's the procedure for getting the Star out of the vault to the tree and back?" I asked, making sure no one in particular paid attention to my and Lucy's conversation.

"Gus, Lon and Regina get it out of the vault on a special trolley, then up onto the loading deck. A town truck takes it to Three Jeweled Angels with Regina riding shotgun. She doesn't leave until it's been locked up in the shop. The Harper sisters only work on it in that locked room. Then Regina stays with the Star from the store to the time it's up on top of the tree. Nobody's tried to steal it while it was on the tree. Same goes for the way back, in reverse."

None of this had appeared in Lucy's notes. Had someone taken those pages out to ensure my failure? "So, the store could make an easy target?"

"Not with the bars and alarms they have."

For a piece of glass with so much security, how had it managed to disappear so easily? "It sounds like a lot of people would know the Star is stored in the Town Hall. And a lot of people have the codes to get into Town Hall. There are a few weak spots where someone could take it."

"I suppose." Her voice sounded strained like a rubber band pulled tight. "You should just tell Regina."

"I can't."

"If she finds out on her own..." Lucy didn't finish the sentence.

Lucy belonged in Brighton. She was loved, wanted, needed. She didn't know what it was like to watch her parents fight over whose turn it was to *not* have her. She didn't know what it was like to watch life from the outside looking in. She didn't know what it was like to create magic and not step into the ring and be part of that magic.

This job was my chance to finally fit in somewhere.

Lucy tipped her chin toward a man strolling with both hands laced behind him as if he were a teacher supervising outdoor recess. "That's Father Lowe. He's the priest at St. Maurice. That's where the legend started, so he might have some information."

"Good idea."

"We'll save you some s'mores," Lucy said and headed toward the firepits.

Like Royce, the good father wore a black overcoat, but a less formal rust-colored beanie and matching mittens that looked homemade. A gift from a parishioner?

I came up to him, then wasn't sure how to address him. Up close, he appeared younger than I expected, more late thirties than late fifties, as I'd assumed from the way he'd patrolled the grounds. "Father Lowe?"

Frowning, he looked me up and down. "Yes?"

I stuck out a hand. "I'm Allegra Livingstone. I took over Lucy Fleming's job at Town Hall. She tells me that you run the Church of St. Maurice."

"I am the resident priest," he said, his voice rolling like a song. The kind of voice that would sound good reading the dullest entry in an encyclopedia. So at odds with his dour looks. He gave my hand a limpid shake.

I pointed toward the bakery booth. "Can I buy you a cup of hot chocolate?"

"No, thank you. I'm fine," he said, even though his cold-reddened beak nose and apple cheeks told a different story. Paying a penance?

"I wondered if you wouldn't mind talking to me about the Christmas Star," I said, leading him to a bench next to the skating rink on the lake. "I'd like to do a special feature."

He sat reluctantly. "I don't suppose you're talking about the Star of Bethlehem."

"Um, no, sorry." I wrapped both gloved hands around the fast-cooling cocoa. "The one that's lit in the town square every

Christmas Eve. I hear that it's the one-hundred-and-tenth anniversary."

A storm roiled on his face. "This town has turned a gift from above into a sacrilege."

"What do you mean?"

He raised his arms, taking in the whole crowd. "These people worship the Star when they should be focusing on the true reason for the season."

Okay, so not a fan of the Star that supposedly materialized in his church. "Isn't honoring the Star also honoring its spiritual origins?"

He dropped his arms and narrowed his gaze at me. "'You shall not bow down to their gods nor serve them, nor do as they do, but you shall utterly overthrow them and break their pillars in pieces.' Exodus 23:24."

That sounded rather violent for a man of peace. Was his hatred of the Star strong enough to destroy it in the guise of saving his flock? Another person to look into.

I smiled at him. "Well, thank you for your help."

"There are better ways of honoring our Lord and Savior than celebrating at the foot of a piece of glass, no matter what its origins."

Still smiling, I nodded and forced myself to walk away as if his words didn't feel like doom.

I was on my way to find Lucy when I nearly bumped into a couple. I took a step back. "Oh, I'm so sorry."

"Allegra Livingstone?" the man asked. His smoke-gray, double-breasted peacoat and his neatly trimmed beard made him look as if he'd just stepped off the cover of *GQ* magazine.

I nodded.

He offered me his gloved hand. "I'm Robin Sims, the earl's nephew."

This was someone worth getting to know for access to the estate. "Hi, Robin."

He turned to the elegant woman at his side, clad in a dark green topcoat nipped in at the waist, making her look super slim, a white wool hat and matching gloves. Her chic outfit made my puffer jacket feel as if I were dressed in a baby-blue marshmallow. "This is my, um, cousin, Kay Spears. She's visiting for the weekend."

"You picked a great time to visit," I said, pumping her free hand. "How are you enjoying our Christmas Village?"

"It's the most wonderful place I've ever seen." She lifted a handful of shopping bags of all sizes. "I've made a dent in my Christmas shopping."

"We like to hear that." I turned to Robin. "Would it be possible to come look at the venue for the gala sometime soon?" The Festival of Lights gala was an annual event hosted by the earl on December 21st. "I took some measurements earlier in the fall and now I need to finalize the plan. I want to make sure everything's on schedule."

"Of course." He had the kind of smile that made you want to smile back. "Drop by anytime. Unless I'm running errands for my uncle, I'm there."

"How about Monday?"

"I'll look forward to it."

I handed him my phone. "Why don't you put in your number so I can call and make sure it's a convenient time."

He did and handed it back.

I sent him a quick text. "There, you have my number in case you need anything for the gala."

His cousin pulled him away. "Robbie, I want to go see those ornaments."

He gave a what-can-you-do hike of his shoulders and trotted after Kay.

I put my phone in my pocket. That took care of one thing on my list—finding a way inside the estate.

I let out a long breath. As much as I loved hanging around

people, at some point, my system hit overload and I needed time alone. I was just about there.

On my way back to Bee, I bought a Christmas Star lap quilt in gold, red and green, a matching pillow and a battery-operated lantern decorated with sprigs of holly, mini-pinecones and a plaid ribbon. Warmth, I thought as I stowed them in the back seat, homey.

But as I drove home, my spirits sank. Other than adding suspects to my list, I was no closer to finding the Star than this morning.

7

"Life is not easy for any of us. But what of that? We must have perseverance and above all confidence in ourselves. We must believe that we are gifted for something and that this thing must be attained."

— *MARIE CURIE*

A lazy snow fell on Sunday morning, the kind that dusted the town to make it look magical. The kind that offered a certain quiet stillness that made you want to slow down and take a deep breath. I glanced at my new quilt and smiled. Maybe I'd snuggle on the couch, play a video of a flickering fire and read a novel for a change instead of working on yet another business report.

I shook my head. After. First, I needed to make at least one step of headway into the Star problem.

With a mug of mushroom-cocoa coffee and a couple of apple cider donuts I'd picked up at the bakery booth last night, I spread my Star notes along the kitchen island, separating the tiny kitchen from the living room, and pored over them. Too bad Fynn couldn't have put a replacement together. I could have checked off the Star problem and gone on to the rest of my mega to-do list.

"Don't think about Fynn!" I said. So, of course, the image of his smiling face filled my mind, and my body started to melt. "No, no, no!"

I forced myself to concentrate on finding a solution for the missing Star.

"You're supposed to help me focus," I told the mushroom-cocoa coffee. That had been its selling point. Although, its earthy taste was growing on me. *There, better.*

Just then someone knocked at my door. A firm, insistent knock. I looked up, frowning. Who would come here on a Sunday morning? I glanced down at my yoga pants and fleece sweatshirt. Not exactly the picture of a professional. On the other hand, it was Sunday morning and, theoretically, a day off.

I opened the door, and as if speaking his name had conjured him up, there stood Fynn, shoulders filling the door frame, face like carved granite, still and serious. Chill, on the other hand, could barely contain his joy. His tail swept the dusting of snow on my tiny stoop at the top of the stairs to the apartment and his front paws tap-danced. He kept looking at Fynn as if he expected a command.

"Fynn?" I said, finally finding my voice. "What are you doing here?"

"Can we come in?"

I opened the door wider. Chill batted his forepaws at me. I crouched and gave his head a good pet, and he rewarded me by bathing my face with his tongue.

"We've been practicing not jumping on people," Fynn said, looking as if he'd rather be anywhere but here.

"Good job, Chihuly!"

I swear the dog actually smiled. He trotted in as if he owned the place, went straight to the sofa, pulled down my new quilt and plopped down on it. I laughed. "Make yourself at home."

"The other reason his nickname is Chill, is that unlike the original Chihuly, this dude is chill," Fynn said, closing the door behind him.

When I thought of Fynn, he was always smiling, laughing. This stony Fynn had my nerves buzzing. I went around the counter island into the kitchen. That didn't help. "Coffee?"

He gave a sharp nod.

"Donut?"

"Uh, sure." He took one of the two high stools on the living room side of the counter. As if he wasn't planning on staying long, he didn't take off his navy parka with its distinctive Canada Goose logo.

I couldn't imagine why he was here, and I didn't know what to do with myself. *Do something, anything.* So, I got out a plate and placed a donut on it, then filled a mug with coffee. Did he still take it black?

"I may have a solution to your Star problem," he said as I slid a mug of coffee and the plate with the donut his way.

"Okay." After the way we'd parted yesterday, I didn't think I'd ever see him again, let alone have him offer a solution. And stupidly, the next word out of my mouth was, "Why?"

His eyebrows lowered as if he wasn't happy with the reason. "I like a challenge."

I nodded, turning away from him to refill my mug. The way he'd said the words staring right into me, I wasn't sure if he meant me or the Star. And that stirred awake something that needed to stay sleeping.

"One of my students is truly gifted with stained glass," he said. "I didn't tell her the specific project but did ask if she'd be interested in doing something a little out there during Christmas break."

A little sprig of hope sprang up. "Really?"

"I'm going to need more specific details." He tilted his head and offered me a poor imitation of the Fynn smile I knew. "Even located some angel aura spirit glass."

"Oh, wow." He'd done research after I left?

He riffled through the many pockets on his parka and came out with a piece of paper. "This is the rough estimate of what it'll cost you for materials."

"Oh, wow." That would pretty much wipe out the savings I'd managed to put away since I'd arrived in Brighton. I figured I needed to sock away as much as possible, in case Regina activated the "no cause" clause. And given that, if I couldn't find the Star, I definitely wouldn't have a job, using up that savings didn't seem wise.

"Still want the job done?" Fynn asked, both capable hands wrapped around the ceramic mug, making it look child-size.

"Let me think." I went to the sofa and sat next to Chill, who plopped his big head on my lap. Petting his curls soothed my jagged nerves enough for me to think. On the one hand, why spend all my savings when I would lose the job anyway? On the other, I didn't want to let Regina down. Plus, I loved Brighton and its people, and I wanted them to have the Christmas they expected. If need be, I could reinvent myself, couldn't I?

"What do you need?" I asked.

"Measurements, better photographs to start with."

I jumped up and paced. Chill whined, his gaze following my zigzag path in the tiny space. "The Historical Society would be the best place to get information. But it's closed on Sundays."

I sat back on the sofa and reached for my laptop, Chill all but climbing into my lap as if to keep me pinned. Reaching over Chill's body, I re-keyed my searches for Brighton's Christmas Star and landed on an entry for a book on Brighton written by the local bookstore owner. "The bookstore opens at ten today. We can get a copy of the book on the Christmas Village. Not sure what it covers but it's a start."

A quick glance at the laptop's clock told me ten was almost an hour away, and I wasn't sure my nerves could survive an hour of Fynn leaning on the counter and staring at me as if I were an experiment gone wrong.

I got up and pointed at the bedroom. "I'm going to go get dressed."

And escape.

I took as long as I possibly could to change into layers for the snowy weather outside. Why had I gone to see Fynn? Why had I started this? Why did I always seem to have to pay such high prices for my every mistake?

∼

THE WALK to the bookstore took much longer than it should have. Chill had to water every single lamp post and every rubbish bin, then sniff every inch of sidewalk in between.

"His nickname definitely fits him," I said, hands in the pockets of my puffer coat, so I wouldn't reach for Fynn's hand out of habit.

Fynn didn't hurry the dog along, just let him lead the pace. Patience was one of Fynn's qualities, one that helped make his art so extraordinary.

"He showed up at the hot shop one day and wouldn't leave. I called the animal shelter, the local vets, and left notices all over town. He wasn't chipped. A month later, nobody had claimed him. So, he stayed." Fynn quirked one side of his mouth. "Can't remember life without him."

Maybe I should get a dog. I could use a faithful companion. Except that my hours wouldn't be fair to the animal. Neither was my uncertain future. "Sounds like you rescued each other."

He gave me an odd look but said nothing.

We made it to the bookstore just as Page, the owner, flipped the Closed sign to Open. She opened the door wide and said, "Good morning, Allegra! Come on in! The book you ordered hasn't arrived yet."

"Just browsing today."

Like Brighton and the bookstore, Page was decorated to the hilt—Christmas light earrings and necklace—lit of course. She wore a green Christmas sweater that would win an ugly sweater contest with its drapings of golden tinsel and red ornaments. A headband featuring a giant golden treetop star topped the outfit.

Page bent down to give Chill a pat on the head. "Who is this handsome gentleman?"

"His name is Chihuly," Fynn said. "Chill for short."

Chill offered Page a paw.

She shook it. "Hello, Chill."

She looked up at Fynn. "And who is this tall drink of water, Allegra?"

"My friend, Fynn. He's visiting for the day."

"Just the day?" Page tutted. "What a shame!"

"Is it okay if Chill comes in?" I patted Chill's head, and he gazed up at me as if he were in love.

Page nodded and smiled. "Of course. We're dog-friendly, as long as he doesn't lick the books."

We all trooped in. Page closed the door behind us. "Can I help you find something?"

"We're looking for a copy of the book you wrote about Brighton's Christmas Village," I said.

Pride lighting her eyes, she swept an arm toward a round table near the door that promoted the book. "Claire and I had such fun putting this book together."

"Does it have anything on the Christmas Star? Fynn is a glass artist, and I wanted him to see it."

"Ooh, that sounds fascinating." Page flipped through the

pages and opened the book to the chapter on the Christmas Star. "We were focusing on the Village, but yes, because the Village, Candlewick Estate, and the Star are all related to the earl, we included a bit about each."

I reached for a copy of the book. "I'll take it."

I paid for the book, then headed toward the small tables in the café where Fynn and Chill already sat.

"He was eyeing the books," Fynn said by way of explanation.

"Coffee'll be ready in just a few," Page said, and ambled behind the café counter.

I pulled my chair closer to Fynn's so we could look at the pages together, remembering all the times we'd sat close studying. He still, somehow, smelled like a sunny summer day. *Don't, Allegra.* I found the chapter on the Star. The photographer had done an excellent job showing it off in all its splendor. "It looks even more beautiful than I imagined."

Fynn studied the photos in silence. My chest grew tighter by the second. I got up and ordered Fynn a plain coffee and me a hot chocolate, then added a couple of fist-size cranberry-orange muffins.

The muffin went down as if it were made of concrete. I didn't know what to do to break the tension between us. A mom and her two children walked in and headed for the kid section. A man, who grunted a greeting at Page, headed toward the history section. A woman, dressed in Sunday best and looking in a hurry, ordered a muffin and coffee to go. Still, Fynn didn't say a word.

We'd made a good team, once upon a time. Conversation between us had come easy. We'd met at Freshman Orientation and just clicked, even though we were in different programs. I'd spent hours helping him put together his art projects, and he'd helped me put on events for the various groups I belonged to.

"Negative space," popped out of my mouth, thinking of

both the Star and the emotional distance between us. I'd sometimes tuned out when Fynn got too deep into explaining his art, but I remembered enough that it had come in handy over the years.

He frowned at me. "What?"

I leaned toward him and whispered, "I can't show you the real thing, but I can show you its form. Would that help?"

8

"Success is most often achieved by those who don't know that failure is inevitable."

— COCO CHANEL

Fynn made short work of moving the bookcase hiding the safe in the Town Hall basement. I used the key and opened the safe door. I hoped against hope that no one would notice our activity. The last thing I needed was to deal with the police. I had to remind myself that I had every right to be here. This was my workspace. I was the Town Administrator. My job mandated I make Brighton and its festivals run smoothly. With the industrial flashlight I borrowed from the workbench, I lit the red box on the table inside.

I motioned for Fynn to lift the cover. "Inside, there's a form in the shape of the Star."

Chill sniffed the vault, then padded away to explore the rest of the basement.

Fynn removed the cover and the watermelon-size rock, making it look like a mere stone. With his fingers, he explored the Star's shape. I had to look away, remembering their feel on my skin, how they'd made me feel loved, cherished. "Does it help?"

"The rock didn't crush the form too badly." He pursed his lips. "It would help more if I could make a cast to get the correct dimensions."

"Could you do that without harming the form?"

His head bobbled from side to side. "There are a lot of ways to make casts, but I think for our purposes and your budget, a paper mold would work. It's just going to take a bit of time."

"It's Sunday. Nobody should come and disturb us. What do you need?"

"Plain tissue paper, a brush and water."

"Won't the tissue paper dissolve in water?"

"I'll paint on just enough water to make the tissue shapeable."

"You've done this before?"

He nodded.

"Okay, let's go to the Country Store. They have a surprising selection of stuff there."

The sidewalks were more crowded now. Storefronts, decked out in swags of greens, white lights and red ribbons, invited passersby in. People waved and said hello as they went about their business. I put on a cheerful smile, but inside I felt like a fraud. If I couldn't materialize a Star, I would ruin their Christmas.

Part of me also worried about being seen with Fynn. Gossip, I learned the hard way, could ruin a career. And if this whole Star business went south, I didn't want him caught up in the mess. He'd worked too hard to get where he was.

"You're fitting in here," Fynn said at one of Chill's frequent stops for pats and compliments.

"It's a nice town. I'd love to stay." Even if I didn't get to keep this job, I could start a new event planning business, couldn't I?

People got married here, had parties here, business events. I'd seen how every festival seemed to bloom side events in and around town. Although, no one would trust me if they thought I was the one who'd lost their precious Star.

Outside the Country Store, Fynn hesitated. "Can Chill go in?"

"It's a dog-friendly town. As long as he behaves, he'll be fine."

Fynn sent his dog a warning look. "Best behavior, Bud."

Chill woofed and wagged his tail.

"The seasonal section should have plenty of plain tissue paper."

As we headed there, Chill got more attention than we did, and he basked in all the such-a-pretty-boys.

Fynn chuckled, sounding more like himself. "That dog is an attention hound."

"He's so sweet, even with the young kids."

I picked up a package of tissue paper. Fynn added two more to my arms. He also chose a pack of brushes containing various sizes and a plastic tub, the kind I would love to soak my aching feet in.

I paid for our items. As if my thoughts were neon signs of my plans of duplicity, my shoulders, and my chest got tighter by the second. Having Fynn there, so close and closed off, didn't help.

"I can't stand this," I said, through gritted teeth once outside, gripping the slippery package.

"What?"

"This." I gestured at his stony face with my chin and the package wobbled in my arms. "You, not talking to me."

He nodded once. "I'm trying to work things out."

"What things?"

"You."

"Me?"

"You left. With no explanation." His exhale sounded like a growl. "I resented you for years. And there you are. Now—" He shook his head, took the package from my arms and strode toward Town Hall.

I trotted after him. "Now what?"

"It's still there."

"The resentment?"

He shrugged, but his gaze reflected hunger. A hunger that tap-danced in my stomach. "Look, let's just take care of your problem."

My turn to growl. Neither of us wanted to get hurt again. This distance was good. Safer for both of us. "Fine. Fine. Let's just get this over with."

In the Town Hall basement, I sat on an upturned bucket, elbows on knees, Chill chilling on top of my feet, keeping them warm. Fynn painted layers of tissue paper with a small amount of water, then gently molded them to the Star form inside the red box and its cover. That infinite patience again, that infinite care. I wanted to know everything that had happened to him in the past eight years since I broke up with him after graduation.

Instead, I asked about now. "How did you end up in Foster?"

He shrugged. "Not quite sure."

"Is it where you want to be?"

"For now."

After another long stretch of silence, he said, "You were right. I needed to go to Spain. I just don't get why you left the way you did."

The million-dollar question. "There was so much going on. Aunt Poppy dying..." Poppy wasn't really my aunt. At one time, she'd been my mother's best friend. Before my mother had managed to destroy that, along with everything else.

"Mom got remarried." To a jerk she would divorce less than three months later.

"Dad only wanted me around when I was planning one of

his events." For free, of course. For a guy worth a fortune, he could be a cheapskate. "Then when I asked him for a testimonial to start my own business, he refused, saying he couldn't be objective. I still didn't know what he meant by that.

"That was also the time when he followed through on his threat of cutting off any financial support if I didn't join the family business." I couldn't see myself pushing papers all day, even if the vision behind the company was important. When you balanced planning parties with curing cancer, I could see his point. It just wasn't my passion.

And then there was Fynn. "You were so happy about the apprenticeship in Spain."

I wanted to cling to him, but it wouldn't have done either of us any good. I needed to let him go find his path. "And I needed to figure out who I was without everyone's expectations molding me."

"How would I have molded you?"

"I didn't want to hold you back, Fynn. You had such a great opportunity and such great potential. And I was feeling like garbage." I petted Chill's head and he sighed. "I took the coward's way out."

"I thought we had a connection. That we could talk about things."

"You would have wanted to take care of me. And I needed to know I could take care of myself. I had so many emotions burning inside." I lifted my shoulders and let them drop. "I had to go."

I left Boston and all the misery it held. "Eventually, I landed in Virginia where I slowly built a business I was proud of."

"Why didn't you call me then?"

"Would you have answered?"

He took in a long breath. "I don't know."

He waved me over. "Come help me. My hands are too big to get into the points."

He guided my hand deep into the Star's point, making my heart beat too fast. Those sensitive hands all over my skin. I shook the image away.

"Go as far down as you can," he said. "Be gentle so the paper doesn't rip. Allegra?"

The feel of his hand on mine seemed to warm the whole box and took my breath away. "Yes, gentle. Got it."

Chill poked his nose between us, and Fynn shooed him off.

We worked together like we used to back in college, in silent companionship. Then I went and ruined the moment by blurting, "I missed you."

His eyes widened but he kept working, adding the last touches to the job. "Okay," he said, arms crossed over his chest, scrutinizing his work. "This needs to dry."

"How long?" Having him here was wonderful. It was a torture. I didn't know how long I could stand it without making a fool of myself. I didn't want him to go. But he needed to leave for my sanity's sake.

He shrugged. "I don't know."

I sighed. "Let's go then."

I closed the vault while Fynn cleaned up and slid the tub and brushes beneath the worktable.

Once we were back outside, I said, "I'll make you lunch."

"You cook?"

I laughed, remembering my failed attempt to make him a gourmet meal our last Valentine's Day together. "I have improved since college, but don't expect much. I haven't gone grocery shopping this week and my cupboards are bare."

Not to mention that I was practically living on canned soup because what was the point of cooking for one, especially after a long day at work?

"Show me the tree the Star will go on," Fynn said. "I have to figure out the collar."

We backtracked to the town square, where the tree stood

right in the middle. Fynn and Chill wandered around the base, checking it from every angle.

"It's a Norway Spruce," I said, watching them from the sideline. "Something like eighty feet tall. It takes about five thousand LED lights to fill its branches."

The tree was perfect—branches, shape, color—from every angle. The Department of Public Works spent hours feeding it and taking care of it throughout the year.

Beside me, Fynn craned his neck up. "The top doesn't look sturdy enough to hold the weight of the Star."

"It isn't. There's a metal pipe secured to the trunk. A crane hoists the Star onto the top of the pipe."

Fynn disappeared into the branches to check out the pipe and came back out with bits of leaves and snow decorating his hair. I fisted my hands in my pockets to keep from sweeping them away.

"What's the verdict?" I asked as I led him back toward the apartment. "Do you think your friend can make a new Star?"

"Student. Yeah, it's possible." Then he frowned. "We may have a problem getting the finished star on my truck. It's bigger than I thought."

I hadn't thought of that. "Oh."

Then another worry hit me. The two halves of the mold were huge. How would we get them into Fynn's truck without being seen? I couldn't afford for anyone to ask questions.

9

"It took me a long time not to judge myself through someone else's eyes."

— SALLY FIELD

After a lunch of canned tomato soup and grilled cheese sandwiches, we headed back to the Town Hall basement with my hair dryer. An hour later, after my blow dryer had overheated and blown a fuse, the paper seemed dry enough. Prying the mold out of the form took infinite patience. Something I didn't have but Fynn did. He somehow unmolded both halves of the paper Star without a single tear or swear. Chill and I watched from the sidelines in rapt admiration.

"Even in paper," I said, "it's absolutely awe inspiring."

Arms crossed over his chest, Fynn scrutinized the paper mold. "I think I can fit both halves under the cap in my truck. I can paste the pieces together at the studio. Right now, I need more of the tissue paper to stuff into the mold, so it keeps its shape during transport."

"There's not much left. Will newspaper work?"

He nodded, already working on gently filling the mold with the leftover tissue paper.

I ran up to the suite of offices on the first floor and retrieved newspapers from the recycling bin.

With infinite care, Fynn finished stuffing the molds. "This'll give it more stability during the drive."

"We'll have to wait until dark to move this."

He raised an eyebrow.

I waved both my arms at the Star halves. "I can't have anyone see this."

If they saw, they'd report it to Regina. If Regina got wind of what I was doing, I'd get fired on the spot. I couldn't let her know I'd failed her. And I wanted, no needed, to stay here in Brighton.

"Right." He glanced at his watch and nodded. "I need to make space anyway."

The three of us hiked over to the municipal parking lot where Fynn's black truck barely fit in a space. Tools of all kinds littered the bed beneath the cap.

"Are you sure it's going to fit?" I asked, holding on to the tools he passed my way.

"It should." He opened the cab door and stowed the equipment on the back seat and floor. All the while, a stew of memories—Fynn smiling at me, laughing with me, making me feel cherished with the wildflowers he left by my dorm room—bubbled away in my chest. It took several trips to get the bed emptied, Chill getting in the way as if he wanted to help, too. Fynn spread an industrial quilted blanket over the bed. Although it was barely four, with the longest night of the year just days away, darkness already loomed over the horizon.

"What now?" he asked, shutting the tailgate.

More torture of having Fynn around and pretending this was just a transaction with no emotions involved.

WE KILLED time by driving to The Farmhouse on the outskirts of town and shopping for snacks for Fynn's ride back to Foster. Because there was no way Fynn and Chill would fit in Bee, we took the truck, and had to rearrange everything in the back seat so the dog could have some space to sit. He vultured his head over my shoulder, insisting I pet his chin. I made a mental note to stop by the bakery and buy some dog treats. I'd see him at least one more time when Fynn brought the fake star back.

At The Farmhouse, we took our time prowling the aisles. Fynn grabbed a handful of venison jerky.

"I see you still have abysmal tastes when it comes to snacks."

"Protein good," he said with a caveman grunt. He jerked his chin at the box with a personal size chocolate tart in my hand. "Better than sugar."

I put the tart back on the table. "You're right. All that sugar probably isn't good for me."

When we got back into the truck, he handed me a bag with a chocolate tart and my heart did a funny roll. "You bought me a tart."

He shrugged, but red crept up his neck. "It's just a pastry."

But it wasn't just a pastry, it was a reflection on his innate sweetness.

At Town Hall, I had Fynn back his truck toward the loading dock in the back alley, away from prying eyes. He'd barely opened the tailgate when headlights, then a spotlight, lit up the area. A police cruiser. *Fudge, fudge, fudge.* I did not need any complications.

"What's going on?" Officer Navarro asked as he swept his flashlight toward us, blinding us. He worked mostly weekends and I didn't know him as well as Micah Shepherd and Chief Hamlin.

"Hey, there!" I groaned inwardly. *Sound guilty much?* "My friend is helping me get some trees up to Candlewick Estate for the gala."

"At this time of the night?" he asked, unconvinced.

"A Town Administrator's job is never done." I sighed as if I was put-upon. "I'm way behind on my to-do list and trying to catch up before Regina growls at me again."

I felt bad for throwing Regina out as an excuse, but she did have a fire-breathing reputation.

Officer Navarro laughed. "The Dragon Lady. Gotcha. Need help?"

"No, we've got it. Thanks. We'll be out of here in a few."

He nodded and went back to his car. This incident would surely go on a report of some sort and, should this whole Star situation go south, it would surface again. I had to hope it wouldn't lead to a jail sentence.

I waited until the cruiser's taillights were gone before heading back in to get the paper molds from the trolley. "Let's hurry and get this done."

"Are you sure this is the best way to handle this missing Star problem?"

I shook my head as I pushed the trolley forward. "It's…all I've got."

"Sounds like it went missing before you got here. They couldn't blame you for it being stolen."

"They would." I'd learned that lesson time and again. Sometimes it felt as if I went through life with a Kick Me sign on my back. "This Star is important to the town, to its history, to its celebration. I don't want them to look at me as the cause of their unhappiness."

"You always did take things too personally."

"Yeah, well, I care."

"You try too hard."

"Thanks Fynn, that's a real nice way to boost a girl's self-esteem."

"I just meant that people would like you fine the way you are."

"Yeah, tell that to all the snotty girls who wanted Allegra-planned parties but didn't speak to her at school as if she had some sort of socially unacceptable disease."

Fynn shook his head but let it go. "I'm here for you, whatever you decide."

And he would be. The realization instantly doused my inner fire.

I helped him load and stabilize the paper molds. Somehow, Fynn managed to slide the Star pieces into the bed without destroying the fragile paper casts.

We stood awkwardly outside the truck, my gloved fingers knitted together, wanting to hug Fynn, knowing I couldn't. "I, uh, really appreciate all you're doing." I shrugged a shoulder. "Considering..."

"I have your back."

I stared into his eyes, saw the old Fynn, and almost cried. I looked away and nodded. "I appreciate that."

"I'll let you know what Emilia, my student, says about how long it'll take to make. If she even can."

I rolled my lips inward and nodded. "Thanks. I'll send you more information after I visit the Historical Society tomorrow morning."

Fynn opened the truck door, hesitated and raked a hand through his dark curls before he turned back to me. "Here's the thing, Allie." He stared at me with a fierce hunger that took me right back to college. "I could never get you out of my head. Eight years and seeing you again." He shook his head and his eyes creased with pain. "It's like it was yesterday again."

I got that. I could feel the ghosts of our younger selves dancing around us. "I know."

He stepped closer. "I can't do this again, Allie."

"I know." We couldn't go back. Not with that boulder of my leaving between us.

And yet, he dipped his head forward and kissed me. And I slipped right back into Allie, melting, sighing, yielding. My arms slid around his neck, holding on as if I were drowning. "Fynn..."

I kissed him gently. My whole being wanted more, but I forced myself to pull away. "You better get going before it starts to snow again."

He nodded, whistled to Chill, who busily watered the snowbank, and disappeared into the truck.

As I watched the truck pull away, a sense of doom leadened every cell in me. I was doing this. I was really doing this. I was having a fake Star made for Brighton. As for Fynn, I didn't know what the future held. But I didn't have to think about that. Not right now.

With a long inhale, I turned back toward the apartment. I was committed now. No going back. I would have to live with whatever consequence came from this star-duplicating scheme. "Are you ready for that, Allegra?"

What if it all went right? What if nobody noticed the new Star? What if the celebration went off without a hitch and the whole town was happy? "Now that would be the perfect outcome."

And something positive to add to my résumé.

"But what if it doesn't?" I asked myself.

I stuck my hands deep in my pockets and tucked my chin down to my chest, trying to leave the doubts behind me. I wasn't a quitter. I could do hard things. But my heart was sinking, and doubt was catching up. This wasn't a mic malfunction, or a catering mix-up. "It's my one chance to stay in Brighton."

Or your one chance to ruin your reputation permanently.

It was also my last chance to make up the hurt I'd caused

Fynn. How, I wasn't sure. But I needed to find a way to let him go, a way that would allow him to move on and have the happy life he deserved without the reminder of the pain I'd caused him.

Hoofing it back to my apartment, I was so lost in my thoughts that I didn't spot the danger in time.

"There you are!" a voice called down to me. "I've been knocking on your door for five minutes."

10

"Learning too soon our limitations, we never learn our powers."

— *MIGNON MCLAUGHLIN*

I looked up the stairs toward my apartment, at the woman dressed in a white cashmere knee-length coat, a red felt hat and matching gloves, that for a second, brought the image of Lady Macbeth to mind. "What are you doing here?"

"Is that any way to greet your mother?"

I stared up at her from the bottom of the stairs. "Hello, mother dear, what are you doing here?"

"Why, saving you, daughter dear."

"Aren't you afraid you'll die here?" I asked my mother as I unlocked my front door, reminding her of the warning about Brighton she gave me as a teenager.

"Desperate times call for desperate measures." She waltzed in, took in the tiny, nondescript space, wrinkling her nose when it didn't meet her exacting taste. The quilt, pillow and lantern that had made me so happy last night now seemed tacky.

"Beggars can't be choosers," I said, meeting her adage with one of my own. She couldn't have picked a worse time for her surprise visit. Which, naturally, was her M.O. I just had to hope that after a day of this bumpkin life, she would rush back to Boston and all its conveniences.

She sighed. "No, I suppose not."

I dropped my messenger bag on the counter, gave *The Confident Woman* a tap through the leather for courage, closed my eyes and counted to ten. Then I pasted on a smile and turned to face her. "So, to what do I owe the pleasure of this visit?"

She attempted a smile, but her lips couldn't move much. Probably due to all the Botox. "When you said you were in Brighton, I had to come."

As opposed to all those other times when I actually needed you. "Why?"

"I had to make sure you were okay."

I wish I could crawl into her head and pluck out the real reason. "Because of the curse?"

She hesitated, then nodded. "Aren't you going to invite me to sit?"

Eliza Campbell Livingstone did as she darned well pleased, never waiting for anyone's invitation. I was usually so good at putting myself into other people's shoes but could never quite get past Mom's overworked skin. "Sit down, Mom. Would you like some tea?"

"That would be wonderful."

She took off her coat and looked around for a place to hang it. With a silent growl, I took the coat, hat and glove from her and hung them, and mine, in the tiny closet. Then I took my time making tea.

She had to have a reason to come all this way. Mom wasn't a country girl; she was city through and through. A hardship was having to wait more than ten minutes for a food delivery, even though her orders were always complicated. And that reason, I thought as I stirred in exactly one teaspoon of honey into her tea, wasn't me.

"Thank you, dear," she said when I offered her the tea.

I'd made a mug of my own just so I would have something to do with my hands. Sitting at the opposite end of the couch, sipping in silence, the ticking of the analog clock in the kitchen, the rattling of the heat register in the living area, the eddy of headlights from car speeding down Main Street all served to tighten nerves already stretched too taut from an afternoon with Fynn. Even the chamomile didn't help.

When I couldn't stand another moment of this non-visit, I plunked the mug down on the coffee table and got up. "Well, it's been nice, Mom, but I've had a long day and I have an early morning tomorrow. Did you already make a reservation at the B&B?"

Mom made a show of looking at her watch. "It's barely six."

"I've had a busy day and I'm tired." I headed to the closet to retrieve her coat.

She licked her lips and carefully placed her mug precisely on the coffee table. "I can't go to the B&B."

"Well, I'm sorry, but that's all we have. The more rustic cabins at Fisher Camp are all full at this time of the year." I reached for my phone. "I'll see if Lilah still has a room available."

"No, dear. That won't work."

"What do you mean?" I asked, index finger poised over the phone to dial.

She knotted her hands primly in her lap and failed to meet my gaze. "The thing is that I..."

"Just spit it out, Mom."

She carefully stroked the skirt of the white wool dress over her thighs. A dress that probably cost more than my weekly salary. "I don't have any funds to pay for a room."

"What do you mean?"

Her face reddened and she stared at her lap as if it contained a treasure she couldn't look away from. "Rudy absconded with the contents of all my accounts."

"Who's Rudy? And what do you mean absconded?"

"Rudy was the man I was seeing." She attempted a frown. "I thought we gave you a better education. Absconded means—"

"I know what absconded means. How could this Rudy person possibly steal any of your assets?"

"He presented himself as a real gentleman." She shrugged. "And then…"

A conversation with Mom was either one-sided or like pulling teeth. "And then?"

"Somehow, he got access to my accounts and emptied them."

"Somehow?" I didn't like where this was going. How could Eliza Campbell Livingstone, the woman who was always in control, fall for a sweetheart scam? "Did you go to the police?"

She stiffened. "Of course not."

That would be much too embarrassing, especially if all her hoity-toity friends found out. "Well, you're going to have to. In the meantime, sell the house to keep afloat. That'll mean cutting back but, as you said, desperate times call for desperate measures. You can rent something cheaper while you try to get your assets back."

She cleared her throat. "The house is already over-mortgaged."

"What did you do?" I was losing patience fast.

"It's not easy being a single woman at my age. Your father's pitiful alimony stipend doesn't spread far, and he keeps threatening to cut it off. So, I had no choice."

"There's always a choice—as you've told me so many times." Keeping up appearances was my mother's main concern, even if it cost her the roof over her head. "Surely, it's still worth something."

"The bank is taking it back due to arrears."

I sat back down on the couch, fearing the real reason Mom had come to Brighton was to make her problem mine. "How could you get yourself in such trouble?"

Her nose lifted ever so slightly. "We didn't all have the advantages you did, Allegra."

"Right, it's not like you came from the wrong side of the tracks and had to fight your way to a better life." I couldn't deal with Mom and the missing Star and Fynn. Not all at once *and* keep doing my job as if nothing was wrong.

"Allegra, I'm in real trouble here."

"I get that, Mom. But I'm not sure what you want me to do about it."

"I do need a place to stay tonight." She looked around the tiny one-bedroom apartment that was nowhere near her standards of comfort. "Perhaps you could lend me the money to stay at the B&B you mentioned."

Considering I'd just Venmoed most of my savings to Fynn to cover the cost of the angel aura glass, that wasn't an option. "I'm afraid that's not in my budget either."

She frowned. "Don't they pay you?"

"They do, but I've had some unexpected expenses."

For the first time, genuine worry leaked into her voice. "Is everything okay?"

"As a matter of fact, no." I sprang up and paced.

"I knew it. I knew that curse was true." She stood up. "We have to get out of Brighton and fast."

"I can't leave. I have too much to do before the tree lighting on Christmas Eve."

"But, Allegra—"

I stopped and faced her, surprised by the firmness of my voice. "I'm not leaving. I like it here. I like this job. I like these people."

"Is a job worth your life?" Her chin joined her nose in cranking upward.

I pulled the front curtain aside and stared at the soft snow still falling on Main Street, streetlights gilding it like glitter in a snow globe. "It's the first place that's ever felt like home."

"You're breaking my heart," Mom said behind me. "Didn't we give you a good life? You went to the best schools, wore the latest fashions, saw places other people only dream of seeing."

I hugged myself. "I know, so greedy of me to want my mother around, to want a hug from her once in a while, to want her to tell me she loved me."

"I was there. I did hug you. And I told you I loved you every night when I tucked you in."

"Maggie tucked me in." Rewriting history was my mother's specialty. I turned back to face her, hoping that maybe I'd see guilt on her face, but no. The history-according-to-Eliza was truth in her world.

Mom blinked as if I spoke a foreign language. "You have no idea how hard I worked to make sure you..."

"To make sure what?"

She gave my question a royal wave. "Never mind, it doesn't matter. Can I sleep here tonight?"

"There's only one bed."

Mom glanced at the couch and closed her eyes. "I'll take the couch."

"Wow, you must be desperate."

"This is no laughing matter, Allegra."

"I'm not laughing." If she wasn't exaggerating and, if this Rudy person had stolen all her assets, then she was in a real pinch. And she was still my mother. "Have you had any dinner?"

She shook her head, and for once, looked as if she was on the edge of tears.

"Come sit. I'll make us something." I riffled through the

cupboards and the fridge and found both still bare. I had planned on going to Stoneley get groceries. Too late now. "I can make you an omelet. Or canned soup."

"An omelet will be fine."

I gathered the limp green onions, the green pepper half, cheddar cheese (which I was sure Mom would complain was too fattening), butter and eggs, and set out to make us both an omelet.

Mom perched on one of the high stools, watching me. "The curse is real, Allegra. And I am truly worried about you."

"The curse seems rather vague." I whisked the eggs with a fork with more fervor than the task needed.

"Yes, well, your grandmother had enough Irish in her to tell a good story."

"Isn't it possible then, that it's just that, a story?"

"The fear in her eyes was real."

I chopped the veggies, forcing myself to slow down so I didn't lose a finger. "I've been here three months."

"Yes, well, it's not Christmas yet," she said with a sniff.

"What does Christmas have to do with the curse?"

"Some sort of star." She tipped her nose toward my chest where the charm hung under my sweater. "That's why she gave me that ugly piece of jewelry."

The mention of the Star stirred the sour soup already sitting in my stomach. I had come to Brighton and the Star had disappeared. Coincidence or correlation? The curse in action? The eggs sizzled when they hit the pan. "The Christmas Star brings good luck to the people of Brighton."

She pointed at the pan. "I didn't realize you were so handy in the kitchen."

"Mom..." Her favorite tactic was changing the subject when it cut too close to something real.

She sighed. "There's a darker story behind the good-luck, public-relations version. And before you ask, no, I don't know that part of the story. Grandma said speaking about it would bring its evil to life."

I cut the large omelet in half, slid each half onto a plate and handed Mom a fork along with a plate. We ate our dinner in silence. I even shared the tart Fynn had bought me with her. After, to prevent any real conversation, we watched a Hallmark movie.

"So unrealistic," Mom said as the credits rolled by.

I switched off the TV. "Don't you think that in a crazy world it's nice to watch something warm, cozy, and safe?"

"I suppose." She reached for my hand and jostled it. "I did enjoy spending this time with you tonight."

Buttering me up so I wouldn't kick her to the curb. "Did you bring a suitcase?"

"In my car."

"I'll go get it for you."

She scrunched at the window and pointed to a white BMW covered with a film of snow beneath a streetlight farther down Main Street. "That's it there."

"You could sell it and buy something cheaper," I said, reaching for my coat.

"Yes, well, let's hope it doesn't come to that."

I nearly chuckled out loud. Even in dire straits, Mom couldn't give up all her comforts. "Because of the snow, I'll have to move it, or you'll get towed."

"Do what you must." She handed me her key fob.

While I was gone, Mom did the dishes, something I hadn't expected at all. Eliza Campbell Livingstone resisted getting her hands dirty. She must really be in trouble. I lugged her giant bag to the bedroom and dumped it on the bed. "I'll let you have the room."

Her gaze went to the sofa, then she sighed. "Thank you, Allegra. I appreciate it."

I made up a bed on the sofa with the extra sheets and blankets, waited an eternity while Mom went through her extensive nighttime routine before I could go through my own five-minute toothbrushing and face washing.

And as I drifted off to sleep on the lumpy, too-short sofa, trying to sort out what I was going to do about Mom, Fynn and the Star, my mother's soft sobs stirred guilt.

11

"It is best to act with confidence, no matter how little right you have to it."

— *LILLIAN HELLMAN*

On Monday morning, after my usual email check and task management program check, I looked up the hours for the Historical Society. While my coffee brewed, I discovered they were closed on Mondays as well as Sundays. My visit there would have to wait another day. Instead, I made an appointment with Robin to go see the venue for the gala. Then I went out and got Mom a muffin for breakfast and had a key for the apartment made for her at the Country Store. I left her a note, then headed off to work.

I wasn't going to lie, getting away from my mother was a relief. As soon as I arrived at Town Hall, I was snowed under an avalanche of vendor contracts for the Chocolate Festival in February, insurance policy renewals and questions from Regina, the staff, and residents, including Pauline Hurst.

She stormed into my office without knocking, demanding I

file her declaration of candidacy paperwork for the March elections. She looked like a washed-out version of Regina—sharp gray coat, smashed-berry cap placed on her dyed blonde bob at a jaunty angle, and enough make-up that she would need a trowel to remove it. Did she expect a television camera to pop out of nowhere to document her filing as if she were a presidential candidate?

Usually, I was more than glad to help a citizen with their problems. I quite enjoyed that part of my job. Since Senator Travis Becker, though, people who stepped all over others to raise themselves up made me want to bite back.

"You'll need to see the town clerk for that," I said, trying to refocus on the insurance document that someone had written in enough over-the-top legalese to give a linguist a headache.

"Lucy always took care of it for me."

I waved to my inbox. Yes, it was a passive-aggressive move, but she was getting under my skin faster than a splinter. "Leave it there, then."

"I insist you file it now."

"I'm swamped right now." As if on cue, the phone on my desk rang.

Before I could pick up the receiver, Pauline put a hand over it. "Do you know who I am?"

Oh, wrong move, lady. "A resident of Brighton."

"I am Mrs. Frederick Hurst." She enunciated every syllable as if she were introducing a star on a talk show.

"Okay." The name did tickle a memory. I had to swallow a groan. Lucy's notes. Apparently, this woman was a giant pain in the behind.

"My husband is a New Hampshire senator," Pauline said with a huff.

Just what I needed, to deal with another entitled senator. "The clerk is better suited to make sure everything is filed correctly for you."

"This is outrageous!"

At that moment, Regina strode in. "Causing trouble again, Pauline?"

"You have no right to try to stop me from filing my declaration of candidacy."

"Nobody's stopping you." Regina waved her arm toward the town clerk's office across the hall. "Lenora, whose job it is to do the filing, will be glad to help you."

Pauline narrowed her gaze, but instead of giving off fierceness, the way Regina did, the move made her look like a rat peering around a dumpster. "You think you're so high and mighty, but your reign is about to end."

"So you've said every election since the 90s." Regina dismissed her comment with a wave of her hand.

Pauline leaned forward. "I know your secret."

"I'm an open book."

Pauline gave a satisfied smirk. "Have it your way, Regina. The truth will come out during my campaign."

Pauline grabbed her declaration of candidacy papers off my desk and marched out of my office, boot heels resonating like cherry bombs against the tile floor.

"Don't mind Pauline," Regina said. "She likes to think she's a hurricane but she's really nothing more than an annoying pop-up shower. How are the plans for the scavenger hunt coming along? It's set to start as part of the Festival of Lights celebrations on the twenty-first."

"Almost done." Hadn't started because of the missing Star. I added that to my to-do list for tonight.

"And the Star?" she asked, and something about the way she looked at me made me wonder if she already knew the Star was missing and was just waiting to somehow blame it on me.

"Waiting to coordinate with Gus and Lon."

Regina tapped my desk once. "Don't wait too long."

"Of course not. I know how important the Star is to Brighton."

And to add insult to injury, just as Regina was about to leave, my mother's voice echoed in the hallway. This time, the growl came out loud.

~

"Mom, what are you doing here?" I was starting to feel like a broken record.

Mom was doing her socialite thing, introducing herself to everyone, shaking hands as if she were running for a position on one of her charity boards. "Eliza Campbell Livingstone. Pleased to meet you. Allegra is my daughter."

"Mom, please, stop." I grabbed her forearm and dragged her into my office, closing the door behind us. With a motion of my hand, I offered her a seat and took mine safely behind my desk. "Why are you here?"

"I wanted to see where you worked." She made a show of scrutinizing my office, most likely redecorating as she went.

"You've seen," I said. "Please go."

One eyebrow tried to rise. "Am I embarrassing you?"

"Kind of." I opened my hands over the sea of paperwork on my desk. "I'm busy, Mom. What can I do for you?"

"I came to see if you'd changed your mind. We could have you packed in under an hour and be on our way."

"To where?"

"Anywhere but Brighton."

"We've been over this. I'm not leaving." I picked up the wad of insurance papers and tried to focus on them. "The curse isn't real."

"But why invite bad luck when you can so easily avoid it?"

"Because—"

Someone knocked at my door, and it took all I had not to snap. "Come in."

Regina, toting another handful of files, opened the door. "Here's the budget—"

I often wondered why she'd hired a Town Administrator when she insisted on doing the lion's share of the work herself.

Regina arched a brow. "Mrs. Livingstone, how nice to see you."

"Likewise," Mom said and, as if she couldn't stand to be lower than Regina, rose from her chair and offered Regina a hand.

On the surface, this appeared like a normal greeting but the undercurrent of something less-than-pleasant flowed between them. Both their faces were frozen into an overly polite mask.

"You've met?" I asked, my gaze ping-ponging between them. When? How?

"A long time ago," Regina said, then turned back to my mother. "Have a pleasant stay." Which sounded suspiciously like, "Please leave."

"Thank you. I intend to." Which I interpreted as, "No way in hell."

Regina left without giving me the budget spreadsheet.

Mom smoothed the sides of her white coat. "Well, I'll let you get back to work. When should I expect you home?"

"I should be there around six."

She smiled but there wasn't any warmth to it. "Have a nice day, Allegra."

I couldn't help myself, after she left, I went to the door and watched her march down the hall toward Regina, standing outside her office as if she knew Mom would confront her.

"What are you really doing here, Liz?" Regina asked, in full Dragon Lady mode.

Liz? No one dared call my mother Liz.

"I will *not* let you or this town have her." Mom's words sounded like ice picks chipping at an iceberg.

"Destiny always finds a way."

Mom leaned forward with a snarl as fierce as any junkyard dog on her face. "Destiny doesn't stand a chance against me."

With that, my mother spun on the elegant heel of her leather boot and strode away, leaving me with a bagful of questions.

Regina watched my mother leave, then went into her office and closed the door with a sharp slam.

Why were they talking about destiny? When could they possibly have met? And why the antagonism between them?

The alarm on my phone warned me of my upcoming appointment with Robin at Candlewick Estate. Maybe, somehow, the Star had ended up there by mistake.

12

"You've got to take the initiative and play your game. In a decisive set, confidence is the difference."

— CHRIS EVERT

Coat on, messenger bag ready, I was about to leave my office for the Candlewick Estate when, out in the hall, Fynn's voice asked about me.

Regina appeared at my office door, Fynn in tow. "This is a place of business," she told me with a haughty voice that rivaled my mother's. "Not a ladies' social circle."

As if, I thought. All these interruptions were not on my to-do list.

"This is Fynn Sheridan," I said as if he were part of the plan all along. "He's a glass artist. I invited him to come look at space in the Christmas Village in case it worked out for an ornament-making demonstration."

Fynn blinked but didn't give away my secret. I was going to hell for lying so much these past few days, but somehow Regina, with her unreasonable expectations, brought out the worst in me. I wanted her to see me as someone competent. And someone competent took charge, didn't they?

"Do we really need an outsider showing us how to do Christmas?" she asked, eyebrows hiking to her bangs.

"He's from Vermont, so not that far away. He was on the cover of *Yankee* magazine last October and would be a good draw for nearby visitors. You were just complaining that attendance was down this year. I was showing initiative like you said you wanted me to do."

Regina tutted. "You need to clear these things with me first."

You can't have it both ways! "The opportunity presented itself, so I took it."

She harrumphed and left.

I wanted to growl. How was I supposed to keep up with her contradictory expectations? I scooted past Fynn toward the door. "Let's go."

Once outside, I stomped all the way to the public parking lot. "It's already been a day and it's barely eleven."

He gave me a strange look, then his eyes lit up with a tease. "So, you saw the spread on the Glass Studio in *Yankee*."

"Just the cover."

He flattened his hand over his heart. "Not sure I can take all this flattery."

"Sorry." I really should be nicer to the guy who might get me out of my current pickle. "Like I said, it's been a day already."

When we got to Bee, Fynn took my elbow and steered me to his truck where Chill barked and danced at the sight of me, cheering me instantly. Fynn opened the passenger door and Chill's tongue reached out for my face.

"Hey, Chill. I'm so glad to see a friendly face."

"What about me?" Fynn asked, climbing into the driver's seat.

"Have you looked in a mirror lately? You look... constipated."

He laughed and turned on the truck's engine. "Where are we going?"

Which brought me back to the present. "Sorry, I didn't mean to volunteer you for a job, but if this Star thing doesn't work out, I don't want you caught up in the mess."

"I do pressed-glass demonstrations at craft fairs during the summer breaks."

"You do?"

He chuckled. "Remember the homemade furnace in my foster family's garage?"

He'd somehow made a furnace from a used propane tank. "You melted glass bottles from people's recycling bins."

"If it helps you, I could set up a demonstration. I have some professional portable equipment these days." He grinned. "Nothing that'll explode."

That explosion had seen him kicked out of a foster home for the last time. "Why?"

He focused on the car parked in front of us and jerked a shoulder up and down. "So where are we going?"

"You don't have to come with me." Chill poked his nose between us, demanding attention.

"I turned in my final grades this morning, so I'm free until January."

I wasn't sure how to interpret that. Was he here because he wanted to spend time with me? Because of the Star dare? "I was on my way to the Candlewick Estate to look at the venue for the gala. And snoop."

"For the Star?"

I nodded. Chill plopped his head on the console between the seats, his tongue reaching for my hand. I ran my fingers through his curls, and he sighed.

"Oh, you know I love a good snoop." Fynn smiled that

crooked smile he always got when I dared him to do something stupid in college. "I'll snoop with you."

A warm sensation washed through me. Then, when sense kicked in, my shoulders, my chest, my hands, all tightened. *Dangerous*, I reminded myself. I couldn't let myself fall for him. Not again. I'd already lost too much this year.

I gave him directions to the estate. He whistled at the big stone house on the hill, overlooking the Christmas Village and Candlewick Lake. "That's some place."

Fynn gave Chill a Nylabone to gnaw on as he lay on his fuzzy blanket on the back seat.

Chill whined.

"He'll be okay in the truck?" I asked.

"We won't be long," he told the dog as if Chill could understand. Chill turned his back on Fynn and attacked the bone. "He'll be fine."

"He really does have attitude, doesn't he?" I said as we headed up the horseshoe entrance to the front door.

Fynn chuckled. "He does."

Someone had gone all out with the greenery and lights and red ribbons, making the imposing house somehow inviting. I pressed the doorbell and a carillon of bells resonated inside. A smiling Robin opened the door. His smile faded at the sight of Fynn. "I didn't expect you with company."

"This is Fynn Sheridan. He's a glass artist. He's here to scope out a demonstration space. We were headed to the Christmas Village, so I thought, two birds, one stone. I hope you don't mind."

"Of course not." He gave a small bow and waved us in. "What did you need to see?"

"The ballroom and the storage room with the props for the Festival of Lights gala."

"This way." He walked with a stiff penguin-like gait through a twist of hallways that transported me to an English manor with their Norwich rugs, wall sconces, and oil portraits of fox-hunting landscapes.

When he opened the double doors to the ballroom, I gasped, taken just as aback by the view this time as last time. Across the room was a wall of windows and French doors that opened onto a flagstone patio and offered views of the Christmas Village and Candlewick Lake in all their winter splendor.

"Wow! That's some view!" Fynn said.

"Isn't it?" Robin said as if he were responsible for the sight. "It's too bad the people of Brighton only get to see it once a year."

"The earl isn't a spring chicken anymore." I strolled to the center of the room and slowly made a 360-degree-turn. Fynn hung back by the doors.

"True." Robin frowned, so close that the overpowering scent of his cedarwood-and-musk aftershave itched my nose. "I'm afraid his health is declining fast."

I'd heard the gossip about the earl in town, how he hadn't really come out of his home in the past year. What losing him might mean to Brighton. "I'm sorry to hear that."

"This may very well be his last gala," Robin said. "So, we need to make it the best ever."

"I always do my best."

"She does," Fynn said, still lounging against the doors.

Robin turned to Fynn as if remembering he was there. "I thought you were a guest artist."

"And a friend."

"Ah." A flicker flashed through Robin's gaze, as if Fynn had just laid down a challenge.

I did *not* have time for this type of complication right now. Not with the Star missing and Regina riding me as if I were an obstinate mule.

"Do you have last year's plan?" I asked Robin, getting down to business.

"Of course. Let me get it for you."

When Robin left, I turned to Fynn. "You had to do that?"

"What?" The innocent look didn't work.

I got my tablet from my bag. I'd already measured the room and added the measurements to my planning program.

Robin returned with a file folder. "Here's last year's plan."

I pored over the plan. "How many people can the ballroom hold?"

"Five hundred."

"That's not nearly enough for everyone. Especially because we'll need space for a dance floor, a band, and a bar." If I didn't want the guests to feel overcrowded, then the numbers would be closer to 475.

"I instituted a ticket lottery this year to meet the fire code," Robin said as if he'd solved a major problem.

"That's fair." But it would still leave many disappointed people. And if there was something I hated, it was disappointing anyone.

"Of course, the board of selectmen and the Town Administrator get tickets."

Technically, I had to be there, ticket or not. And having a large slice of Brighton in one place would make it easier to ask questions about the Star. "Thank you, I appreciate that."

"You are the magician behind the scenes." His wide smile would most likely have another woman swooning, but I was too tense with everything going wrong to feel flattered.

Fynn snorted, then pretended to be entranced by an oil portrait of the original earl above the stone fireplace.

"What are the load in/load out details?" I asked, ticking off boxes on my venue checklist.

"Sorry?"

"When can the vendors start setting up and when do you need them out by?"

"Given the earl's poor health, I'd like it kept to a minimum. How long will it take to set up?"

"We'll need at least a full day, preferably two."

"That's not going to work. You'll have the day of."

Thanks for your flexibility.

I studied last year's layout and kept seeing Fynn in my peripheral vision. He was making it difficult to concentrate. But Fynn and his eye for space and all his talk about art in college had served me well in setting up events that had a wow factor.

"Here's what I have in mind." I slid a finger over the stage on the app and moved it to a new spot. "I think we should move the stage from here to here."

Robin stood too close to me, poring over the page. "Why break with tradition?"

"I'd like to invite as many people as possible." I drew lines on the plan with a finger. "The caterers come out from there. They have to cross in front of the stage to get to the buffet tables. This way, not only do the servers become less visible, but the guests will also get a better outside view."

Robin shrugged. "It'll be dark. It won't matter."

"The Christmas Village will be lit up and so will the lake after the Festival of Lights tree lighting earlier that evening. It'll look like they're watching a snow globe."

"Yes, I see that now." He pondered the view, then smiled at me. "You have a wonderful eye for details."

"Thank you. Plus, it will allow us to invite more people." I closed the app. "Can I see the storage area for the props?"

He led us to a basement filled with locked rooms like some sort of Bluebeard den from the old fairy tale. All those locks would make snooping for the Star more difficult.

From the pocket of his tweed jacket, Robin took out an old-fashioned set of keys and opened one of the doors.

Fynn gave me a signal to distract Robin. I gave a small shake of my head. He sent me that crooked dare smile. I almost groaned out loud.

Robin and I went through the white trees, the blue-and-silver decorations, the snowflake lanterns, the boxes of linens and boxes of white lights. At some point, Fynn lifted the keys and disappeared. *Please, don't get caught.* I wasn't sure I could come up with a believable explanation. These past few days notwithstanding, lying wasn't in my nature.

I worked hard to keep Robin focused on the decorations with a myriad of questions, scribbling notes on my tablet, then edged my way to the topic of the Star. "What do you think about the Star?"

"What do you mean?" Robin asked, clearing the top of a crate.

"It's the 110th anniversary, and I was thinking of having a special recognition at the lighting ceremony on Christmas Eve."

He shrugged. "I don't know much. Just some family lore."

"Like? I've heard the townspeople talk of it as a good-luck charm. Others have mentioned a curse. As an outsider, it's been hard to get people to open up."

"Yeah, I know how that goes." Robin sat on one of the decoration crates and invited me to join him. "I've been trying to help out Uncle Harry and all I get is suspicions."

I sat down next to him. "What's suspicious about you caring for your great-uncle?"

"They think I'm after his inheritance, but it's all in a trust for the town, so I have nothing to gain."

Interesting tidbit about the trust. Was there a way to break it? Was that why Robin was so solicitous toward his great-uncle. "Family takes care of family."

"Exactly."

Mom popped into my mind, and I shook her image away.

"Is the Star stored here?" I made a show of looking around. "I would love to take a peek at it. I hear it's magnificent."

Robin's mouth flattened. "I haven't seen it anywhere."

"That's too bad. Where do you supposed it's stored?"

"I'd assumed here because it's so precious." He shrugged as if he'd looked for it and failed to find it. Which, of course, made me wonder why he'd looked for it in the first place.

I pretended to write down more notes about the props. "What do you do when you're not taking care of your great-uncle?"

Pride straightened his shoulders. "I designed a personal financial planning app that I sold last spring to a major financial planning company. I've been looking for my next project since. Then a few months ago, my mother heard that Uncle Harry needed help, so I volunteered."

If he'd sold his app, then he'd probably made money and didn't need the Star. He was most likely a dead end, as far as Star stealing was concerned. Out of the corner of my eye, I spotted Fynn.

"Okay," I said with a sigh. "I think I have everything I need."

I rose, making my messenger bag fall on purpose and spill part of its contents. I crouched down to pick up the pieces.

Robin joined me. "Allow me."

"I've got it," Fynn said. He kneeled by my bag and returned Robin's key ring to his jacket pocket.

Robin saw us to the front door. "If you need anything else," he said, offering me his hand and holding mine just a tad too long. "Please don't hesitate to call or visit."

The subtext said, "Without Fynn."

"Thank you." I shook his hand and had to tug a little to get it back. "You've been very helpful."

I waited until we got back to the truck and Chill had finished washing my face. "So? What did you find?"

Fynn drove around the semi-circle entrance and back down the steep driveway. "Only that the owner collects a lot of junk."

"No Star?"

"No Star."

Another dead end.

When he got to the bottom of the driveway, Fynn asked. "Where to next?"

"Might as well go see if we can find you a spot to show off your glassmaking skills."

The clock to Christmas Eve ticked louder with each passing day.

13

"Start rewarding yourself for accomplishing small things. Celebrate those wins and use them to catapult you forward into your most courageous, confident version of yourself."

— FROM *"22 HABITS OF A CONFIDENT WOMAN"*
BY LOGAN HAILEY

With Fynn and Chill following me like a shadow, I opened the door to the apartment after a day that seemed to go on forever to find the scent of roast chicken filling the space. I frowned. "Mom?"

Her head popped up from behind the counter where she was making a racket looking for something in a lower cupboard. "Hi, Allegra. Supper's almost ready."

"You made dinner?" The queen of ordering out and losing in-home cooks due to her pickiness made dinner? I dropped my bag by the door. Chill trotted in and went to say hello to my mother, who greeted him with surprising warmth, given her reason for not allowing me to have a dog growing up was that they were dirty animals.

"I'm perfectly capable of reheating. I got us a rotisserie chicken, red potatoes and green beans from that grocery store in the next town over." She took in Fynn. "Good thing I got the large containers. Nice to see you again, Fynn."

"Mrs. Livingstone," Fynn said with a nod.

"I thought you were broke," I said.

She cleared her throat. "I found a few bills in your night table drawer."

Money I rewarded myself every time I did something hard. Money I was saving for a massage at the Spa in Stoneley. "Mom! I don't go through your stuff."

She tsked. "You used to love sitting at my vanity and playing with my makeup."

"I was, what, six at the time? Plus, not the same."

"That's neither here nor there." She waved to the stove as if it were a grand prize. "I provided dinner."

While I lamented the loss of the massage I'd looked forward to rewarding myself for getting through the Christmas festival season, Fynn, amusement all over his face, took my coat and hung it in the closet along with his. With a sigh, I shook my head. What was done was done. And not having to make dinner after the day I'd had was a blessing.

Chill, nose working as if he were on the hunt, sat by the oven, taking in the good chicken smells in big gulps. Mom flitted from cupboard to the counter, setting a table of sorts on the counter.

"How was your day?" she asked, adjusting forks and knives just so on red placemats I'd never seen.

"Long." I sat on one of the stools. How much time had Mom spent going through the apartment? She seemed way too familiar with where everything was. Good thing I didn't have a diary hidden under my mattress like I had as a teen.

"Fynn, what are you doing in town?" She folded pieces of paper towel as if they were linen napkins.

He grinned. "I'm going to do a pressed-glass demonstration at the Christmas Village this weekend."

"Oh, that's wonderful!"

After lunch, we'd spent the afternoon scoping out the Christmas Village for spots where he could fit his portable glass-blowing equipment and finally settled on Santa's Workshop. He'd give a couple of demonstrations in between the crafts for kids and sell his pressed-glass ornaments in Santa's shop. The arrangement seemed to please him—and Santa. And part of me was glad he'd stick around for a while. The other part wondered how I'd make it through without making a fool of myself and kissing him again. Having him around could prove dangerous for my well-being.

In spite of some of Mom's Botoxed skin apparently having softened, the rest of dinner was an exhausting affair with all of Mom's nosy questions to Fynn. Good-natured as he was, she could wear a man down. I couldn't blame him for wanting to escape.

"I'm staying at a friend's apartment above his studio," he said. "I should go check in with him." He ruffled Chill's head, and the dog wagged his tail. "I've got to feed this guy soon."

"Of course." I silently pleaded with him not to leave me alone with Mom.

He just smiled and shook his head. "I'll see you in the morning."

He lifted a hand in my mother's direction. My mother, who was doing dishes for the second time in as many days. "Have a good evening, Mrs. Livingstone."

"You, too, Fynn. So good to see you again."

After he left, Mom said, "I always liked that young man."

I snorted. "You said you thought I could do better."

"I wanted you to have options and not settle so young like I had to."

Rewriting history again. "You'll have to entertain yourself. I have work to finish."

On the clean counter, I spread out paper from a roll I'd bought at the Country Store and a box of colored markers.

Drying her hands on a kitchen towel, Mom settled on the stool next to mine. "What are you doing?"

"I have ten days to put together a scavenger hunt."

"I can help."

I tilted my head. "You can?"

"Don't sound so surprised. Where do you think you learned how to plan parties? I used to take you with me to planning meetings. And you'd play under the table while we worked."

"I did?" I didn't remember Mom taking me anywhere, not even to doctor's appointments.

She lined up the colored markers in order of the rainbow. "Until you got bored and decided you would rather stay home with Maggie than spend time with me."

"I'm sorry." Why was I apologizing? I hadn't done anything wrong. "Are you sure you want to help?"

"I'm not leaving Brighton without you, and you insist on staying, so…" She lifted a shoulder and let it drop. Where was this motherly ferocity while I was growing up? "I can't just sit here and do nothing. I'll go stir crazy."

Sitting still wasn't in my mother's nature as evidenced by the whirlwind nature of our relationship while I was growing up. She'd storm in, talk at me for a minute, then whirl right back out, reminding me of the Looney Tunes Tasmanian Devil.

"This isn't the same as one of your charity dinners."

Her nose cranked up. "I've planned plenty of scavenger hunts."

"You have?" I asked, doubtful. Of course, I had no idea how she filled her days.

"I have." She got up and dug through her purse for her

phone. "It used to be much harder but, now that there are apps that do most of the work, it's a breeze."

"You know how to use apps?"

She pinched her lips flat but kept scrolling through her pages of apps. "What do you take me for?"

"Someone who doesn't know much about electronics, given how many times you've hung up on me 'by mistake.'" I made air quotes.

"As I said, this is easy. Even a child could do it." She perched a hip on one of the high stools. "What kind of hunt are you going for?"

"I didn't even know there were types."

"Who's the Luddite now?" She laughed and, it was such a rare happening, that I couldn't help staring at her. "Outdoors? Indoors? The favorite one at home is Selfies Around Boston. You could do a Festival of Lights hunt. An ornament hunt. A light hunt."

I put up a hand. "Okay, okay. I get the idea."

I scrolled through all the messages Regina had sent me and found the one on the scavenger hunt. "Regina wants—"

My mother swatted the air as if the mention of Regina bothered her like a gnat.

"What's with you and Regina?"

"Nothing." She shook her head, a quick-quick motion that suggested there was plenty. "What does *she* want?"

Yep, definitely something. I shook my head. *Let it go, Allegra. Don't let yourself get sucked into Mom's drama.* "Something that lasts from the Festival of Lights on the twenty-first to Christmas Eve, so a hunt that lasts four days. She wants to hand out the prize at the tree lighting on the square."

"Then I suggest the selfie challenge. You can send the participants scrambling all around town for Christmas-specific items."

That was perfect, actually. "And it would be a way to include Stoneley and Granite Falls landmarks."

We spent the evening brainstorming scavenger hunt ideas, and by the end had a long list of Christmas items, landmarks and winter themes that would keep the most avid of hunters busy. They would earn their prize of a basket full of goods and services donated by local merchants.

"So how does this app work?" I perused the list of hunt items, checking it twice.

My mother picked up her phone and showed off the app. "You give your hunt a name, put in all the hunt items in here, pick your colors and themes and out pops your hunt. The hunters register, take a selfie with the hunt items and post them on our hunt page. That gives you an email list for next year. The first one to get all the items wins the prize. After you enter the items, there's practically nothing left to do. You post—"

"Look at you with the tech talk."

She chuckled. "You post the link, people sign up, upload their selfies, and the computer does all the sorting and counting." She flipped her phone down on the counter. "The downside is that they do charge a set-up fee."

Mom's charity events always had generous funds. "I'll see what's left on my Christmas budget."

"Look at you, talking budgets."

I smiled. I couldn't remember any time when things had been so easy between Mom and me. It's what I'd wanted for such a long time growing up. "That was a really good idea, Mom."

"I do have them sometimes."

She looked small and sad and vulnerable. Not qualities I usually associated with my mother. I reached over and hugged her. "Thanks."

"You're welcome." She pushed me away. "Now, go get ready

for bed. You look like you're doing to drop at any moment. I'll set up everything and send you the link so you can pay the fee."

And there we were, back to normal.

I hurried through my nighttime routine and by the time I got out of the bathroom, my mother was in the bedroom with the door closed.

On my tablet, I stared at the calendar. Fourteen days until Christmas Eve.

Between Regina, Mom and Fynn, I'd made zero progress on finding the Star.

14

"Once you become self-conscious, there is no end to it; once you start to doubt, there is no room for anything else."

— MIGNON MCLAUGHLIN

When I left for work the next morning, the Star was still on my mind, a thorn I couldn't extract. Fynn and Chill waited at the bottom of the apartment stairs and fell in step next to me as I headed to Town Hall.

"So, what's on the agenda today?" Fynn asked while Chill insisted on licking my hand.

"Work. I'm so behind." I'd had nightmares about a to-do list that kept unspooling forever and being chased by a giant glass star.

"Anything I can do to help?"

I stared at him, unable to figure out why he was being so helpful. The awful thing was that I wanted to ditch work and spend time with him. I didn't even care that I'd be letting down Regina. "The Historical Society opens at ten. How about I meet you outside Town Hall just before ten and we can walk over together?"

"Sounds like a plan. Chill and I will get the lay of the land."

"There are trails off both Candlelight Lane and Lakeshore Drive if you want to take him for a run in the Brighton Woods. Or there's the dog park next to the sports field off Birch Drive."

Running was how Fynn had controlled his frustrations while in college. His life hadn't been as privileged as mine. He'd always had to worry about where money for the next meal would come from, keeping up his grades to maintain his scholarship, working while studying to pay for housing. He'd hated it when I offered to pay for dates. And I'd hated letting him pay, knowing how hard he had to work. So, we'd ended up doing cheap dates—ice cream pints from the CVS, French fries from the local greasy spoon, student activities on campus.

I typed in the Brighton page URL on my phone and showed him the trail maps.

"Chill could use a run." He scrubbed a hand over Chill's head, and Chill gazed at him adoringly. *I get the appeal, Chill.*

I sent Fynn the link.

We stood awkwardly at the bottom of the granite stairs to Town Hall. I hooked a thumb toward the double oak doors. "I should go."

His smile held an enigma. "I'll see you in a couple of hours."

He turned, whistling to Chill, who whined and hesitated. "Come on, Chill."

After an inquiring lift of his brow in my direction, he trotted after Fynn.

That dog, I thought and smiled.

Then I sighed. *That man.*

I shook my head and hurried inside where Regina already sat in her office. As I strode by, she said, "Allegra, a word, please."

I inhaled, pasted a smile, stiffened my spine and entered

her office. What had I forgotten to do this time? "Good morning, Regina."

She gave a sharp nod. "How are the preparations for the gala coming along?"

"Everything's on schedule." At least everything on that front was under control. "Tickets are sold out. Menu and caterers are set. Band's confirmed. The set-up team is good to start bright and early on the day of the gala to keep the disruption to a minimum for the earl."

"I'm glad your out-of-town guest isn't keeping you from doing your job."

Did she mean Mom or Fynn? "Of course not."

"See that it remains that way. Christmas makes or breaks Brighton."

And the missing Star would definitely break it.

∽

THE HISTORICAL SOCIETY made its home in the boarding house where the earl had first lived after he'd landed in Brighton. Somewhere along the way, the white Greek Revival home with the front porch was renamed Spencer House. The downstairs housed the museum showing off Brighton's history. The upper floor held rental offices that helped support the museum.

I pushed the black door open, setting off a bell above my head. The scent of musty paper, dusty antiques and lemon wood polish filled the air.

"What are you looking for here?" Fynn asked, stamping the snow from his boots on the welcome mat.

"Other than details on the Star for you? I'm not sure. The Christmas Star's been part of Brighton for over a century. Maybe if we know more about its history, we can figure out who would want to...you know."

He nodded and commanded Chill to sit and stay on the porch while we went into the main room.

Agnes, the gnome of a woman who curated the museum's displays, seemed old enough to have lived its history with her thin white hair twisted into a low bun, her roadmap of wrinkles and her red long-sleeved, high-necked swing dress that most would classify as vintage.

"Welcome to Spencer House!" Agnes said, rising from her desk. Her smile smoothed out the wrinkles and added sparkle to her eyes. When she put on her round glasses, I realized where I'd seen her before—playing Mrs. Claus at the Christmas Village on weekends. "Would you like a tour?"

"We're actually looking for information on the Christmas Star." I placed a hand on Fynn's upper arm, and wished I hadn't when my body wanted to lean into his. "Fynn Sheridan is a glass artist from Vermont, and I wanted to show off our town treasure. With the Lighting Ceremony coming up, I'm also doing a write up for the website, so I need details."

The lie came more easily every time I said it.

"Ah, the Christmas Star. Such an integral part of Brighton. You've come to the right place." Agnes bustled over to a side room and a display case filled with photos. She launched into guide mode. "Do you know the history of the earl?"

"Some." Mostly contradictory gossip.

"He was a businessman," Agnes said. "His family immigrated from England after some sort of misunderstanding with the king that cost them their land. The family owned a cloth mill in Massachusetts along the Merrimack River between Lowell and Lawrence. He was taught by his father that profits were more important than people." She tutted. "That led to a disastrous mistake that cost the lives of one hundred and ten workers at the mill."

"What kind of mistake?"

"Apparently, some workers had taken to sneaking off early,

so he'd started locking the doors. To make things worse, he was cutting corners to keep the profits high to please his father. One day one of the machines caught on fire." Agnes' hands moved around her, bringing the fire to life. "Bales of wool and cotton, bolts of fabric, looms all went up in flames, along with the people working the factory floor."

"That's horrible," I said. "How come the earl is so beloved then?"

Agnes lifted the display case's cover and picked up a photograph of a young man with a drawn face, eyes filled with sorrow that reached through the camera to the onlooker. "The earl's story is one of redemption. The death of all those people weighed heavily on his conscience. His father rebuilt the mill, but the younger earl couldn't stand the sight. He gave away his share of the family fortune to the families of the people who died."

She placed the photograph back in its spot. "He tried to escape the pain of his mistake by leaving home, but the tragedy followed him wherever he went. He wasn't welcome anywhere. When people found out who he was and what he'd done—" she tsked "—he was forced to leave."

"So how did he end up in Brighton?" I shifted my messenger bag to the back and leaned forward to examine the display more closely. "Why was he allowed to stay here?"

"Legend has it that he found his way to Ransom—that was Brighton's previous name—on Christmas Eve. The Reverend Father Bright found him in the last pew after the midnight mass service, all but dead. He listened as the earl poured out his heart. The man's honest remorse touched him. Because the Reverend Father vouched for the earl, he was allowed to stay."

"What does all of that have to do with the Star?" I waved a hand over the photographs chronicling the earl's life in Brighton.

Agnes pinched her mouth. "This is where to story gets a little murky."

"Oh?"

"In one version, the Star just appeared in a flash of light that lit up the sky for miles. And the earl, awed by its beauty, vowed to change. He promised that as long as the Star shone on Christmas Eve, he would make sure that the town thrived. He had a knack for business and kept his word. The Star has shone every single Christmas Eve, and Brighton has thrived." Her smile turned impish. "Of course, this is the version we like to promote. It has more pizazz."

Correlation didn't imply causation, but I kept my doubts about magic lights to myself. And, of course, the magic angle did make for a good story.

Local legend also said that if the Star didn't shine, bad luck would befall Brighton. And I'd get the blame because they would see me as the one who lost their precious Star. "You mentioned another version of the story?"

Agnes lifted a photo that showed the earl and another man standing side by side, the Star between them, a woman on either side of each man. "In the other version of the story, the earl had the Star built by a local craftsman as his promise to help the town thrive." Her voice softened. "The earl has more than kept his promise. There's no other place like Brighton."

This version of the story made more logical sense. Magic worked great to stir curiosity and draw in tourists, but it didn't really exist. And if a real person created the Star, then Fynn's friend could recreate it. The important thing was to have a Star present for the tree lighting on Christmas Eve.

"Who's the artist?" Fynn asked.

Agnes squinted at the fuzzy black-and-white photo and her voice hardened as if she held a grudge against this long-ago dead man. "Amos Thannen, originally from Germany."

"You don't like him?" I asked.

She shook her head. "He put a curse on Brighton. If the Star doesn't shine, the town will die."

"That seems a little drastic," Fynn said.

Agnes sniffed. "We don't take our prosperity for granted. And curses, if enough people believe in them, can come to pass." She shivered. "I dread to find out what would happen if the Star didn't shine."

I swallowed hard. Yet another reason to make sure Brighton got its Star back. Because the people of this town *did* believe in the curse. And as Agnes said, it would trigger the nocebo effect, where a negative outcome occurred due to belief.

"And the women standing behind them, who are they?" I asked. There was something familiar about the small woman standing next to the earl. Not so much in her looks but in how she stood, as if she wanted to disappear into the background.

Agnes' arthritic finger pointed to the side of the earl. "That's Nell Brochan. Her mother ran this house, which was a boarding house back then. Nell took care of the earl while he recovered after his collapse in the church. Then she went with him as his housekeeper after he built his own cabin." Her finger moved to the woman standing next to Amos Thannen. "That's Sarah Bright, the Reverend Father Bright's sister. She took care of her brother and later married Amos. The couple left soon after this photograph was taken. Apparently, the earl and Amos had a falling out. That's when they say Amos cursed the earl and Brighton. No one ever heard from Amos or Sarah again."

Bad blood, payback, retaliation for perceived harm. Those were all good motives for the theft. But why now? Why so long after the original pain point of leaving Brighton? "Do you know what their argument was about?"

Agnes shrugged. "No one knows for sure."

"Do you think it had something to do with the Star?" I asked.

"I have no idea, hon. It all happened before my time."

"Of course." I tilted my head, studying the photograph. "Amos looks familiar. Does he have family still living in town?"

"Not that I know of."

"What about the Reverend Father Bright, does he still have family in town?"

"He left soon after his sister did." Her features pinched. "Just after the town was renamed to honor him."

There was something odd about the exodus of the priest and the artist so soon after the earl decided to stay in town.

"Rumor has it that someone tried to steal the Star once." I tried to sound as casual as I could. "Is that true?"

"That happened, oh, twenty-some-odd years ago." Agnes replaced the photo in the case and closed the cover. "They were caught in the act."

"Why did they steal it?"

"Who knows? Because it has brought Brighton so much good luck, there are those who would like to gather that good luck for themselves. What they don't understand is that the Star was a gift to the earl and its 'magic,'" —she made air quotes— "works only for the earl or one of his descendants. It works only for Brighton."

That connection to the earl put his nephew Robin at the head of the list.

"Who tried to steal the Star?" Fynn asked.

She smiled as if she'd bitten into a lemon. "Some no-good-kins from Stoneley."

Royce Tanner had worked for the town of Stoneley for at least twenty years. And he'd mentioned how he'd wished he'd thought of the Star story. Could he have engineered a theft attempt? He was already at the top of the suspect list. I needed to find out more about him.

Agnes led us to a leather-covered album. She donned white cotton gloves and handed us each a pair she plucked from the pocket of her dress. "This album contains photos of the Star over the years."

Each photo was dated with a handwriting that could pass as calligraphy. "The earl has said more than once that the Star belongs to the people of Brighton. It's a symbol of hope and renewal for the community. He never meant it to belong to one person like some people think it should."

"Like who?" I asked.

"The earl's niece for one. The earl never married and never had children, so he doesn't have any direct descendants, but there are plenty of people who try to claim kinship with the hope of getting their hands on the Star and his fortune."

Success seemed to bring out the leeches. They could have used the energy expended on trying to get something for nothing to build their own successes.

"His hope was that it would guide lost souls home," Agnes went on. "He believed that as long as the Star shone, it would protect the town and bring it prosperity."

"The craftsmanship is superb," Fynn said. "A real masterpiece. I wish I could see the real thing."

"You'll have to wait until Christmas Eve." Agnes pointed her chin at the album. "The Star is made from a rare type of crystal-infused glass. It's what makes it look as if it's glowing from the inside."

Was that the same as the angel aura glass Fynn mentioned?

Fynn bent closer to the album, studying the Star. "Do you have anything that shows the construction more clearly?"

"What?" Agnes asked, her Mrs. Claus smile bright with laughter. "You want to copy it?"

He launched her his best smile, one I hadn't seen since I'd found him again, and my heart answered with a yearning that made me reach for it. "As an artist, I'm curious, that's all."

Agnes bustled to a drawer where she withdrew a sketchbook that looked as if it was about to fall apart. She carefully laid it on the table at the center of the room and gently turned the pages until she found what she was looking for. "Here are some drawings made by Amos Thannen."

Fynn sent me a look over Agnes' head. The sketches showed the Star's collar and armature—exactly what Fynn was looking for.

He took out his phone. "May I?"

She hesitated, then shrugged.

Fynn took pictures of the sketches. "Thank you."

"Yes, Agnes, thank you so much for your time," I said. I wasn't sure that anything I'd learned brought me closer to finding the Star, but at least its history was clearer.

"Make sure you sign the visitor's book before you leave." She winked at me. "You know how the town budget works. If I can't prove that we get enough visitors, my funding will get cut."

I laughed. "I don't think you have to worry."

We headed over to the podium by the door where the guest book, along with a pen on a string waited. As I scribbled my name, I noticed a series of entries.

"Look!" I whispered, and pointed at a name, one that showed up at regular intervals. I took a photo with my phone and flipped back through the book, noting that Royce Tanner had visited at least once a month for the past year.

"Who's Royce Tanner?" Fynn asked.

"A prime suspect." I turned to Agnes, who'd taken her seat at her desk. "Agnes, why is Royce Tanner visiting Brighton's Historical Society? Doesn't he live in Stoneley?"

She shrugged. "He says he's doing family research."

"Was his family originally from Brighton?"

"It's a possibility." The antique phone at her desk rang and she answered it. "Brighton Historical Society!"

"What are you thinking?" Fynn asked as we exited Spencer House.

"I'm not sure." I needed time to let all the little pieces of information marinate.

Chill had taken a spot on the wicker couch on the porch. His tail thumped at the sight of us. Fynn dug out a dog biscuit. "There's a good dog."

Chill made quick work of the treat and followed us down the short brick path. Having been a good dog for so long, he took off on the lawn and romped in the snow, coating his hairy feet in icy balls of snow, looking like a yeti. Fynn whistled, and Chill took the long way around to meet us on the sidewalk.

As we made our way back toward Town Hall, the wind bit my cheeks, but I hardly noticed. "Do you think a descendant of Amos Thannen might want the Star back?"

"Anything's possible," Fynn said. "Are you any good at genealogy?"

"No." I groaned. "But I know someone who is."

15

"You wouldn't worry so much about what others think of you if you realized how seldom they do."

— ELEANOR ROOSEVELT

To get out of the way of foot traffic, I pressed into the alcove leading to the Knit and Piece. Herded by Chill, Fynn crowded in next to me, his heat radiating all the way down to my bones. I looked up, his lips so close all I'd have to do is lean an inch forward to kiss him. I tamped down the thought and concentrated on finding my phone in my bag. Chill's tail beat a tattoo against my wool pants while he tapped paws with Rona's white Great Pyrenees dog across the display window glass.

"Mom?" I said when she answered. "Where are you?"

"Some place called Bob's House Brewery and Pub."

This type of establishment was so below my mother's standard that I couldn't help asking, "Why?"

"I'm testing the scavenger hunt, and this is one of the stops you chose."

Right, I had. Bob's House featured an old-fashioned phone booth he'd remodeled to look like a bob house, complete with hole in the ground covered with acrylic ice. It made for a popular selfie spot. "Stay there," I said. "We'll be right there. I'll buy you lunch."

"Not to look a gift horse in the mouth, but lunch? Here?"

"Kenny's a great cook."

"If you say so." Doubt filled her voice.

"We'll be there in five."

Fynn and I hoofed it to Old Town Road, Chill crossing and recrossing our path, thinking this was a fine game.

Once there, I made a quick scan of the room and found Mom sitting at one of the long wooden tables, her posture perfect, as usual. Seeing her made me straighten my own spine. Kenny placed an ornate drink in front of her, and Mom chatted with him as if he were an old friend. For all her faults, Mom had a way of putting people, even strangers, at ease.

Taking a deep breath and digging for a smile, I strode toward her. What surprised me was the drink. Liquid the color of a brown ale filled a beer stein. A skewer of orange slices and a dollop of cream decorated the whole. Because her mother had been an alcoholic who died of liver failure at a young age, Mom never drank. And that had led to way too many lectures about the evils of alcohol during my teens.

"What's this?" I asked, peeling off my scarf, hat and gloves, and taking a seat across the table from her. Fynn led a reluctant Chill to the dog play area in the corner by the bar where Kenny's two rescue Dachshund-mix dogs spent the day hoping to meet new playmates.

"Is that any way to greet your mother?"

I sighed, noticing she'd borrowed my one cashmere sweater, an end-of-season gift to myself a few years ago. "Hello, mother dear. How are you?"

"I'm well." She tipped her chin at her glass. "This is a signature mocktail Kenny created just for me. He's calling it the Eliza."

Of course, he was. "It looks delicious. What's in it?"

"Something called chocolate chai. The oranges bring out the exotic spices in the tea and blends well with the chocolate." Mom waved a hand at Kenny behind the bar. "She'll have one of these." She turned to Fynn, who sat next to me, close enough for his heat to reach right through my sweater and creep up my neck. "And you?"

Fynn gave the drink a doubtful look. "I'll pass."

"Your loss." She took a sip of her drink and carefully placed it back on the coaster. "So, what is so pressing that we need to ingest grease for lunch?"

I studied the menu, "Kenny makes a killer salad with microgreens he grows in his kitchen."

"Really?"

"You'll love the warm bowl with quinoa, roasted sweet potatoes, spinach and cranberries." Kenny's menu contained what you'd expect at a brewery—nachos, burgers and wings—but also healthier options like hummus and veggies, salads and flatbreads. Not to mention, he was famous for his twelve-layer chocolate cake. Which was what I craved to order but wouldn't. I didn't need the sugar rush to spike my already ragged pulse. Or my mother's disapproval at my poor dietary choices. She prided herself on having gained *not so much as an ounce* since her wedding day. Never mind that she'd had a baby somewhere in there.

We ordered, and Mom studied my outfit. "Is that what you're wearing to work today?"

"I have a lot of running around to do." My sweater, jacket and wool pants were appropriate for the job. Regina had never complained.

"People judge you within seconds, you know." Mom tried to hike an eyebrow. "Are you sure you want to convey that casual of an impression? You hold a position of influence. The town has given you a lot of responsibility for someone so young."

She still saw me as the teenager I was when I left home twelve years ago.

"We're in Brighton, not Boston." I swallowed a groan by sipping the mocktail she'd ordered for me.

"Still, it doesn't hurt to put your best foot forward," Mom said.

"I think she looks wonderful." Fynn smiled at my mother and took my hand beneath the tabletop, squeezing it in reassurance, instantly relaxing me.

She cocked an eye at his jeans and navy ski sweater that heightened the breadth of his shoulders, obviously finding it lacking. "Yes, well..."

"And she knows what she's doing. Her events run smoothly."

She gave a dismissive flick of her hand. "And how many events have you gone to?"

"You'd be surprised."

"Fynn's well-known in his profession." You'd think that in her current cash-constrained condition she'd have a little more compassion for others, but no, apparently not. She was still a judgmental snob.

"What have you sold lately?" she asked, because selling was more important than creating in Mom's book. The only thing with meaning to her seemed to be money.

"Mother!"

Fynn let her critical comments roll off his wide shoulders as if they were nothing but annoying rain drops. "You've heard of the Glass Garden at the New York Botanical Gardens?"

She nodded, toying with the straw in her drink.

"The Wildflower exhibit is mine."

"Oh." She was impressed but there was no way she'd ever let Fynn know.

"Aw, wildflowers?" I said, my voice going gooey.

He tilted his head and gave a shy shrug while red crept up his neck.

Mom's gaze ping-ponged between us. She wouldn't ask, and I wouldn't tell her that wildflowers were Fynn's love language in college. I'd open my dorm room door in the morning and find a flower or two he'd picked somewhere. They never failed to cheer me, and I'd carry them with me all day. A pang of yearning for those simpler days hit me harder than I expected, and I choked on a mouthful of mocktail.

"I see," Mom said, though she had no idea. "What—"

Before the barbs got too sharp and dug into Fynn too deeply, I interrupted. "I wanted to ask you about genealogy."

"What about it?"

"Remember how you looked up Dad's family?" And made me suffer through lectures on the importance of my roots, how lucky I was to have come from such good Boston Brahmin stock, filled with Winthrops and Warrens and Winslows and governors and magistrates. How I should appreciate my history. Although, come to think of it, she never mentioned her own family's history.

"Of course," Mom said, pleating the side of her placemat.

Our meals arrived. Mom studied her salad as if it required a permit for excavation.

"What's the best way to find out if someone's related to someone else?" I asked, digging into the best crab bisque I'd ever eaten. Fynn attacked his burger with gusto.

Mom pinched her lips and dug into the edge of the salad. "Other than ask them?"

"For now."

Mom launched into a lecture on genealogy that had me forcing myself not to roll my eyes. Ask my mother for the time and she would tell you how to build a watch. Fynn sent me a knowing smile, and I almost laughed out loud remembering how Fynn used to love setting her off on tangents just to see how far she'd go.

"What exactly do you need?" she asked, nudging a cranberry aside.

I told her about our find at the Historical Society. "So, you want to figure out if this Royce Tanner has connections to Brighton?"

"Yes." On my phone, I showed her the photo I'd taken of Nell, the earl, Amos and Sarah with the Christmas Star. "And also Nell Brochan, Amos Thannen and Sarah Bright."

My mother's perfect complexion seemed to blanch a little under her foundation. She picked at her salad, swirling a piece of sweet potato around her plate. "Don't you have enough on your plate right now without going on wild goose chases? I thought you had a gala to prepare for and a scavenger hunt and a tree lighting ceremony."

Two tree lighting ceremonies on two different days in two different places. "It's important."

"This kind of research can be quite complex, you know."

Why was she trying to put me off researching strangers? It made no sense. "Which is why I'm asking *you* how to go about it efficiently."

Mom's smile tightened as much as the Botox would let it. "Well, I can look for you later. Right now, I'm busy finalizing this scavenger hunt for you."

"I'm not asking to do it. Just how I should go about it."

"Allegra." Her tone had that broken glass-sharp edge that could turn cutting any second. "I don't want you to get overwhelmed by this research. You tend to take on too much, and I worry about you, especially because this job seems to mean so much to you."

I pushed away my bowl of soup when heartburn gripped my chest. I knuckled the pain, making it worse. "I appreciate your concern, but if it wasn't important, I wouldn't ask."

Asking her had seemed the most expedient way to find the information I needed then, but now I triple-guessed myself. In her eyes, I couldn't do anything right. "It's fine, Mom. Don't worry about it. I'll ask at the library."

"Well, now you're making me sound like an ogre." She pushed aside her barely touched salad. "You wanted this scavenger hunt ready to launch in ten days. For that to happen, every item needs to be checked and rechecked."

"I'm just asking you how to go about doing the research in an efficient way."

"Fine," she said, her chin hiking. "I'll do your research, but you'll have to do the scavenger hunt check yourself."

What had just happened? My head was spinning so fast, I wasn't sure if I was coming or going. Mom reached for her phone and went through how to do the check on the app so it could go live on time.

Once she was done, she said, "Give me the names again."

I dug through my messenger bag and took out a small notebook. I ripped a page and wrote down the names. "Sarah Bright married Amos Thannen and moved away from Brighton somewhere around the early-nineteen hundreds. I'd like to know where they went. Sarah Bright was also the Reverend Bright's sister. Nell Brochan's mother ran the boarding house where the earl stayed after he arrived in Brighton and then served as his housekeeper once he'd built his own home."

Mom took the piece of paper and snorted in an unladylike manner. "Housekeeper, pah!"

Fynn and I exchanged a where-did-that-come-from look.

"As a reminder, the app can't go live until you pay the fee."

"It's on my to-do list."

She stuffed the paper in her purse, then turned her attention to Fynn. "So, tell me about what you're working on now."

Unfazed, Fynn bit into his burger and chatted easily about the work he was doing at Foster College. I went up to the bar and paid for our lunch, feeling once again as if I'd fallen short in my mother's esteem.

She doesn't believe in me. I'd always been a disappointment to her.

My mother's phone rang like an old-fashioned rotary phone. "Oh," she said, a warm smile for the first time since we'd walked into the pub. "Excuse me, I have to take this."

She stood and headed toward the ladies' room.

"That was odd." I picked up my coat.

Fynn took my coat and held it for me. "Everything about your mother is odd."

"True."

Fynn nodded toward the bob house. "Let's get that first selfie out of the way."

"No, it's okay. I can just take a photo."

"What's the fun in that?" He took my hand and led me to the booth. "If we're going to do this, might as well do it right."

Laughing, we crammed together into the booth. I somehow ended up sitting on Fynn's lap, one arm tight around me, making me feel warm and safe as if I were in a cocoon. Close, way too close. I didn't want to leave.

Trying not to think about Fynn, about wrapping my arms around him, about kissing him, I took a selfie and uploaded it to the scavenger hunt app. "One down, twenty-three more to go."

16

"I laugh at myself. I don't take myself completely seriously. I think that's another quality that people have to hold on to... you have to laugh, especially at yourself."

— MADONNA

While we ate lunch, the skies had grayed, promising snow. I tugged my pink wool hat down over my ears against the crisp December breeze. I pulled out my phone and clicked on the scavenger hunt app. *It's Beginning to Look a Lot Like Christmas* chimed out as the hunt logo appeared.

I glanced at Fynn who was trying to clip on Chill's leash, Chill fighting him every inch of the way, tail wagging, tongue flapping in my direction.

"He really likes you." Fynn smiled up at me and my traitorous heart gave an unexpected leap. Yep, he still had it, the ability to render me stupid with just one look. *Dangerous*, I reminded myself. *Falling for that smile is dangerous.*

"Ready to start?" I forced my tone to stay casual, even though the warmth in Fynn's eyes made my stomach flutter. I had a job to do if I wanted to prove myself to Regina and, well, keep my job.

"Ready when you are," Fynn said. "Where to first?"

Once back on Main Street, I oriented the town in my mind and chose the nearest clue. "'At this time of the year, Santa needs a little help.' There's a photo of the giant present that's out in front of the post office." I pointed toward the brick building on the other side of the street that was once a train station.

Fynn and Chill fell in next to me, Chill's leash loose between us while the dog led the way as if he knew where he was going. The dog greeted every passerby like a friend and lapped up the compliments and pats. At this rate, we'd never get the check done in time.

Awkwardly, I leaned into Fynn to take that selfie in front of the blue-and-white present with a red bow. He chuckled. "You're going to have to come closer if you're going to fit us both in the frame." He reached for my waist and smooshed me closer, making my coat suddenly feel too hot. We had twenty-two more of these selfies to take. At this rate, I wouldn't survive the afternoon. Chill insisted on joining us, paws on Fynn's thighs, making him look like a hairy child, and us dissolve into laughter.

"That dog has FOMO," I said, stomach hurting from laughing so hard.

Fynn scrubbed Chill's head, and Chill leaned into the pats with an inane grin on his face. "He's an attention hound."

After I pulled the phone back, Chill barked at me as if he wanted to see the photo, his leash tightening and shoving me closer to Fynn. "Sorry."

"No problem," Fynn said, his voice sounding rusty.

"Two down."

We moved through town, from the library to the stationery store to the bookstore, to one of the three churches in this small town—the one where the Star supposedly appeared. There, as we took a selfie in front of the nativity scene, the Reverend Lowe came running out, coatless and shaking a fist over his head.

"What do you think you're doing?" Even though his skin hung thin over his cheekbones, small jowls hung from his lower jaw, red and trembling.

Chill braced in front of us, tail and ruff up, teeth exposed, growling a warning at the priest not to come any closer.

I pasted on a smile. "We're just taking a photo of this beautiful nativity scene."

"I won't allow it." He backpedaled away from the reach of Chill's jaw. "I know you're up to something with all your talk of the Christmas Star and tree lightings." His hands flayed about like flags in a gale. "I refuse to be part of whatever false god you're chasing. This is a place of worship. A place of peace. A place of solace."

"Of course, Father Lowe." I took Fynn's hand, making a show of heading toward the sidewalk. "We'll be on our way."

He crossed his arms over his chest and made sure we stepped off church property. Chill sent him one last bark.

"Good dog," I said, patting his head. "That is one angry man."

"Not exactly a man of peace," Fynn said.

"No kidding." I glanced at the app. "At least we got the shot before he chased us away. Maybe I should change that stop. I wouldn't want anyone feeling threatened." There were at least two other churches in town. I peered down at the app. "Next stop, the Country Store."

I was checking the photo we'd taken in front of the reindeer at the Country Store's window when Mrs. O'Connor waved me down. "Allegra! I've been looking for you all day! I must talk with you!"

Mrs. O'Connor had to be in her eighties, yet still managed to buzz around town as if she were decades younger. She was known for her helpfulness, keen observations and sharp wit. She had no compunction about letting me know how I was doing on a regular basis.

"Hi, Mrs. O. How can I help you today?"

"Allegra, dear," Mrs. O'Connor said, her voice warbling with excitement, "I saw something peculiar last night. I tried speaking with the police about it. They didn't take me seriously, and I doubt they will look into the matter. Then I sought out Regina, but the Dragon Lady was too busy spewing fire to listen."

Christmas was a pressure-filled time at Town Hall. "I have time. Do you want to go into the bakery to warm up?"

She shook her head, gaze darting all around her as if someone could overhear. "I don't want the wrong people to hear this."

Intrigued, I leaned in. So did Chill, begging for a pat. Fynn pretended interest in the storefront window's display. "What did you see, Mrs. O?"

"It was just after midnight, I was taking my nightly stroll through the town square, admiring the stars, you know," Mrs. O'Connor said, petting Chill's ear, and he all but purred.

"I don't like the idea of you being out so late all alone."

"Well, it's the only time I can get the town to myself without having to stop and chat with every busybody around."

I pinched my lips so as not to laugh. Mrs. O was most likely the one starting those conversations. I'd ask the night shift officer to drive an extra patrol around the square to keep an eye on Mrs. O. The last thing the town needed was finding a little old lady frozen like a popsicle on the town square.

"I was sitting on the bench in the gazebo," she said, "admiring the decorations on the tree when I saw a strange, luminous glow emanating from the hilltop in the direction of Candlewick Park."

"Was it the nightly light show on the lake?"

Mrs. O'Connor paused, brow lowering as if trying to keep her temper in check. "No, dear. It happened *long* after the Christmas Village closes. It was a soft, pulsating light, casting a shimmering aura over the trees and the night sky. It had streaks of green, blue and purple, swirling and intertwining in the darkness. It was as if the air itself was infused with...magic." She shivered. "I felt the vibration over my skin like a chill."

Did she wear a pacemaker? Did I dare ask? Could this mysterious glow be connected to the disappearance of the Christmas Star? No, that was crazy. I was grasping at mist when it came to figuring out where the Star had gone. Mrs. O had most likely been cold from sitting outside on a bench in the middle of the night.

"Do you think maybe it was the aurora borealis?" Fynn said, turning from the window and placing a hand on my low back, making me forget Mrs. O for a second. "The news said they're active right now."

Mrs. O'Connor's spine straightened, her forehead pleating and her voice taking on an edge of fire. "Oh, no, young man. I know what I saw. What I felt." She leaned closer to me, whispering now. "Legend says those lights appeared when the angels gave the earl the Christmas Star. It's the way the Star glows every Christmas Eve. If the Star's light is glowing now, then something is terribly wrong."

A strange sensation of heat and light filled my body, then a hum. Fynn's nearness? I shook it off. "Okay, I'll check it out. Thank you so much for letting me know."

"I knew I could count on you, dear." Mrs. O'Connor patted my arm. "You have a good heart."

She slanted Fynn a doubtful look. "You're not from here, are you?"

"Visiting."

"Then I shall forgive you for your impudence."

He gave one nod. "I appreciate that, ma'am."

I gave her a stern look. "No more midnight romps alone until I investigate those lights, Mrs. O. Promise me."

She blew out a breath. "All right. Please, let me know what you find."

"I will." After giving Chill a smile and a pat, she zoomed away.

"What do you think that was about?" Fynn asked as we resumed our trek.

"I don't know. She's sharp for her age. Not much gets by her. I don't think I have a choice, though. With the Star missing, I'm going to have to go to Candlewick Park tonight and see if I can find what's going on."

"Not alone, you're not."

My heart skipped a beat in anticipation. *Dangerous*, my mind reminded me. "I'll be fine."

"Maybe so, but I'm still going."

I sighed. I knew Fynn well enough that he wouldn't let this go, especially after Mrs. O's warning of something feeling off. Maybe feeling that impossible yearning was my penance for hurting him. "Okay."

At the bakery, the massive gingerbread house that had graced the front window, making a perfect selfie stop—and was the clue for the bakery stop—had disappeared.

"Oh, no!" I pushed through the door. Fynn stayed outside.

"This dog has a sweet tooth," he said, signaling Chill to sit. "I wouldn't want the place destroyed."

"Maeve makes dog cookies."

He hesitated, then stepped in, tightening his hold on the leash.

The scent of gingerbread and chocolate greeted us. "Hey, Maeve," I said to the woman behind the counter. She wore a headband decorated with gingerbread men and women to contain her dark curls. "What happened to the gingerbread house in the window?"

"Mrs. Hurst bought it." Maeve leaned down to place a tray of chocolate-drizzled pecan tassies in the display case. "I tried to talk her out of it, because now I'm going to have to redo my window." She hiked a shoulder to her ear. "But she offered me an insane amount of money for it."

Of course, it had to be Mrs. Hurst and her pushy manner. "I had it as a stop on the scavenger hunt."

Maeve reached into the display case and brought out a gingerbread girl and tipped her head. "Sorry..."

"How about having them take a selfie with a cookie instead?" Fynn asked, nodding toward the gingerbread girl.

I accepted the cookie. "Perfect."

Chill jumped up, big paws reaching to the top of the counter where his tongue reached for a tray of pecan snowballs.

"Chill, off!" Fynn tugged on the leash. "Those aren't for you."

I scratched Chill's ear. "Are you hungry? Maybe he needs a snack."

Fynn chucked his chin at the three glass jars filled with dog bones. "I'll take a large bone for this guy."

"Hang on a sec." Maeve disappeared into the kitchen and came back with a gingerbread man-shaped dog cookie. "I need a taste tester."

She came around the counter, and Chill offered her a paw. "Such a gentleman."

"How much do I owe you?" I asked, pulling out my wallet from my bag.

"On the house." Maeve's eyes twinkled. "I foresee many

gingerbread cookie sales in my future. When does the hunt start, so I can make sure to have enough stock?"

"Regina will release it during the tree lighting ceremony at Candlewick Park on the twenty-first."

"Perfect! That gives me time to bake."

On our way back out to the sidewalk, I broke off half the ginger girl cookie, gave a piece to Fynn, and took a bite. "These are the best cookies I've ever had."

"I can tell." He laughed and gently swept crumbs from the corner of my mouth. His gaze focused on the task a little too intensely, and a panicky feeling zinged through me.

Danger, Allegra. Danger.

Pulse uneven, I cleared my throat and looked down at the app. "Next on the list is the town square gazebo."

The gazebo's entrance twinkled with fairy lights in the building dusk. Soft snowflakes wafted down like feathers, sticking to everything they touched, giving the square a magical look as if we were standing inside a snow globe.

The white of the gazebo and the warmth of the fairy lights reminded me of the arch at the debutante ball my mother had insisted I attend my senior year in college. She hadn't wanted me to invite Fynn.

"Do you remember the ball?" I asked Fynn.

He groaned. "How could I forget!"

"Do you understand the hoops I had to jump through to get you invited to this ball?" Mom said, tugging on the itchy white dress that made me feel fat and ugly. *"The money your father had to spend to secure a table?"*

"You forgot to ask me if I wanted this."

She nodded at the seamstress who jabbed the dress, and me, with pins. *"The point of this ball is to meet men of your caliber."*

"Are you saying Fynn isn't good enough for me?" Because he was the best person for me. He loved me the way I was, never asking me to change.

"I'm saying an artist can't possibly support you in the way you were raised."

"I'm going to support myself."

I'd won. I'd invited Fynn. But Mom had also been right. Even though Fynn had made the most handsome man in the room in his rented tux, he hadn't fit in, and I'd felt bad for him. I hadn't wanted any of these entitled, upper-crust, well-connected boys who found only faults in me; I'd wanted Fynn—the one person who made me feel...happy. To my mother's utter dismay, Fynn and I had snuck out of the ballroom and enjoyed the evening outside by the pool.

"I still have the white rose wristlet you bought me," I said, blushing a little at the admission.

"Yeah?" The twitch of his lips had a vulnerability I found endearing.

I nodded, then focused on the town square before I got lost in memories again. "I think that's it for today. We still have half the list to go through. Sites in Stoneley and Granite Falls. So far, it looks like everything worked perfectly." I tipped the app in his direction, showing him the gallery of twelve selfies we'd taken, each photo getting progressively goofier. "I'll have Mom change the gingerbread house to a gingerbread cookie. And possibly the church to avoid Reverend Lowe's wrath."

Chill whined at our feet. I bent down and patted his curly head. "I had a lot of fun today."

"Me, too."

"Thanks for playing along." The wind kicked up, needling my neck. I reached up, patting my throat. "Oh, no. I lost my scarf somewhere."

"Let's retrace our steps."

Of course, we found it at our first stop: the pub. Chill trotted to the play area to greet his canine friends.

Kenny lifted the pink scarf from beneath the wooden bar. "Found it under the table."

"Thanks!" I nudged Fynn with an elbow and pointed my chin at the end of the bar.

Royce Tanner sat there, using the wall to hold himself up, talking at Kenny, who managed the occasional *uh-huh*, while serving the rest of the customers parked on stools.

"Hi, Royce," I said, wrapping my scarf around the collar of my coat. "Everything okay?"

He narrowed his gaze as if it took a moment to place who I was. "You! This is all your fault."

"Okay, what exactly is my fault?"

"All of it." He slurred his words. "All this Brighton this, Brighton that. Stoneley's just as nice and we're just a stop on the way home."

"Talk to Meredith Mills Carpenter. She's the Tri-Town coordinator. If you want more events, she can arrange something."

He scoffed. "The Star deserves what it got."

"Which is?" Was Mrs. O right? Had she seen the Star's aura glow?

Royce lifted his whiskey tumbler, sloshing out amber liquid. "Getting buried with all the trash at the dump."

I frowned. "What did you do to the Star, Royce?"

"Wish I could take credit." He laughed like a demented doll and raised his now-empty whiskey tumbler. "Good luck with your tree lighting ceremony Christmas Eve."

Fynn moved in on Royce. "You'd better start talking."

Royce laughed. "You don't scare me."

Fynn lifted Royce right off the barstool and held him up, feet dangling a few inches off the floor. *Impressive*, I thought. Who knew glass blowing could build such muscle?

"Your Star is gone," Royce said with a mean little smile. "It's been gone a while and none of you idiots noticed. And now Brighton will die. Like it should have a century ago. I just wish..."

"How do you know it's gone?" I asked.

Royce signaled Kenny for a refill. Kenny ignored him. "Overheard some hoodlums talking about stealing it last Christmas."

"Who?" Fynn asked, tightening his grip on Royce's crisp white shirt.

"Don't know. Never seen them before. Or since."

Fynn caught Kenny's attention and let Royce back down on his stool. "I think he's had enough."

"I've got his keys. Already called him the taxi."

Outside once again, Royce's confession about the stolen Star whirled in my mind. If the Star had ended up at the dump a year ago, then it could be buried under a mountain of trash. Unless Fynn's friend could come up with a new star, I was doomed. I waved a hand vaguely toward Town Hall. "I should get going. If I don't check in with Regina, she'll worry. I've already gotten several texts asking me where I was."

"Yeah, it's getting late. I should go feed the beast." Fynn tugged Chill closer, gaze lingering on mine in a way that had me melting. "What time do you want to meet to go to the Christmas Village to check on those lights?"

I needed to pull up armor around me. When this visit ended, I didn't want to have to cobble my heart together again the way I had the last time, even though I'd been the one to leave.

"I have to check in at work. I'll text you." I pointed toward the municipal lot. "I'll walk you back to your truck."

As I watched the truck pull away, wishing I could be with Fynn and Chill, my phone rang. I expected to see Regina's name, but Mom's avatar popped up.

With a sigh, I answered. "What's up, Mom?"

"Allegra, come home! Now!"

The urgency in her voice had me frowning. "What's wrong?"

"You'll never believe what I found." Her voice held a note of gloat.

"So, tell me." I headed toward Town Hall to check in with Regina.

"No, not over the phone."

And Mom called me dramatic. "I'm on my way."

17

"Your real work in life is to fill yourself til your cup runneth over so that you're never grasping and need, clamoring and insecure."

— OPRAH

After a quick check-in with Regina, I picked up a pizza for dinner. The scent of tomatoes, basil and garlic wafted between Mom and me on the counter between the kitchen and the living room. She had a pile of papers arranged in a fan on one side and my computer open to some sort of genealogy software.

"Ugh, no wonder you're so tired if that's how you eat every night," Mom said, accepting a plate nonetheless.

"You're welcome." I went to the fridge and got out the fixings to make a salad. "Can you spill your find now? Or do I have to start pulling teeth?"

"Well, it's quite fascinating." Mom's voice had an animation I hadn't heard in a long time. "I followed the Bright family tree. I had to go backward before going forward to make sure I had the right branch." She stopped to take a lady-like nibble of pizza. She frowned. "This is good."

As if I would feed her poison. I rolled my eyes and shook my head. "Go on, Mom."

"Yes, well. As you can see here." She pointed at the screen showing boxes and lines. "Amos Thannen seems to have simply disappeared. But when I did a search on his image, this showed up." The black-and-white photo on the screen showed someone that looked a lot like the Amos in the photograph at the Historical Society. "But one photo isn't enough, so I looked for more and found these."

The screen filled with half a dozen family photos—a woman who looked like Sarah Bright and two little boys, who appeared to be twins, hanging on to Sarah's apron.

"The names didn't match, of course, and I can't be one hundred percent sure." She clicked her tongue as if saying that, of course, she was sure. "But the first names do match. They simply changed the family name to Tanner."

"Tanner, as in Royce Tanner?"

"Exactly!" The fierce glow in her eyes told me she had more. She handed me a chart, finger jabbing at the sheet of paper, making it impossible to read. "They moved to San Francisco where Amos used his skills at the forge to make something or other for the building boom. And..."

Lips pressed tightly together, she practically bubbled over with excitement, leaning into the pause to create anticipation.

I sighed. "Mom, just spill it."

"Regina Buchanan and Royce Tanner are second cousins." She dropped the words like a bomb. "Their great-grandfathers, Amos and Sarah's sons, Walter and Ward, were brothers."

"Regina and Royce are related?" Which meant that both were also related to the legend of the Star through Amos Thannen. Was that why there was so much animosity between them? Regina had somehow cashed in on the family legend of the Star, leaving Royce behind?

"Yes!" Mom looked ridiculously pleased with herself, and bit into the pizza again as if she hadn't eaten in a week.

Why had Amos and Sarah's descendants come back east? Had they, like me, grown up with the legend of the Christmas Star? Except theirs had included how they got robbed of their legacy whereas mine focused on the curse? Did they want it back? Then why wait so long to steal it? None of this situation was making sense.

Except that Royce had said someone had stolen the Star last Christmas. Someone that wasn't him. Which meant it had gone missing for almost a year.

"Wait, does that mean that we're related to Amos, too? What with great-grandma's dramatic flair for the Star story with a curse?" Was that why Mom and Regina couldn't stand each other?

"No, of course not." But something about the way she suddenly felt the need to neaten the papers had me wondering if there was something to my question.

"So where did our family's story come from?"

"I have no idea."

"And you're not curious? You, who looked into every detail of Dad's family all the way back to England?"

She chewed on her pizza. "I gleaned enough from family stories to know there was nothing to be proud of. My father was a gambler who had a habit of losing. He had another family he was never going to leave for the likes of my mother. Do you really want to dig into that?"

Which, of course, made me even more curious. Could I figure out how it worked and do some snooping myself? After Christmas. After I'd figured out this whole Star mess.

With a jab of her finger, she clicked out of the genealogy

program. "But knowing that Regina and Royce are related helps you with the missing Star, doesn't it?"

I nodded, uncertain as to how exactly it helped other than give them motive. "That's great work, Mom."

She beamed like a child starved for a compliment.

"You'd make a good detective," I added, pushing away the pizza when the heartburn returned.

"Yes, well, that wouldn't pay the bills."

And there she was.

Mom closed the computer's cover and stacked it on the pile of papers. "I met a wonderful woman today, and she invited me to attend their annual Christmas basket committee meeting tomorrow."

I was glad she'd found something to keep her busy—and out of Town Hall. "That's right up your alley."

She smiled. "It is. Pauline—"

"As in Pauline Hurst?"

"Yes, you know her?"

"I sure do." She was a thorn in the Town Hall's side.

"Anyway, I'm meeting Pauline at the Community Center at ten tomorrow morning, so I won't be able to continue with the scavenger hunt check."

"That's okay, I can finish it." I was used to getting dropped off my mother's to-do list when some better offer came along.

I swallowed hard, wondering if Fynn would want to finish the job with me. The survival part of me hoping he couldn't. The masochistic side hoping he would. "We're halfway done."

I got the phone from my pocket. "Could you change the photo of the gingerbread house to this one with the gingerbread cookie? Apparently, your new friend bought the house."

"Yes, she's donating it as a raffle item. Isn't that so generous? For every basket someone helps fill, they get a ticket with a chance to bring the house home."

Okay, so maybe I'd misjudged Pauline's intent when it came

to the gingerbread house. She was still not my favorite person. "We'll also need to change the church stop. Reverend Father Lowe is going to scare away the scavenger hunters."

"Easy enough." Mom gathered her plate and used napkin. "We make a good team, don't we?"

Watching her expectant gaze, it occurred to me that, beneath the outer cactus spines of her personality and the aura of having her life together, Mom had the same confidence problem I did. "We do."

~

FYNN PARKED the truck at the edge of the fairgrounds, the headlights casting long shadows in the parking lot. Wind swayed the tree branches still lit with fairy lights and scudded puffy clouds across the dark sky. This close to midnight, the vendor tents were all dark, their red, white and green banners rustling in the breeze. No happy fairgoers strolled through the aisles or skated on the shallow lake. No cinnamon scent filled the air. No Christmas music piped out of the speakers.

I glanced at Fynn, his profile illuminated by the bluish glow of the dashboard, softening the rugged lines of his face. Chill popped his head between the front seats, his tongue lapping at my cheek. He looked from me to Fynn as if asking what came next.

"I should take him out," Fynn said, turning off the engine and breaking the awkward silence between us that had my nerves popping since he'd picked me up. The more time I spent with him, the more time I wanted to spend with him, and that was asking for trouble.

With a *woof* and thump of his tail against every surface of the cab, Chill scrambled over the seat before Fynn finished opening the driver's-side door. He didn't wait for Fynn to get out of the way before jumping out, his claws scraping against the metal frame.

Outside, the air was thick with the promise of more snow, an ironed-shirt crispness that filled my lungs. Chill bopped my hand with his nose as if saying *you're it* and took off barking as if wanting me to join his game of tag. Sticking my hands in my pockets, I glanced all around me, the midnight cold seeping through my layers. I was glad Fynn had offered to come along. "It's so weird to see this place empty."

"Which is why I didn't want you coming here alone," Fynn said, rounding the truck.

"It's not—"

"Boston, I know. But safety first. The buddy system exists for a reason."

"Is that what you are, my buddy?" I smiled at him, the words catching in my throat like sharp bites of ice.

Something hot and hungry flashed through his eyes. "Let's go with that."

The part of me wired for survival moved my feet away from Fynn toward Chill, busy sniffing at the snowbank by the entrance gate. As we approached, he bounded right through the slats of the gate, his tail wagging like crazy. We followed, my shoulder knocking into Fynn as if I had a hard time keeping my balance.

"Do you really expect to see anything tonight?" Fynn asked, his voice a warm contrast to the cold night.

I shrugged, running my hand through Chill's curls when he joined us, his fur thick and warm against my gloved fingers. "Mrs. O may be old but she's sharp. If she said she saw something, then she saw something. I somehow doubt it's anything magical, though." Chill took off again, sniffing. "Given that the Star is missing, and the lights are similar to what the town sees on Christmas Eve at the lighting, I need to check it out."

"I still think she saw the aurora borealis." He craned his

neck, looking at the clouds, hanging low and heavy. "Doubt we'll see much tonight."

"Still worth a shot. Maybe the clouds will clear up."

"Ever the optimist." He sent me a crooked smile. "Remember the time we went star gazing at the top of the Mars Center in the middle of winter?"

I chuckled, the memory bittersweet—the cold night, Fynn's warm arms, the belief that nothing could ever separate us. "Not our best idea. Orion's still the only constellation I can ever find."

I didn't mention how often I thought of him when I happened to glimpse Orion in the night sky.

"Same," he said, his gaze lingering on my mouth before sliding away.

I wanted to say more, to tell him how much I missed our time together, but what was the point? I'd lost that right the day I left without an explanation. I waved a hand vaguely to our right. "Let's hike the Woodland Walk. It'll help keep us warm while we wait. Plus, it's pretty."

Fynn whistled to Chill, who screeched to a halt, stared at Fynn and changed course to lead the way through the woodland trail filled with pines decorated in various Christmas themes.

Our steps crunched on the snow, stirring up my anxiety again, making my movements stiff and awkward. The silence between us stretched and filled with heaviness. I didn't know how to be around Fynn anymore. I wasn't Allie. At least not the Allie he remembered. He'd had fun with that Allie. That Allie had believed that, in spite of everything, the world was still a good place. That Allie had believed she could somehow bring joy to people. I kicked at a pinecone. Chill chased it and brought it back.

But that Allie had also hurt Fynn deeply.

Chill nuzzled my hand as if he knew I needed reassurance.

Then I remembered the handful of dog biscuits I'd bought at the bakery and stuffed in my pocket and gave him one.

"I've missed this," Fynn finally said, matching his pace to mine along the trail. "Being with you, going on your adventures."

My heart ached at his words, the pain a dull throb. I missed it too—the easy companionship, the comforting feeling of belonging. "You mean misadventures."

With a tip of his head, he acknowledged the less-than-stellar outcomes to most of my dares back then. "You certainly made life interesting."

I wasn't sure what to make of that. Interesting was good, wasn't it? He'd somehow made me feel as if I could do anything.

This Allegra was more restrained, less sure of herself, even when it came to events. This Allegra second-guessed herself at every turn. This Allegra spent too much time worrying and fearing the next anvil that would fall on her head and finally crush her. I didn't want to be that way. I didn't want to worry about what Senator Becker, Regina... my mother thought. I wanted to wake up like that naïve girl, eager to see what each day brought.

I glanced at Fynn, his profile as handsome as an ancient idol's. Somehow, I wanted to bridge the gap between who we'd once been and who we were now. Could we still fit? *Don't go there, Allegra.*

I pushed my fists deeper into my pockets and frowned. I couldn't erase what I'd done, not unless I found a way to pluck the memory and pain out of his brain. That hurt would always stand between us, a bomb that might detonate at any time.

The night seemed to press around me, and my chest grew a knot the size of the Star, making it difficult to breathe.

"You made me feel like a normal guy," Fynn said.

"Because you were."

"My father died when I was thirteen," he said. "Car accident on his way to work."

I nodded. I'd heard the story. His mom had died not long after and, with no family, he'd ended up a ward of the state.

"I never told you that my mom killed herself."

"Oh, Fynn." My heart ached for the boy dealing with two major deaths so close together.

"So, when you left, it brought up all those old feelings of..." He shrugged as if he couldn't quite figure out how to name those emotions.

"Abandonment?"

He nodded. "They all came back."

"I'm so sorry, Fynn. I—" But nothing I said would take away the pain.

As we rounded a curve in the path, a gust of wind sent a flurry of snow falling from the pine branches above, showering us in white powder. I shrieked as the snow snaked into my collar and melted. Hiking my shoulders to stop the icy rivulet, I stumbled, reaching out instinctively. Fynn's strong artist's hand caught my arm, steadying me, a reminder of how safe I'd once felt in his arms.

"Careful," he said, his voice, close to my ear, rumbling all the way down to my chest.

"Thanks," I said, voice barely above a whisper, hands grasping him too tightly.

When I was back on my own two feet, he shifted, holding on to my hand, and we continued strolling the path winding through the trees. *Dangerous*, I reminded myself. I should take it back, keep the distance between us. Safer.

"I truly am sorry, Fynn," I said, eventually unable to contain the pressure that built with every step. I took back my hand and rubbed my gloves together to make up for his lost warmth. "For the way I handled things in college."

"I know." His gaze searched mine, the pain I'd caused still there, a shadow he couldn't hide.

Regret and guilt tasted like unsweetened cocoa all the way down my throat. "I truly never meant to hurt you. I just..." I shrugged, returning my hands to my coat pockets, so I wouldn't reach for his. "I was scared. Of how much you meant to me." I tipped my head and shook it. "We were so young."

He made a gruff noise. "That sounds like your mother."

I couldn't deny that her warning had echoed through my mind. Given how young she'd married and how her marriage had ended on such a bitter note. I'd wanted both of us to be sure. I'd just gone about it the wrong way. "It's more than that. I didn't want to be the cause of your resentment the way I was for both my parents. You have true talent, Fynn. You needed that scholarship and that apprenticeship to hone it. I would've held you back. I should have explained all of that."

"You could have come with me."

"Do you think either of my parents would have funded that trip, given how they felt about my choices?"

Even more than lack of funds or parental approval, the love I'd felt for Fynn made me fear that I'd lose him once his career took off, just like I'd lost Maggie when I'd turned sixteen and Aunt Poppy that last year in college, and anyone I seemed to care about. After that, after Fynn, it just seemed easier to check out of loving someone rather than risk losing them. And Fynn deserved to be happy. He deserved an open-hearted partner. I wanted happiness for him even if it cost me mine.

"And now?" Fynn asked, an edge to his voice. "Would you come with me?"

"Now..." My voice sounded fragile like an icy thread on the verge of breaking. Come with him? As in go to Vermont? All of me vibrated with a YES! Except... "I don't deserve another chance."

Fynn reached a hand out, dragged one of mine out of its

protective pocket and held it firmly yet softly, his touch, even through our gloves, warm and steady. "Seeing you again..." He flattened his mouth and gave a sharp shake of his head. "Do you want...would you want...to try again?"

Hope sprang so fast and full that it made me dizzy and I swayed on my feet. "You forgive me?"

He stopped and the motion turned me toward him, our breaths mingling in the frosty air. "I want to, Allie. I really do. But it's going to take time."

I got that. I wouldn't trust me either. I studied the snow at our feet, the snowflakes crusting the toes of our boots like a miniature chain of mountains, that suddenly seemed insurmountable. Could we somehow make a relationship work?

"We're only an hour apart," he said, fragile hope in his voice. "We can take things slow. See where things go."

I nodded fast like a branch in a hurricane, wanting this so much that it nearly burst out of me. Another chance with Fynn. "I'd like that. A lot."

He tucked a strand of flyaway hair back into my wool hat. Then his fingers lingered on the nape of my neck, crisping static electricity up and down my spine. Our faces were near, so near that a breath could close the distance.

He made a gruff sound, almost like a growl. Then he wrapped his arm around my shoulders and pulled me closer. Our bodies met at an awkward angle, misaligned as if they didn't remember how we fit. Then he shifted, and my whole body sighed as we slid perfectly in place like nesting dolls.

My heart beat so loud, it was all I could hear. He leaned forward that last little bit and our mouths met, an achingly soft touch that melted away the years. *Dangerous to hope, to want so much*, my brain tried to warn me. Then it went offline, and my heart gave in to the moment.

He broke the kiss, rested his chin on top of my head. His heart thumped against mine like an echo.

Another chance with Fynn. I would get another chance with Fynn. This was the best Christmas present ever. I wouldn't blow it this time. I would tell him how I felt. I would keep the lines of communication open so that what had happened eight years ago would never happen again. I wouldn't blow my second chance at happiness with the man I loved. Yes, loved. Then, now, forever.

A sudden rustling in the bushes nearby made us both jump apart. A flash of something big and fast flew through my peripheral vision. Chill barked and chased after whatever was in those woods. The sound of his barks echoed in the air.

"Did you see that?" I whispered, hanging on to Fynn's coat sleeves with both hands.

"Looked like a deer."

We followed Chill's trail in companionable silence, Fynn still holding my hand, his touch a reassuring anchor. That's what he'd always done for me—made me feel strong, solid, as if I could do anything.

The sky stayed stubbornly overcast, a dark blanket covering the stars, especially now that Chill was leading us away from the lit trees. We came up to him at the stone bridge over the narrow river between Brighton Lake and Candlewick Lake. His eyes shone with excitement, his tail a deranged metronome.

As I caught my breath, something thrummed through my veins, a subtle vibration that started beneath my feet and moved all the way up to my head. "Do you feel that?"

"What?"

"The vibration. It feels like it's coming from the stones."

"I don't feel anything, except cold. Chill!" he called to the dog who, nose to the ground, chased after the deer's trail once more. "Come!"

Chill glanced at Fynn and kept going.

"That dog!" Fynn jogged after the dog, finally catching up with him before he disappeared into the woods again.

Leading the dog with a hand on his collar, he made his way back to me. "That'll teach me to trust him off leash."

"There is a leash law in the park," I teased, suddenly feeling as if my skin had been stripped, leaving me raw, vulnerable... breakable.

Snow fell in fat flakes that melted on my cheeks like tears.

Fynn shook off the layer of snow settling on his wide shoulders. "Looks like Mrs. O's mysterious lights are a no-show tonight."

"Looks like it."

"Are you ready to call it a night?" He searched through his pockets and pulled out a leash.

A glance at my watch told me it was close to 1 a.m., long after Mrs. O had seen the lights. "I suppose."

"I'm heading back to Foster tomorrow," he said, hooking a leash on Chill's collar. He glanced up, a pleased shine to his eyes. "Got a text from Emilia. She's making good progress on the Star, but she needs some help. While I'm there I'll make the collar. I'm hoping I can bring it back for you by the weekend."

A gift as big as his heart.

"Oh, wow, that would be fantastic." Disappointment at his not being there to help me with the rest of the scavenger hunt check filled my whole body. I told myself I needed this break to regain my balance. That we needed to go slow so I could regain his trust. Plus, having a star for the lighting ceremony on Christmas Eve would be a huge relief.

"You have those pressed-glass ornament demonstrations on Saturday and Sunday."

"Can't miss those. I'll bring back some ornament stock, too. For the Christmas Workshop store."

Chill's leash in one hand, mine in Fynn's other hand, we made our way back to the truck. I couldn't help glancing back at the bridge, still feeling the echo of that hum in my bones.

18

"While it may seem counterintuitive, getting out of your comfort zone is a great way to get more comfortable. As you try new things, you feel more empowered and courageous."

— FROM *"*22 HABITS OF A CONFIDENT WOMAN*"* BY LOGAN HAILEY

Flynn came back on Friday after lunch for his promised pressed-glass ornament demonstrations later that day—minus the star replica.

"No star?" I asked when I met him in the parking lot at the Christmas Village.

"No star. There's still a lot of work to do." He brought out his phone and showed me the progress. He was right. It was coming along nicely but it was nowhere near finished. "Emilia's doing a great job. Only an expert's going to be able to tell the difference." He planted a kiss on top of my head. "By next Friday, I promise."

Another week of dodging Regina so she couldn't ask me if the Star had made it to Three Jeweled Angels yet. I'd have to get creative. Good thing all the Christmas activities gave me a bagful of excuses. Still, I could put her off only so much longer.

"Let's get you set up at Santa's Workshop," I said.

I hopped into the truck and was greeted by Chill's tongue. "Hey, there, mister. I missed you."

"Just him?" Fynn teased.

"I might have missed you a little, too."

He laughed that full-throated laugh of his that made every cell in my body smile.

I helped Fynn set up for his glass ornament demonstration at the Christmas Village, Chill getting in the way at every turn. The physical distraction kept me from obsessing about the Star or thinking about Fynn and a possible future with him. While the forge heated up, I bought him a bowl of chili that we ate sitting on a bench by the lake, Chill sitting between our legs, enjoying all the activity around him. Skaters zipped and fell and picked themselves back up. Happy sounds filled the air. A contentment I hadn't felt in a long time settled over me. I wanted to hold on to this feeling, capture it under glass like a snow globe, so I could revisit it whenever I needed a boost.

The joy on Fynn's face as he worked the demonstration that night redoubled my belief that I'd made the right decision eight years ago. He was meant for this. He was both a natural teacher and a gifted artist. He'd needed to hone his skills—without me in the way.

The impression grew over the next few days as he repeated his demonstrations on Saturday and Sunday, garnering *oohs* and *aahs* from the crowd as he molded the molten glass into pieces of art that would become treasured ornaments families would take out year after year to add to their trees.

While he stowed his equipment in his truck on Sunday night, I bought one of his pressed-glass ornaments—a winter scene depicting the Christmas Village entrance. It would serve as a reminder of our time together here. Not that I'd ever forget.

At the apartment, his goodnight kiss, tender and hungry, made every cell in me heat up with need.

"I'll be back as soon as I can," he said, even as he held on to me.

"Yes, please." One of us had to move, so I took a step back and reached for the knob on the apartment door.

As I watched him head to his truck, I patted the glass ornament through my bag, feeling its solid circle, lying alongside my copy of *The Confident Woman*.

A piece of him I could hold on to when he inevitably left for good.

∼

FYNN and I talked on the phone every day. He sent me photos of the progress on the fake star. The ease between us was starting to feel like it had eight years ago. All that only made me miss him more.

At least Mom was too busy running around with her new friend, Pauline, to add to my stress level. I barely saw her when she returned at night, too tired to talk. Which suited me fine because she would read the guilt I was trying so hard to hide and needle me until I confessed. Mom tended to wield secrets like weapons, using them with precise lethalness, so I didn't want to give her something she could hold over Regina. Or me.

And Regina seemed too busy with her own projects now that the gala and Christmas Eve were just around the corner to remind me about the Star. So, even though the days were long, I was making progress on my to-do list.

By Thursday night, my nerves felt like frayed rope. But the Christmas Village sparkled with lights and decorations and the good weather had drawn in enough townsfolks and tourists to please Regina. Children laughed. The carousel spun, piping out Christmas carols. The aroma of gingerbread wafting in the air reminded me I hadn't anything since breakfast.

To keep up my energy, I should fill my belly with chowder or stew. But the smell of gingerbread pulled me toward the bakery booth where I ordered a thick slice of still-warm bread.

Leaning against a lamppost by the carousel, enjoying the children's glee, I spotted Pauline Hurst with her perfectly coiffed hair, her tailored smushed-pea colored coat and beige hat, standing by the entrance gate. She stood out like a cactus at an orchid show. I frowned. What was she doing? Why was she handing out flyers?

I stuffed the last of the gingerbread loaf in my mouth and chewed as I strode Pauline's way, glancing all around for any signs of my mother. Those two had spent the week figuratively joined at the hip. Mom was nowhere in sight, which was a worry in itself. What was she up to?

With this being my first Christmas Festival, I couldn't afford for anything to go wrong, especially because of the missing Star. I didn't need Pauline stirring up trouble.

As I got closer, someone dropped one of the flyers on the ground. I picked it up. She'd made a full-color pamphlet exalting all the reasons she should replace Regina on the board of selectpersons in March. I crumpled the flyer and stuffed it in my pocket.

"Mrs. Hurst," I said with as much politeness as I could muster when I reached her. "I understand that you're excited about the town elections in March, but this isn't the time or place for campaigning. The Christmas Village is for holiday magic, not politics."

Pauline narrowed her gaze at me, annoyance crossing her face. "Allegra," she said, every syllable dripping with condescension. "Every opportunity is the right opportunity to engage the community. After all, my husband and I have done so much for this town. It's only right that as many people as possible are reminded of all I could continue to do for the town as an elected official."

"And Brighton is thankful for all you and your family have done for the town, but I must insist," I said, hoping the haughtiness of my words matched hers. "The Christmas Village is for families to enjoy the holiday season. Please put your flyers away."

"Just who do you think you are?" She pressed a flyer into an unwilling passerby's hand. "You have no authority here. Don't forget where the real power lies in this town. One word from me to my husband, and you'll find yourself without a job."

Not unless she could convince the earl and Regina. And given how Regina felt about Pauline, she'd keep me on to spite the woman.

"It's my job to create a magical experience for everyone who visits the Village." I pointed at the pile of flyers in her hands. "Those don't belong here. Please respect the purpose of this space."

People stopped and pointed, wondering what was happening. Knowing that causing a scene wasn't going to win her any goodwill, Pauline relented. She stuffed the flyers in her bag and sniffed. "Mark my words, you will regret this."

As Pauline stormed off, I couldn't help wondering if her need for influence and attention might have driven her to steal the Star. Did she plan on making it reappear on Christmas Eve, anointing herself as a hero in the process?

Pauline didn't stomp away far. She stopped by the information booth at the head of the main drag and pulled out her phone. Curious, I moved in closer, pretending to inspect knitted goods in a neighboring booth.

"I want her gone," Pauline said, her words shaking with rage. She jammed her free hand so far down into her coat pocket, I thought she might rip the lining. "After Christmas will be too late!"

Out of the corner of my eye, I spotted someone leaning against the side of the skate rental booth. But instead of looking at the skaters on the rink, his gaze connected with mine. A crooked smile spread over his face. Lon, Gus' stepson. I'd seen him helping Gus hang lights around town. He stood there with his too-long hair and all his inappropriate biker leather on this cold night. Making sure I watched him, he headed for Pauline. He leaned in close, speaking to her in a voice too low for me to hear.

She sniffed, then handed him the wad of flyers. Then she headed toward the parking lot. After she was out of sight, Lon dropped the flyers into a nearby trash barrel.

I walked up to him. "What was that all about?"

"If I were you, I'd stay away from that witch."

"Good thing you're not me."

"She's harmless but her husband isn't."

I snorted. "It wouldn't be my first encounter with a vengeful senator."

"He collects information on people and uses it as a weapon."

"Good thing I'm an open book."

Lon tilted his head. "He knows your secret."

With that he strode away.

"Hey, what secret?" I called after him.

But Lon didn't turn back, just kept going deeper into the Christmas Village until he disappeared. Did he know more than he'd let on? If he was so chummy with the Hursts, did he know what happened to the Star?

I tried to find him to get clarification, instead I got caught up in the buzz floating around the Village.

"What's going on?" I asked Dalia, who manned her card booth. She'd stuffed her dark hair into a light-blue and white cap with a snowflake design.

"Apparently Father Lowe just up and left, leaving the

church in a lurch for Christmas services." She neatened up a display of scrap paper cards for all occasions. Ordinarily, the bright colors and patterns would have held my attention.

"Why would he do that?" I asked. The man had seemed filled with anger and overly protective of his church.

"Rumor is it's because you were putting too much emphasis on the Star, and he felt all the highlight on the commercial—" she made air quotes "—side of Christmas drowned out the true meaning of the season."

Or maybe he'd stolen the Star, and I was getting too close for comfort to the truth. I had to find him. "Do you know where he went?"

She shrugged. "No one does, not even the diocese."

I frowned. "That can't be good."

"Plus, it ruins the Christmas Eve flow." She adjusted the woolen shawl with the same snowflake pattern as her cap over the shoulder of her coat.

"What do you mean?"

"First the town gathers for the tree lighting and gratitude ceremony, then we all head out to midnight mass services, filling all three churches."

Keeping up with all the traditions of the most important day of the year in Brighton was of utmost importance with the Star missing. Normal, everything had to feel normal. I couldn't let one rebellious priest keep the town from gathering.

19

"Instead of beating yourself up for your mistakes or flaws, give yourself a generous dose of grace. Your insecurities can only have as much power as you give them."

— *FROM "22 HABITS OF A CONFIDENT WOMAN" BY LOGAN HAILEY*

Fynn brought back the Star early Friday morning. We snuck it into the basement before the rest of Brighton stirred. Each step through the loading dock echoed like a mini-explosion as we rolled the Star to the elevator, making me fear getting caught in the act.

Of course, I could always say that, because I was running so far behind schedule, I'd recruited Fynn's help to get the Star to the jewelry store. Except, of course, that they didn't open until ten. I didn't like lying and I'd lied so much lately, I was afraid I'd say the wrong thing to the wrong person.

"Where's Chill?" I asked, to distract the too-fast track of my thoughts.

"He stayed home with Emilia and her boyfriend." Fynn chuckled. "With the gala, it just seemed easier."

"Well, tell him hi when you see him again. I miss the big doofus." The dog had a way of grounding me I could use right now.

In the basement, we somehow wrangled the Star back into its red metal box without breaking it, our breaths steaming the cold air with the effort. The thing was much heavier than I expected, though with all that glass, I shouldn't have been surprised.

"It's magnificent," I said, watching the angel aura glass shimmer under the flashlight's beam.

"Emilia did a great job." He pointed to the panels. "She even added some dust to look like it had stayed in storage all year."

"Nice touch." I rolled my lips inward, trying to keep my too-fast breath from sounding like a freight train in the narrow space. This would work. It had to work. "I can't thank you enough for doing this for me."

"I know how much staying in Brighton means to you." Fynn's brows furrowed.

I reached for the box cover, and he helped me guide it in place over the Star. "I haven't felt at home anywhere since...our time together."

He leaned a hip against the table and tipped his head. "Have you thought of what happens if they figure out it's not the real thing?"

I shrugged, trying to appear nonchalant while my pulse tripped in double time, and headed out of the vault. "I'll get fired."

The knot in my chest tightened at the thought.

"And you're okay with that?" He closed the vault door behind us, metal clanking like a warning.

"No, but I won't have a choice." I wanted to stay in Brighton more than anything, except maybe being with Fynn.

He tilted his head, studying me. It took all I had not to squirm. "Okay."

"Okay, what?"

"I've got your back."

With that, some of my anxiety quieted. I wasn't alone.

Christmas Eve was only a few days away. The tree lighting ceremony *needed* a star, fake or real. Pauline's husband had stirred up trouble, and Regina had stood up for me. The priest was still missing. Lon was nowhere to be found. And I was sure he knew more than he'd let on. I busied myself locking the door and pocketed the key. "I might still find the real Star in time."

"We'll keep looking."

What if Fynn is right? And we don't find it? How would I explain the duplicate? I thought as we climbed the basement stairs.

What if I told Regina the truth about the Star? That would not go over well. I could see her face now, disappointment swirling in her dragon eyes. She'd believed in me, given me a second chance, and I'd let her down.

She'd fire me on the spot, leaving the gala in the lurch. Not that Lucy couldn't do a good job, but I'd done all the prep, I knew all the details, and she'd be playing catch-up. And dealing with Baby Autumn already had her stressed.

After the gala, I told myself, heartburn so strong I thought something might be wrong with my heart. *Not your heart*, I told myself, *your conscience*. I had to have a big win under my belt before ruining Christmas for the whole town. This gala needed to run without a hitch, not just for me, but for the earl, especially if this gala was his last.

"What's going on in that head of yours? I can hear the wheels turning," Fynn said.

"This is such a mess."

He wrapped an arm around my shoulders. "We'll get through it."

Back on Town Hall's main floor, bright with Christmas trees and wreaths and thousands of colored lights, but still empty of people this early in the morning, offered a cheer that didn't match my chaotic insides. *What-ifs* came and went like a train with never-ending cars.

Fynn hooked a thumb over his shoulder. "I need to get the mini-forge to the Christmas Village and set up again."

I took in a big, pine-scented breath, and nodded. "Okay, I'll meet you there after I get the star to the jewelry store."

I headed toward my office to phone Gus but, of course, Regina called me from her office. Just how early did she get in? Had she heard our star sneaking even though the loading dock was at the opposite end of the building? No, or she'd have investigated.

"I just got a call from the Harper sisters," she said, hands tented in front of her on her desk. "They still haven't received the Star."

I swallowed the knot in my throat, and it joined the ball in my chest. Thank God they hadn't called yesterday. "I'm trying to coordinate with Gus, but he's been busy."

She tipped her head, gaze stabbing me as if she wanted to cut me to pieces. "I just finished speaking with him. He and Lon will be at the vault in an hour. Be there."

Sweating a lake under my coat, I gave her a too-tight smile. "Of course."

When I went back to the basement an hour later, Gus and his stepson Lon waited by the vault door. Gus, with his white beard, solid body and twinkling eyes, looked just like you'd expect a grandfather to. Lon, on the other hand, looked as if he belonged in a biker gang with his heavy engineer boots, leather jacket and tattoos running up his neck. I speared him with a look that said I had questions. All I got back was an enigmatic smile. Somehow, the cold and musty air seemed stronger, the light starker.

"Hi, guys," I said, voice ultra bright. I got the key from my pocket and worked the lock. "Sorry for the delay."

"No problem," Lon said, skewering a crooked smile at me while his gaze ran up and down my body, making me shiver in a not-good way. I was glad I'd worn my puffer jacket and not my good coat.

"It's my first time doing the transport." I pocketed the key while Gus urged Lon to open the door. "How does it work?"

"We'll get the box onto this trolley," Gus said, thumbs hooked through his overall straps, supervising Lon as he moved the platform inside the vault. "Then put it on the truck and drive to Three Jeweled Angels."

"Sounds easy enough." I chuckled and the sound gave off a Chuckie-vibe to my ears. *You have to calm down.*

"We've had a lot of practice," Gus said, but his gaze flickered at me as if something was off. I worked up a smile and tried to make myself useful, but only got in the way.

Gus and Lon stood one on each side of the box and slid it onto the trolley—the reverse of what Fynn and I had done earlier this morning.

I held my breath. *Don't look inside. Please, don't look inside.* I didn't want to be around if anyone realized it wasn't the correct star.

As they rolled the box to the elevator, the knot in my chest grew. What if the fake star wasn't convincing enough? Too late to worry about that now.

And Fynn's question came back: *How will you handle it if they do?*

No earthly idea.

I pressed my lips again and took in a deep breath. Nothing I could do about it now.

"We'll meet you at the loading dock." Gus pressed the elevator button and the doors creaked closed.

I raced up the stairs, legs feeling as boneless as overcooked lasagna. Regina waited at the loading dock, red coat, black hat and gloves on, ready to bodyguard the Star to its destination.

The elevator clanged to a stop. Her voice cut through the noise. "I'm not pleased with how long it took you to get this simple task done."

"I've had a lot on my plate, including getting the scavenger hunt up and ready for Saturday's unveiling," I said, trying to keep my voice steady.

She harrumphed, breath steaming from her nose like her namesake dragon. "Using an app was a good idea."

What would she say if I told her the idea was Mom's. I almost chuckled at the thought and had to clench my teeth tight not to.

"I can ride with the Star," I said, needing to know it got to its destination and hoping to corner Lon and ask him questions. Regina didn't need to see the Star until Christmas Eve.

She shook her head. "You have more pressing things to do than to ride along with the Star."

My heart sank, but I plastered on a smile. "Of course, Regina. I understand."

My conscience twisted. Lucy's warning to tell Regina before she found out on her own echoed in my mind.

Lucy was right, of course. I should. *Come clean. Do it now. Before it's too late.*

I gathered my courage. "There's something—"

"Not now," Regina said, striding to the truck's passenger side. She slammed the door. "I left today's agenda on your desk."

"Lon," I started as he locked the cargo door. "I have questions."

"Sorry, babe. Got to go." He jogged to the cab.

I pressed a hand to my burning chest. Fine. I tried. I could deal with this.

I had the gala of my life to put on.

And the town expected their Star for the tree lighting.

So, I would give them a star.

∼

Between checking and rechecking my task management app, going over my gala checklist and making phone calls to confirm that all my vendors would show up at their assigned time tomorrow, I kept waiting for Regina to accost me and accuse me of switching the Star. For her to fire me. Instead, she flooded me with more to-dos for my list.

The growing knot in my chest and the restlessness irritating my nervous system drove me to keep moving at all times like a toy with a broken Off switch.

I just had to get through the gala tomorrow night.

Then the three days until the Christmas Eve tree lighting ceremony.

20

"Your success will be determined by your own confidence and fortitude."

— *MICHELLE OBAMA*

On Saturday, I hit the ground running, doing my best to put Fynn and his kisses, my guilt, out of my mind. I couldn't let *anything* distract me today. Today would make or break me. Today was my most important event since the fiasco with Senator Becker. Today, I would either become part of Brighton, or remain forever an outsider.

This event had to run perfectly. Not just because this was my job, but because this was most likely the earl's last gala. I had to make it the best he'd ever attended. Even though I'd never met him, I felt a certain connection with him. We were both outsiders who wanted to make Brighton home.

Given Robin's request to keep the chaos to a minimum for his sick uncle's sake, I'd arranged for the whole set-up to happen today. I stepped into the ballroom, clipboard in hand, and glanced down at the schedule. The schedule was tight, and

I had to hope that nothing would go wrong. *Yeah, right. Like that's ever happened before.*

I checked the contents of my rolling emergency kit. I had scissors, tapes of all kinds from double-sided to duct in an array of colors, Sharpies, large gallon bags, sandwich bags, quart bags, envelopes and pens, and zip ties and pins of all kinds to make any necessary adjustments to not only various parts of the décor but also to help out with clothing failures like a broken zipper.

Speaking of the devil, Robin appeared at the ballroom doors, wearing dress slacks, shirt and tie, as if he were going to a business meeting rather than guiding vendors to their assigned areas and helping to supervise their set-up.

"The decorating team is here," he said.

"Right on schedule." I should have met them at the loading dock. Part of my job was to stay two steps ahead of the next to-do on the list. *Please don't let this be how the day will go.*

I closed my eyes and took three calming breaths, then followed him to the storage area where the silver trees, giant snowflakes, miles of fairy lights and blue and white decorations were stored. "Thanks for agreeing to be my right-hand man today."

His smile showed unnaturally white teeth. "The pleasure is all mine."

I handed him a walkie-talkie. "This will be the best way to keep in touch today."

He pressed a button. "Testing, testing."

The room filled with static and an ear-splitting shriek. I winced.

"Guess it's working." He showed me his bright, white teeth.

I handed Robin a copy of the floorplan design. "Make sure they follow it to a T. Everything's calculated to the inch."

Still smiling, he saluted. "Yes, ma'am."

"I'm way too young to be a ma'am." I chuckled.

He gave a roguish nod. "Allegra, then."

Maybe if I wasn't so worried about today, I could let myself be enthralled by his charm. Except that he wasn't Fynn.

The AV and lighting set-up followed soon after. I was glad for all the busyness, keeping me going and keeping me from thinking about the whole Star mess.

I scarfed down a protein bar for lunch. Before I'd taken more than two bites, the tables and chairs arrived promptly at noon. But as soon as the first stack of chairs came out, I realized we had a problem.

"Where are the rest of the chairs?" I asked the driver and showed him the work order. "There should be twice as many."

"Sorry, lady, I just deliver the stuff."

"All right, then. Go ahead and unload the tables." At least they'd gotten that part of the order correct. "Hold the chairs. I'm going to make a call."

I called the rental company, who assured me that, yes, I had ordered the Chiavari chairs, but no, I couldn't get anymore, because there were none in their warehouse at the moment. They'd sent me an email earlier in the week and when I hadn't answered, they'd assumed all was okay.

That was on me. A stupid beginner mistake. *Don't. Now's not the time to beat yourself up.* I flipped through the haystack of emails and, yep, there it was. "You're sure you can't get me any more?"

"Absolutely positive."

I didn't like this setback one bit. The last thing I needed was people looking for chairs.

"It's fine," I told myself, desperately attempting to hold back the growing knot in my chest. "It's not a deluge. Just chairs. I'll think of something."

I did a quick online search, and no one nearby had any chairs.

Call Tessa, I told myself. We'd met at an event planning

conference when we were both starting out. We'd been good friends. She was one of the few people who'd reached out to me after the Senator Becker debacle. And, if I remembered correctly, she lived near Manchester.

I swallowed my pride and dialed Tessa's number.

"Hey, friend!" Tessa said. "It's been a while since we touched based."

"I'm sorry about that," I said, "especially because I'm kind of in your area now. In Brighton."

"Oh, love those festivals."

I sat on a stair and curled up around myself, heart beating too fast. "I, uh, I'm calling to ask for a favor."

"Spill it."

"Tonight is the Festival of Lights gala at Candlewick Estate and because of a mix-up, the rental place only sent half the chairs I need. Do you have a trusted vendor who might be willing to help me out?"

"How many do you need?" she asked.

I told her, and she said, "Let me make some calls. And don't be a stranger. Let's get coffee soon."

"Thanks, Tessa. You're a lifesaver."

"What are friends for!"

The decorating team worked like a well-orchestrated hive, setting up the trees, tables, chairs and place settings. The catering team had taken over the kitchen and were setting up the stations on the buffet table that would later brim with food. The florist arrived with the snow globe table centerpieces.

Regina barged into the ballroom, carrying a table centerpiece. "This isn't the design I approved."

I groaned.

She plucked at the decorative arches around the snow globe that she herself had chosen and approved several months ago. "They're much too tall. People will have to keep ducking around the centerpiece to talk to each other. This is unacceptable."

She's nervous, I told myself. *This event is a big deal for her, too. And she wants everything to be up to Brighton's usual standard.*

The knot in my chest now buzzed. During my interview back in September, she'd told me I wasn't her choice for the job. For the past three months, I'd bent over backwards to make her every request come true, so that she would trust me, trust that I could get things done in an efficient way. I thought that she had grown to trust me. Her sudden lack of confidence in me stung. But I couldn't afford to let it show. Especially not today. "I'll handle it right away."

Regina gave a sharp nod and charged to the stage where the AV team was setting up the mics. I found the florist and told Piper of Regina's concern. I took out my scissors and reached for the arch of greenery. "How about if you cut the arch here and here, and rearrange the greenery like so?"

"Not as pretty," Piper said, pulling up miniature shears and green ties, "but if it'll keep the Dragon Lady from breathing down our necks, I'm okay with it."

"You're a lifesaver, Piper."

I made the rounds, checking on progress. Lucy, who'd offered to help this afternoon while her husband looked after the baby, called me on the walkie-talkie as I fixed a falling snowflake in the foyer. "The AV team needs you now. They've run into a snag. The mic system's down."

"See if you can find Robin," I said, tacking the snowflake in place with putty. "He knows the estate better than I do and will know where to go to fix the problem."

"Will do. Sounds like it may delay the set-up."

"Let's hope not too long." I made a note on my tablet to circle back.

"Allegra!" Regina's voice echoed down the hall as she bulldozed in my direction. She tugged on my sweater's sleeve and pulled me toward the ballroom. She pointed to the buffet table where a giant snowflake reigned, flanked by carved pillars that would hold a dozen votive candles each, refracting light. "Should the ice sculptures be out?"

Why was Regina in such a state today? I'd never seen her so flustered. She was taking fire-breathing to a whole new level. And I was making too many rookie mistakes. "They should still be in the freezer. They're going to melt much too quickly. I'll take care of it."

"Thanks."

She gave a sharp nod. "It's imperative this gala smoothly."

"I know."

Each new glitch chipped a dent in my confidence. What if this turned into another Senator Becker fiasco? *Then you'll do what you've always done. You'll pick yourself up and start over again.*

The prospect made my heart sink. I was so tired of moving, of reinventing, of starting over. I just wanted to stay in one place for long enough to make real friends, build a real home. Was that so much to ask?

As I headed to the kitchen to see about having the ice sculptures moved, I ran into Robin.

"How's the electric problem?"

"An overload. I've called an electrician and he promised to get here within a half hour."

"Thank you." On impulse, I hugged him. One less problem I had to deal with.

His cheeks pinkened. "You're welcome."

I didn't know why I ever thought he'd stolen the Star. He was going out of his way to make this event a success for his uncle's sake. And that brought up the fact that with everything going on, I hadn't made a dent into figuring out who might have stolen the Star or investigating Royce's mysterious thugs.

The afternoon turned into evening much too quickly. But all the hard work paid off.

The ballroom looked magical with its trees and fairy lights and winter wonderland decorations. Tessa had come through and found a vendor an hour away that could help me. The chairs had arrived just in the nick of time. I made a note to send her a thank you gift. The electrician had fixed the electrical short and the mics were up and running. Regina's voice could boom her welcome to every corner of the ballroom. Not that she actually needed a mic. The band had set up on the stage, ready to regale the gala guests. The scent of hot appetizers wafted from the kitchen, setting my stomach gurgling.

As the crew and volunteers dispersed after the final run-through, Lucy sidled up to me. "You did good, Allegra. The place looks fantastic."

"Thank you so much for all your help. I couldn't have pulled it off without you taking over half the checklist." Out of the corner of my eye, I noted the curtain to the cloak room needed tying back.

"Thank *you*. It was so nice to get out and feel like a human with a brain." She gave me a hug. "We make a good team."

"We do. You're staying, right?"

She lifted a hand to her chest with a tell-tale milk leak. "Got to get some relief."

Regina cornered us. She nodded a greeting to Lucy, then glared at me. "Well, it looks like you pulled it off, Allegra. Let's just hope the rest of the night goes smoothly. I need to go get ready for the Festival of Lights tree lighting at the Christmas Village. I'll see you here at promptly at seven thirty."

Where did she think I was going? Regina grabbed her coat and left, plowing forward as if heading into battle.

Lucy turned me around and pointed me toward one of the staging rooms. "You have half an hour to get into your gown and freshen up before you do the final check. Make sure you eat something. Is Fynn coming tonight?"

"I invited him, but big parties like this aren't his thing." Having him here would be a huge distraction, and I couldn't afford any, so his absence was probably for the best.

"But you'll be here and, given the way he looks at you, I'm sure he'll show." Lucy gave me a hug and escaped. "Call me tomorrow. Let me know how everything went."

Three more days until Christmas Eve. I had no idea if Fynn planned to stay for the lighting of the fake star or leave tonight. Some part of me still held out hope that I'd find the real Star and save Brighton's Christmas. But I couldn't think about that now. I had this gala to get through.

By 7 p.m., I was dressed in an ice-blue, ankle-length dress for my role as Town Administrator, the estate glowed, and the air bubbled with champagne-like excitement. I needed to relax my event brain and stop looking for things out of place, like that chocolate fountain that wasn't quite straight. The first of the guests trickled in by 7:30. My hands shook. From cold, I told myself, not guilt.

I drew in a long breath, wiped my hands along the side of my dress, and pasted on my hostess smile. "Hello, welcome to the Festival of Lights Gala."

I collected tickets and answered pre-emptive questions, the main one being, *where's the bathroom?*

Robin stood next to me, magazine-handsome in his tux, greeting guests in his uncle's stead. He certainly made an impression—as if he belonged in the role of estate host.

My position as both the event planner and Town Administrator would give me the opportunity to talk to guests, and maybe uncover something about the missing Star. I had a golden opportunity to gather puzzle pieces and, hopefully, put them together.

I had the fake star, but I really wanted to give Brighton the real one.

I looked down the line of guests strolling up the walkway. I somehow doubted Royce's thugs would queue up for the gala. Then my heart fluttered and sank. Behind the board of selectpersons and their spouses, stood Fynn, handsome as ever in his tux, my mother's attention-getting red sequined arm hooked through his.

What was she doing here?

21

"Owning our story and loving ourselves through that process is the bravest thing that we'll ever do."

— BRENÉ BROWN

"Mom, what are you doing here?" I asked my mother, who stepped into the estate's foyer and the reception line as if she had every right to be there.

Her smile widened. "Is that any way to greet your mother?"

I swallowed a groan, noticing Fynn grinning in my peripheral vision. How had she roped him into escorting her? "Hello, mother dear. What are you doing here?"

She drew a gala invitation from her tiny red-sequined purse. "Pauline gave me a ticket."

How did Pauline get an extra ticket when they were supposed to be distributed through a lottery? I took it from her, as well as Fynn's. "How fortunate for you."

"Especially considering that my own daughter didn't offer me one."

"The gala is for residents." I ignored the fact that I'd given one to Fynn, who wasn't a resident.

She shrugged. "You won't leave so, apparently, I'm one now." She squeezed Fynn's elbow. "I ran into Fynn in the parking lot, and he kindly offered to escort me."

Fynn sent me a look of apology over Mom's head.

"Lucky you." Our argument was holding up the line. I gave her a tight smile. "Enjoy your evening."

"Oh, I plan to." She swept away, towing Fynn in her wake, as if this was her event and she was the center of attention everyone had been waiting for. She'd have her work cut out for her with Regina and Pauline also vying for the part.

"I'll see you later," Fynn whispered. His fingers brushed mine, lingered for a second before my mother's gravity dragged him away.

Pauline and her husband arrived soon after. Frederick Hurst looked like the quintessential well-heeled businessman in his tux, close-cropped hair and air of privilege I recognized from my own father. Pauline stood out in her hummingbird-green dress and pirate-trove of gold jewelry dripping from her neck. She handed me her velvet cape.

I handed it back to her with a small smile. "The cloak room is to your left. I will take your ticket though."

Pauline turned to her husband. "You're going to let a party planner talk to me like that?"

"Event planner," I said. "And Town Administrator."

Lightning in her gaze, she opened her mouth to protest, but her husband interrupted, took the cape from me, exchanged it for their tickets and, hand at the small of her back, urged her forward. "Let's keep the line moving, Pauline."

Kay Spears, Robin's cousin, climbed up the stairs, elegant in a white, off-the-shoulder dress under her coat. He greeted her with a kiss on the cheek that seemed too intimate for a cousin. *None of your business, Allegra.*

Yet another non-resident who'd somehow gotten a ticket. Of course, as a relative of the host, I suppose I should let that go. But how many others had wrangled an illegal invitation? Would that put us over capacity? The last thing I needed was the fire department to show up and shut us down.

"Nice to see you again, Kay," I said.

Her gaze swept the foyer. "Wow, this place looks great!"

"Thanks."

With the bulk of the guests now mingling in the ballroom, I headed that way to make sure everything was set for Regina's welcome address. Later, the earl would make an appearance, and give a speech about all Brighton had accomplished this past year.

Soft music, from the trio on the stage, added atmosphere without impairing conversation. The bar held a steady business. Waiters wove seamlessly through the crowd with plates of appetizers. So far, so good. My gaze swept the room for things that in need of attention—the trash can by the bag needed a fresh bag, that tape by the stage needed tamping down, a candleholder too close to the edge of the buffet table needed to be moved before someone knocked it over.

I spied my mother regaling guests with stories. Fynn's gaze caught my eye. He gave me an encouraging nod.

On my way to the kitchen to check on the buffet, I stopped to collect a lone earring from the floor. Someone would be looking for this. Crouched like that, I overheard Kay and Robin arguing in a side hallway.

"Your uncle's too soft." Kay's voice floated my way. "He's giving away too much of his wealth to the village and forgetting his own family."

I pressed against the wall, blatantly listening in to her exchange with Robin.

"Yeah, I'm tired of hearing how great Harry is. I could run this business so much better." Robin's voice held a hard edge I'd never heard before. So much for being the devoted nephew. "Were you able to find a way around the trust?"

"I'm working on it."

"We don't have much time."

"I know, Robbie. I know," she said, her tone grating. "Were you able to get closer to this Allegra person?"

"I tried but that brute that follows her around like a puppy's been making my task difficult."

"Well, pour on the charm. You're good at that." She snorted as if she were immune to it. "Like you said, we don't have much time, and she seems to hold the key."

The key to what?

The swish of Kay's dress told me she was heading my way, so I rose and slipped into the bathroom, then locked the door behind me. There, I did a search on Kay Spears on my tablet and learned she was a lawyer with a high-price firm in Boston. Was she Robin's cousin at all? Why was Robing trying to get close to me?

I had no time to ponder the exchange. Just as I came out of the bathroom, Regina cornered me. "There you are. I've been looking for you."

"Even hostesses have to use the bathroom."

"Yes, well, the earl has requested your presence in the solarium."

To make sure all was set with his speech? "Okay. Where's that?"

"I'll take you."

After leading me through a warren of hallways, she left me standing by a set of double doors that looked like the ones in the ballroom. She turned to leave, then glared at me over her shoulder. "You're fired, by the way."

"Wait! What?"

She turned around, fire in her gaze. "You. Are. Fired."

"Why? I thought I was doing a good job."

"Did you think I wouldn't notice that you gave me the wrong star?"

Heat flared up my neck and surely turned my cheeks crimson. How could she? Emilia had done such a wonderful job. "I—"

She put up a stop-sign hand. "Don't. There is no acceptable excuse for your subterfuge." She nodded in the direction of the doors. "Don't keep the earl waiting."

My worst fear had come to life. Not only was I fired, but I also had to go face the earl with the consequences of my actions. Heart jackhammering in my chest, I knocked on the door.

Fired, I was fired. I'd have to leave. I'd have to start all over. A weight landed on my shoulders and pressed down. I wasn't sure I had it in me. No amount of re-reading *The Confident Woman* could stir up enough self-confidence.

And yet, what choice did I have?

"Come in," a voice called, sounding both brittle and commanding.

I swallowed hard and pushed the door open.

Lights showcased the forest of exotic plants filling the room. An earthy smell, along with that of strong tea, perfumed the air. The muted sounds of the gala traveled through a window cracked open a few inches.

The earl sat in a fern-upholstered club chair, a brown afghan draped over his knees. He wore a black suit that belonged to another era. But it suited him, made him look dashing despite the pallor of his skin beneath his neatly trimmed, mostly salt beard.

He gestured toward the chair across from his, a marble-topped side table between them. "Sit, Allegra."

He knew my name? Of course, he did. He was the one who'd requested Regina hire me. Against her wishes. And I'd let him down.

I sat primly on the edge of the chair, feet together, hands in my lap, part of me prepared to flee given the opportunity. I should thank him for the opportunity he'd given me, but my throat was so dry no word would scrape through.

He lifted a light-blue Wedgwood teapot with gold trim and silently offered me a cup.

I shook my head, afraid I'd choke on the liquid.

"You're probably wondering why I asked you here," he said.

I tried for a smile, but it felt like a grimace. I nodded.

He attempted to pour himself a cup, but his hand shook too much. I reached for the pot, poured, and offered him the cup. He gave a nod of thanks.

"Do you know the story of the Christmas Star?" he asked.

Of course, he wanted to talk about the Star, how Christmas was ruined because I'd failed. I forced my fingers to stay still on my lap, forced myself to look at the earl. "I've heard several versions."

"None of which are the real one."

22

THE EARL'S STORY

"I have led a good long life," Harry said, taking in the young woman sitting, prim and properly, on the chair across from his in the solarium, looking for all the world as if she expected the sky to fall on her head. He understood the feeling. He had put off this meeting as long as he could, yet had wanted it to happen much earlier.

He would ask too much of her, and his greatest fear was that she would walk away.

"Geologists say that energy vortices crisscross the earth," he said.

She lifted a brow in question. But the legend was as good a place to start as any.

"Rumor has it that those swirling centers of energy lead to healing or even enlightenment. You have no doubt heard of places like Sedona, Stonehenge and Easter Island. But there also exist hundreds of lesser-known sites."

He laughed. "I never used to believe in such things, but I have had a lot of time to study. The winters are long in Brighton."

She gave a quick smile as if she was not sure where he was

heading. He had rehearsed his speech, but seeing her in the flesh, he had not expected the rush of love, knowing and regret, nor the instant connection. He was getting to be a doddering old man.

"Brighton happens to sit on an intersection of ley lines that make it seem alive with energy." Searching for an explanation as to what he had experienced all those years ago, he had a geological survey done sometime in the late 1930s. "Visitors leave not quite knowing why they felt so good in Brighton. A fact, of course, Regina Buchanan, Brighton's most fearless advocate, uses to her advantage to make Brighton a thriving tourism center."

"She is fierce."

He laughed. "That she is. But she is also one of the kindest, most generous women I have ever met. She has given up much to serve Brighton."

Allegra nodded, fast and rigid like a marionette with an inexperienced handler, not quite believing his words. He would not either, which was why this confession was so difficult. She *had* to believe. Or they were all doomed.

"Legend has it that an angel appeared to me one Christmas Eve, one hundred ten years ago, and offered me, a sinner, grace. Do you know who St. Maurice is?"

She shook her head.

"The patron saint of cloth workers." He lifted a hand, waving the troublesome gnat of conscience away. "But I am getting ahead of myself."

He lifted his cup from the saucer and sipped, buying time, really. This was not going as he had rehearsed. "Some people say the church is situated on that Brightonian energy vortex, and that is why my healing transformation took place."

The geological survey showed otherwise, which was why he had the estate built on this piece of land rather than in town. He had foolishly thought that if he resided atop the epicenter of the vortex, he would be spared. That what he had experienced was the hallucination of a dying man. The years—and his work—had taught him otherwise.

And the Star, of course. He could not deny its presence. Or its power.

"The truth is that on that fateful Christmas Eve, the church was locked, and the Reverend Father Bright was ill with a fever and in bed in the small house across the street. The pews of the church were filled with the bodies of parishioners, dead from influenza."

He looked out through the dark window, saw himself on that cold night, starving and frostbitten. He remembered the horror of seeing those dead bodies lying on the pews. The sight carried him back to Spencer Mills, to the burned bodies laid out like cordwood by the river.

"I had reached the end of my rope," he said, and his voice rasped as if he were still breathing that smoke-filled air. "I laid down on a granite slab behind the church. I had planned on letting the elements have their way. To end the misery. I deserved that fate for the sins I had committed. As steward of the people in my employ, I had failed them."

And he was a coward. Instead of facing what he had done, he had run, hoping to escape the guilt. But no matter how fast he ran, it kept pace with him. "One hundred and ten souls died that day because of me."

The weight of that failing still pressed on his heart. Not even all his good deeds since then could erase the permanent black mark.

"That is where the angel appeared to me, outside, on a rock." Harry remembered the clear night, the ribbon of stars in the sky, the frigid air burning his exposed skin.

"Have mercy on me," he had whispered into the night.

The scent of snow and pine had surrounded him. But the silence, the profound and absolute silence, was what he remembered most. He had not felt anything like it since that night.

Then a rod of lightning had pierced the sky and descended, cracking down on the rock at his feet. Light filled the clearing behind the church as if it were midday. The coward he was should have been afraid, but as weary as he was, he welcomed death.

Until that angel had appeared.

Twice as tall as any human, dressed in robes the color of clay, and woven wings that spanned the clearing. Love had poured down from the angel. A love so accepting as he had never experienced. A love so pure that it had turned him into a crying mass of regretful flesh.

"The angel's voice boomed inside my head. 'When you wake on the morrow, the lost souls will reappear in the bodies of the dead of this town. As long as your heart remains true, the Star will shine every Christmas Eve for a full day and those lost souls will live another year.'"

Harry gave a wry chuckle. "'What star?' I asked, for I did not perceive a star anywhere, except for the millions in the sky. Instead of answering my question, he kept talking as if I had not said anything. 'One year for every soul you took.'"

My heart still ached at the thought. "One hundred and ten."

The memory of the warning, of his most recent failure parched his throat. "'Should the light not glow on Christmas Eve, you will know you have failed. You will die...and all the souls of Brighton will die with you.'"

He slaked his great thirst with a gulp of tea. "Now, I no longer cared what happened to me. But I had already had one hundred and ten souls from the fire weighing on my conscience. I did not want the responsibility for their lives a second time."

He had scrambled to his knees, hands intertwined at his heart and begged release. "The obligation was too much. I could not go through that pain again. But the angel kept going. 'Should you make it to a hundred and ten years, your debts will be repaid, and the souls of Brighton and Spencer Mills will live on.'"

Harry's hands shook at the memory. He tried to place the cup and saucer on the table, but the path wobbled. Allegra reached for the cup and saucer and took them from him, her touch warm and tender. She had a kind heart. He had seen the evidence these past three months as she managed Brighton's affairs with aplomb. He had made the correct choice, no matter Regina's early reservations. Even she was impressed by Allegra's work ethic.

"A vortex of light spun, making an unearthly noise," Harry continued, remembering the ungodly fear that had wracked him thinking hell was opening up beneath him. He wished he still had the teacup to steady his hands. "And then, as quickly as it had come, the vortex receded into the stone below me. At my feet lay the Star. Its heart pulsed with a golden light, making the glass alive with unimaginable colors." He shook his head, reliving his awe. "Magnificent, simply magnificent."

Trapped in the glass were swirls that he somehow understood were souls, souls that would remain captive until he could free them with his repentance. Tears had flowed down his cheeks. The angel had walked through the walls of the church and blown a breath onto each of the dead. One hundred and ten.

"From the church arose the moans and cries of the dead waking. Their lives, the souls of those who had died in the fire, they were my responsibility now. I had a choice to make. And as much as I wanted to die, I could not let another one hundred and ten people perish because of my selfishness. I had to find a way to wash away the stain on my own soul by freeing theirs."

"*As the generations grow*," the angel had warned him, "*more souls will depend on you to hold the Star's charge.*"

"That's when I swore on all that is holy that I would do good by these people. That I would earn back their freedom."

"*Pain is inevitable,*" the angel had told him. "*Suffering is optional.*"

The first few years, Harry had suffered terribly, struggling to fulfill his mission. That first year, the Star barely held a glimmer. "Then in 1929, the first year of the big depression, I couldn't do enough, and that Christmas Eve, the Star failed to glow. People started dying."

The angel had appeared to him once more and warned him that he was wasting his second chance. Death would not save him; it would send him to an eternity of suffering. "The angel told me to gather the villagers and let them add their gratitude to my deeds to help charge the Star."

So, Harry had. And the Star had found enough charge to glow. He had then understood that he needed the villagers as much as they needed him. And that had changed the course of his actions. "That is how the Christmas Eve Star lighting ceremony started, why it is so important. I redoubled my efforts after that fateful Christmas. That's when I started the Christmas Village and the festival."

Her skin blanched and her eyes widened. "One hundred ten years. *This* year."

He should not be surprised that she recognized the import of the year.

"Oh, no," she said, and a visible shiver wracked her body. Her gaze met mine with such distress that I reached out to her. She pinched her lips, then swallowed, and holding on tight to my hand, said, "The Star. It's gone."

23

"Stay afraid, but do it anyway. What's important is the action. You don't have to wait to be confident. Just do it, and eventually, the confidence will follow."

— CARRIE FISHER

"I am aware that the Star is missing," the earl said matter-of-factly.

He reached across the marble side table and placed his free hand over our clasped hands, somehow slowing my runaway pulse. If what he said was true, then the missing Star spelled doom for the whole village. And me creating a duplicate had achieved nothing, except emptying my bank account.

I'd expected a dressing down on my inability to do anything right, for him to fire me all over again, even though Regina had already taken care of the task for him. "Regina told you."

He took his hands back and swept one down the length of his body. "My body has told me so."

This story wasn't real. It couldn't be. Angels appearing, offering conditional grace. The dead coming back to life. A Star that appeared out of nowhere. A Star the earl said he could feel. And not only that, but a Star he also depended on to stay alive and keep the village thriving. Why was he playing me like this? What would it get him?

"What about Amos Thannen?" I asked, remembering the photo from the Historical Society of both men, standing by the Star. "I thought he built the Star."

"Amos was fascinated by the Star. Obsessed even." The earl sighed. "I allowed him to study it for his art's sake." He gave a slow shake of his head. "But that was a mistake. When he wanted to take it apart to discover the source of its light, I had to rebuff him. Then, one night, I caught him in my home, tools at the ready to destroy the one thing that was keeping us all alive."

Agnes at the Historical Society had mentioned a disagreement between the men that had caused a rift. "That's what the argument between you was about."

"We both said words we regretted. Yet, both of us were too proud to admit a mistake." He tipped his head downward. "I still had much growing to do."

"Why did Amos leave?" One argument wasn't big enough to send someone running all the way across the country. Especially back then when travel wasn't as fast or easy as it was now. Of course, running away was my own M.O. Rather than face conflict, rejection, I left.

"Because of the broken trust between us," the earl said. "It is not a proud chapter in my history. But he did well for himself in California, created a life and family."

"You kept track of him?"

"Of course. He was, at one point, a friend. I wished him well."

Keep your enemies in sight? "Did you know both Regina Buchanan and Royce Tanner are related to Amos?"

He arched a brow.

"Of course you did." My toes curled inside my flats from me forcing my feet to stay in place. "Do they know of their relation to the Star?"

He nodded. "Regina understands the import of the Star, which is why she does everything in her power to protect it and Brighton. Royce, on the other hand, is focused on the power of the Star without understanding that he could not wield any of it. The Star is not corruptible. It is cooperative."

"Do you think Royce could have stolen it or arranged to have it stolen? He mentioned how it's been missing for a year, how some thugs stole it last Christmas and destroyed it."

"I have had him investigated and found no evidence that he was involved in the theft. Also, if he had destroyed the Star, I would be dead and most of Brighton, including you, would have disappeared."

Not super reassuring. I got up and paced. Could the Star not shining really cause people to just disappear? "Who else came up on your radar as a possible suspect?"

"Let us just say I was thorough."

I stared at him for a moment. "That would also have been good information to have three months ago."

"I did not want to prejudice you."

"So, instead you had me duplicate your efforts?"

He tipped his head. "When you say it that way."

"That's a lot of wasted time." I tried to order my thoughts, ping-ponging between utter disbelief and damage control. Except no amount of scissors, tape or pins could fix this issue. "Let me get this straight. You've investigated possible suspects and have come up with nothing. And yet, you think that I can somehow find your Star?"

"The Star shines but once a year and recharges my body for another year." He plucked at the jacket that I now realized hung too loosely on his torso. "Since last Christmas, my body has grown weaker instead of stronger. At first, I thought that perhaps I had a bout of the influenza that was going around. But the doctor could find no sign of illness. And my body kept getting weaker. In late spring, I had Regina check on the Star. That is when she found it missing." He gave a wry smile. "I know what you are thinking. A hundred-and-thirty-four-year-old man is bound to grow tired."

"One hundred and thirty four?" For some reason, even after his story, I'd thought that he was a descendant of the earl. How could nobody have mentioned this before? "You're the original earl."

"The one and only." His smile was small and sad.

"How is that possible?" Did the rest of the town know? How had that never come up? So often I'd heard people refer to the original earl as if more than one had managed the estate.

"It is purgatory, my dear."

He signaled for me to sit down, but I couldn't. I had to move, or my mind would fly right out of my skull. He and Regina had known the Star was gone. Had that been a test? One I'd obviously failed because Regina had fired me. But how else was I supposed to have reacted.

"I have trusted a few select people in each generation with the story, because I could not do all this by myself," the earl said. "They became Brighton's guardians and helped me with my goodwill projects, helped Brighton thrive. The tree lighting on Christmas Eve is more than a ceremony to entertain the masses. It is a matter of survival for the descendants of the native villagers. If the Star does not shine, we will all disappear from history as if we had never existed."

"As in erased from people's memory?"

He nodded.

I collapsed into the chair. I would die before I'd had a chance to really live. I would never get married. I would never have children. I would never have a home of my own. I would never get to know what it feels like to truly belong somewhere.

I thought of Fynn, of him not remembering our time together. Time, that to me, was most precious. Considering how I'd hurt him, was this a kindness? Would his life turn out better without me in it?

And my father? If he'd never met my mother, if he'd never had me? How would his life have evolved? Would he have made a happy marriage? Would he love and want his children?

The happy whisper of music coming from the gala made me want to cry. No friends, no family, no clients would remember the role I'd played in their lives. No one would remember the joy I'd added to their special moments with my events. I would never again get to create unique occasions for anyone.

I pressed a hand against my tight chest. The thought of no one remembering me hurt. As if I didn't matter.

As if I were nothing.

"If you've known for over six months that the Star was missing, why the charade of having me bring it to the Three Jeweled Angels?" I asked, carefully modulating the anger roiling inside me.

"Why did you not come to Regina or me as soon as you realized the Star was missing?"

I snorted. "I didn't want to disappoint."

The story of my life. Try to do good. Try to impress. Try to be what others wanted me to be. I should have realized by now that all it led to was disappointment. On both sides.

"Our intention had been that you would come to Regina, trust her, and she would share—"

"Really? You thought that toying with someone as if she were a mouse was a good idea? Do you know what I've gone through since I found out it was missing? How I've blamed myself even though I wasn't even here when it went missing?" My hands flew around me like lightning, punctuating my words. Then I pointed toward town. "I had a *replica* made just so Brighton could have its Christmas!"

This was beyond ridiculous. Regina had led me to believe the missing Star was my fault. She'd fired me because of the missing Star.

"Would you have believed me if I had told you this story last September?" he asked.

I didn't believe it now. "At least I would have had months to find the Star rather than days."

He tipped his head in acknowledgement. "Age does not confer absolute wisdom. I do apologize for my method. I needed to know that you were the right person to take over as guardian of the Star. Without prejudice. I did not want you acting just to curry favor the way my nephew does. You have to understand how dire the situation is. How having the right person at helm is of utter import for Brighton's future."

"I don't understand how lying helps the situation." I needed to go somewhere, anywhere but here. To just walk out that door and leave the earl and Regina and Brighton to figure out their own mess. The worst part was that, if any of this was actually true, I couldn't leave. Because wherever I was when the Star failed to shine, according to the earl, I would disappear.

He stared at me with something tender and aching in his gaze. "I brought you here with the hope that you could help recover the Star."

"Knowing the plan would've helped." Plans, schedules, timelines were what made an event successful. Not last-minute winging. I lifted my arms in a helpless manner. "I've been looking for the Star for weeks now. There's only three days left until Christmas Eve. If you haven't found it in six months, what makes you think I can find it in three days?"

"You are of my blood."

24

"When you're different, sometimes you don't see the millions of people who accept you for what you are. All you notice is the person who doesn't."

— JODI PICOULT

I snorted. Me? Related to the earl? If Mom knew she was related to an earl, she would have exploited that fact to cement her place in society. Instead, she had to depend on my father's name and continued business success to keep her in designer dresses and Botox. "I don't think so."

"Did your mother not tell you the story of the Star?" the earl asked.

"She told me Brighton was cursed and to stay away." Which I now wish I'd done instead of being stubborn and defying her.

"What she did not understand is that running from your destiny will not change it. That was explained to her several times."

I stopped my pacing and faced him, fists so tight my short

nails bit into my palms. "Several times? What? She knows about the Star and our relation to it?"

"Long ago, I made the mistake of confessing the Star's origin to Nell, the woman who nursed me back to health after the priest found me outside the church on Christmas morning. When I moved to my own home, I offered her employment. Over time, we became...more than friends." His old eyes, somehow still looking sharp and clear, looked up at me. There I read his love for the woman he lost. "Nell is your great-great-grandmother. She had a daughter named Dorothy, who had a daughter named Judith, who had a daughter named Liz, who had a daughter named Allegra."

So what if he knew our genealogy. My mother proved that anyone could learn—or pay—for that information. "Eliza. My mother's name is Eliza."

"That is her story to tell." He batted away the fact as if it were unimportant. "The story I told Nell scared her. She left me. She thought that if her child did not live in this cursed village, then she would be safe." He looked down as if the stone floor suddenly offered something of interest. "She would not. The curse, as Nell put it, would have followed her. She did not realize that I would do anything to protect her and our child."

The curse language certainly sounded familiar. "Why didn't you go after her and explain?"

The mournful strains of a violin from the ballroom stirred the quiet of his silence. "Just as those souls could not escape the factory floor when the fire broke out, I cannot leave the borders of Brighton."

"Wow, this is...too much." Did that mean that because we were related to the earl, Mom and I were stuck here now that we'd come to Brighton?

As if reading my mind, the earl said, "You are not the sinner. The restriction was for me to feel what it was like to be one of my employees unable to escape the fire. You are free to leave whenever you want. Although, I am hoping you will stay."

I sniffed. "I'm not sure Regina will let me. She fired me."

"She does not hold the key to your future. You do."

"I still don't understand how I'm supposed to help you find the Star."

"Let me continue with the story." Again, he gestured for me to sit, and I stubbornly refused. With a weary sigh, he went on, "I hired a private investigator to locate Nell, but he could not. Back then, disappearing was much easier. Especially for a woman who could change her name by marriage, which Nell did several times over. Every five years, I would hire someone new. Looking for Nell gave me the idea of tracking down descendants who left the village and offer them a way to make a living in Brighton, so that whatever happened, we could all be together."

He looked at me with such tenderness that it softened all the hard lines grooved into his face. "Then, fifteen years ago, I located you."

That was quite the hop, skip and jump from Nell to me. "How?"

"The private investigator located the DNA analysis your mother had done online, trying to trace her own father."

Who, according to my mother and grandmother, didn't exist. So much for privacy. "Okay, why me? Why not my mother? Why didn't you ask *her* to look for your Star?"

"Because circumstances have closed her heart."

Life had a way of doing that. "Mine's pretty closed too."

He just smiled as if he had some sort of inside track to the workings of my heart. "I sent Regina to speak with your mother fifteen years ago."

Was that what had started their animosity? "I'm sure that went well."

He laughed. "Your mother is as fierce as Regina and would not let you go. Not for any price."

"You tried to buy me?" And, most surprising of all, my mother refused?

"It was a measure of last resort. I had invited your mother to live here with me, to have you grow up understanding your legacy. For you to learn how to run the estate from the ground up, so to speak. Prepare you for your future."

Whoa, run the estate? Me? I shook my head and redoubled my pacing.

Fifteen years ago, I was a confused and angry teen. Mom was single. Divorced from my father for a decade. Although she never said anything, I knew she worried about money, about my father cutting her off from living in the lifestyle she'd become used to. I'd also overheard her many times use me as a pawn to keep the funds flowing into her bank account. That particular tactic had worked until my father cut me off after I refused to join his company.

With money, status, and power so important to her, why had she not jumped at the chance to become the next earl? What was a female earl? Was there even such a thing? I shook my head. *Not important, Allegra. Focus.*

"That still doesn't explain how you think I can find the Star when you can't," I said. Because it was becoming abundantly clear that I couldn't give either the earl or Regina what they wanted, just as I'd never been able to please my own parents.

I was never meant to become part of Brighton, to make a life here. To belong here. I was just a means to an end. The event planner brought in to stage an elaborate experience. Then what? Had Regina planned on firing me all along after Christmas? Use the down-and-out event planner, and toss her out like cold catering leftovers after she was done? That made her no better than Senator Becker.

"Will you trust me, Allegra?" the earl asked.

I paced from the sago palm to the banana tree, really wanting to stride right out those glass doors and keep going, all the way out of Brighton. My mother was right. This place was cursed. Yet, something held me in the room. The need for answers after so many years of questions? "How can I trust you when you and Regina have lied to me from the moment Regina called me on the phone last August?"

That call had given me such hope. The apple festival, the dog adoption festival, the harvest festival had all rebuilt my shaky confidence in my event skills. I was starting to make connections with vendors. The successful festivals had given me the feeling that I could belong here. But all that was nothing but an illusion, a slight of hand, a false hope.

"I have seen how you care about Brighton and its people," the earl said. "You belong here, Allegra. You are my sole heir."

"What about Robin?" This wouldn't come as welcome news to Robin, especially after he'd invested all those months of care.

"He does not possess the proper mindset. He and his lawyer friend are seeking a way to take over my estate. But he cannot. When the Star shines and I can finally move on, I want all I have achieved in Brighton to go on. And only someone with a pure heart and a connection to the Star can carry on my life's mission, my legacy. Robin has neither. You have proven worthy. You are not afraid of hard work. And you have grown to love Brighton and its people."

I huffed and continued pacing. Mission, legacy, a fight over an estate I didn't even know existed five minutes ago. I didn't want any of it. I just wanted Fynn. The realization stopped me cold. Fynn, I loved him. Always had. Always would.

And, now, I could never have him.

I turned to face the earl, fists tight. "What if I don't want any of this?"

"This is the hundred-and-tenth year. The year all these souls will be freed. Or die," the earl said. "Once my debt is paid back, you will be free to do as you choose with my legacy. I do hope you will stay and carry on my mission."

He gestured toward the chair. "Will you please stay? For now. Will you please allow me to teach you how to tune in to the Star? Will you please help me locate it? There is still time to save us all, Allegra."

He was putting too much pressure on me. If I said no, then all these souls would become my burden. At this point, I'd already lost my job. My relationship with Fynn would surely fall apart when I tried to explain this...mess. So, things couldn't get any worse, could they? Unless you counted disappearing from history on Christmas Eve.

"Will you try something with me?" he asked.

I gave a reluctant nod.

"Sit. Please."

I sat on the edge of the chair, knees tight together, hands knotted.

"Move the chair so that we are facing each other."

I did, then sat back down, hands pressed hard against my thighs to keep my legs from jittering.

"Close your eyes."

I did, but they blinked back open.

"It is easier to feel the Star with one's eyes closed."

"Feel the Star?" This was getting too woo-woo, and I'd never been into woo-woo. I'd never trusted anything woo-woo. Growing up, some of my friends went to see psychics, had their cards read, their fortunes told. I always took such things with a large grain of salt. Hard work led to results. Not woo-woo. And I'd worked hard to build a business and a reputation since my father cut me off.

"Close your eyes, Allegra." The earl's voice was gentle, hypnotic.

I swallowed hard and did. He took both my hands in his, our palms flat, facing each other's.

"Breathe in slowly through your nose to a count of four. Hold for a count of eight. Then slowly let your breath out through your mouth to a count of sixteen."

I followed the sound of his breath, allowing myself to mimic him.

"The Star has a vibration all its own," he said a few minutes later, when the breathing had me feeling lightheaded. "It is weak right now, but as you are healthy, you should be able to tune in to it."

I focused on my hands, felt nothing but the cold of the earl's fingers and the warmth of his palms pulsing against mine, growing warmer. Was that the vibration he was talking about?

"Get out of your mind and into your heart," he said. "The Star is not logical. It is pure love."

More woo-woo. I had no idea how to stop thinking, how to get into my heart.

"Pretend, Allegra. Pretend to breathe through your heart. Focus on love."

Even though my eyes were closed, I rolled them and swallowed my doubts. Focus on love. That popped up the image of Fynn and his mischievous smile that made his eyes shine and his whole face glow. His laughter echoed inside me. I wanted a future with him. I wanted that chance. How would thinking of Fynn help me tune in to the Star?

But then, I did feel something. A low thrum through my bones like sitting near train tracks and feeling the roll of the wheels travel through your bones and muscles.

My eyes flew open, and I yanked my hands away from the earl's.

"You felt it," he said with triumph in his voice. "I knew you would."

My pulse raced and I wrapped my arms around my middle. Just like on the bridge that night with Fynn, looking for Mrs. O's mysterious lights. The hum that had started at my feet and wormed up my body before disappearing. Fynn hadn't felt it. But then he'd been focused on catching Chill. Had I felt the Star then?

"It's weak," I said, shaking as if I were outside without a coat. "Getting weaker."

"Because you can feel the Star, I believe it is still in Brighton."

25

"Optimism is the faith that leads to achievement. Nothing can be done without hope and confidence."

— *HELEN KELLER*

"I've looked everywhere," I said, leaning forward in my chair, pleading with the earl to understand that I wasn't cut out for the job. The peaty scent from all the potted plants in the solarium raised nausea. The regulated humidity clung to my skin, making the air feel too thick to breathe. "I couldn't find it. That's why I had a duplicate made."

"Tune in to the Star once more, Allegra. Its strength is weak, but it is there. It must be somewhere close."

I took in a long breath, tried to relax, to tune into the Star. A thread of heat, a small pulse like the beat of a heart wove through me. I tried to hang on to the sensation, to figure out where it came from, but the thread weakened, its heat, its heartbeat waning, then breaking. "It's getting weaker and more difficult to follow."

"Which makes it even more imperative that you find it soon."

I was caught in a finger trap. I couldn't not look for the Star. Yet I didn't have the skill to find it.

The earl reached for my hands once again and his bony fingers grasped my fingers like claws. "You must not share the Star's secret with anyone."

"Why not?" I pulled my hands away from his icy grasp and rose, needing to get away from the earl and the guilt he was trying to spur. "People have a right to know something that affects them."

"I would wager that people would scoff at the notion that they could simply disappear because the Star did not shine. And if they did believe, alarm would surely ensue. The more scattered people are, the more people who witness the disappearance, the more questions will be asked. For the villagers' sake, it will be much better for all concerned if they stay together."

Shaking my head, I paced, the heels of my flats clicking on the stone walkway. I could understand how he would think the news could cause panic. His beloved Nell had left him, thinking she could protect her daughter that way. Instead, Nell had lived in dread of the curse, passing on that fear to the generations that came after, including my own mother. The weight of that fear, my own nest of doubts, and now the responsibility of saving Brighton. It was too much to bear.

"I have to tell Fynn," I said, facing the earl and staring down at him. "He deserves the truth."

I owed him that after he'd offered me a second chance. And I had to have a conversation with my mother about the fact she'd known about this Star business for fifteen years and had never said a thing, other than to never step foot in Brighton for fear of death.

"I implore you not to," the earl said, and a lightning of pain tore through his gaze, hunching him over. "Do you want to be responsible for the deaths of half the villagers?"

"Aren't I anyway if I don't find the Star?"

"We can contain the panic."

"How?"

"I have faith in you."

Something I was lacking in myself. His words, heavy with responsibility, made my resolve waver. No, I didn't want to be responsible for anyone, let alone a town full of strangers.

But Fynn popped into my mind with his smile that lit up his eyes and his unwavering support since I'd found him again... and his love that had somehow survived all these years of me ghosting him. He'd offered me a second chance. I wanted that chance to earn his trust, his love, more than anything else.

And now that Regina had fired me, I was free to leave Brighton and go wherever I wanted, including Foster, Vermont. Nothing tied me here.

My palm flattened over my chest, even as my steps quickened, then slowed.

Except for the Star.

"I understand your concern," I said, knowing how much he and the villagers stood to lose. How much I stood to lose. "But I have to tell Fynn. He deserves to know."

The earl's expression softened. "How do you think he will react to the possibility that you will disappear in three days' time? He is loyal. He will try to save you, even though there is no possibility of saving anyone tied to me and the Star. And if he tells anyone in his misguided attempt to save you..." His frail hand rose, shaking.

The implications hung in the air between us, heavy and foreboding. The secret was a burden, one that couldn't be shared lightly. But I trusted Fynn. I couldn't keep this from him.

Tears burned, but I blinked them away. "I just...don't want to lose him a second time. Surely, you of all people will understand that. You told Nell because you felt it was important for her to know all of you, to keep her in the loop of what was happening to you."

"And look how that turned out." The earl's gaze took on a look of pity. "I lost Nell *because* I told her my secret. If I hadn't, my heirs would have lived here in Brighton and grown up with their legacy." He reached for me, but I moved out of his reach. "You have the chance to choose differently. You must decide if your love for Fynn is strong enough to withstand the secret you must keep."

Knees rattling like a pile of poorly stacked dishes, I took a deep breath. By telling Fynn, I risked unleashing a chain reaction I couldn't control. But keeping the secret would destroy our relationship.

"The burden of leadership is heavy, Allegra." The earl's gaze begged me to understand. "You must protect Fynn and Brighton, even if it means sacrificing your own happiness. Finding the Star is not just a matter of love, but of life and death for a great number of people in Brighton."

I let myself fall into the chair and took a deep breath, the decision feeling as if it were out of my hands, as if I had no control over my future. *The Confident Woman* had lied. Confidence didn't come simply by holding the belief that you were enough, not when your abilities didn't match up to the task. Expansive postures, talking with a deeper tone, and showing up weren't enough. No amount of affirmations could get me to believe that I was powerful enough to handle anything life threw at me.

The earl was right. I couldn't risk a chain reaction of panic I couldn't control. Keeping the villagers together, no matter what happened on Christmas Eve, was better for the whole. I had to stop being so selfish. My heart wept at the thought of losing Fynn once more. I wrapped my arms around my waist, doubling over, trying to keep myself together.

"I'll find the Star," I said, as much to myself as to the earl. My resolve surprised even me. I looked up, meeting his hopeful gaze. *Be bold. Take a risk.* "And I'll keep your secret for now. But promise me something in return."

His spine stiffened. "And what might that be?"

"If I find the Star and it shines on Christmas Eve, you'll explain the situation to Fynn, why I couldn't tell him what was happening, why I had to wait. He deserves to know the truth, especially if I'm to take over your legacy. Because, if this turns out with a positive result, I'll have hurt him all over again, and he'll refuse to listen to me, so you'll have to explain that you made me promise silence."

The earl considered my words, then nodded. "Agreed. But until then, you cannot tell a soul."

I swallowed hard. By keeping Fynn in the dark a little bit longer, I was choosing to protect him in the only way I could.

I rose to leave. The earl caught my hand, his fingers cold and hard against mine. "Remember, Allegra, the path you choose will shape not just your future, but that of Brighton's."

His warning followed me down the hallway like the whines and whistles of a nor'easter wind. The Star was out there, weak but still sending out feelers. I had a job to do. I would find it.

∽

THE WEIGHT of the earl's secret nearly crushing me, I returned to the ballroom. I could hardly breathe, and it took the whole way back to find a smile and pretend all was well. Regina may have fired me, but I was still legally responsible for this event. I would stay until the last vendor left. I would finish the job. I would do it right.

The ballroom shimmered in the glow of the fairy lights, electric candles and ice, turning it into a magical winter wonderland. The chandeliers hung like stars, casting intricate patterns on the polished marble floor. Bright music invited dancers to the floor. The scent of sweet and savory treats and pine boughs filled the air. I wove through the crowd, smiling, nodding, greeting—ensuring everything was perfect. People danced and chatted and ate. Everyone seemed to enjoy the event.

I noted once again the filling garbage can by the bar and made a note to have them emptied. One of the candles in the ice sculpture no longer glowed. I'd have to check the batteries. Did those wires near the stage need another swipe of tape?

I spotted Fynn in a small circle listening in on a conversation between Aaron Carpenter, a local woodworker, and Gabriel Conley, a local metal artist. As if Fynn sensed my gaze, he turned and smiled at me. He came toward me, looking handsome and confident.

Fynn extended a hand toward me. "May I have this dance?"

"So formal," I joshed, one hand wrapping around my waist, the other curling into a fist so I wouldn't chew my nails.

"Your beauty brings out the gentleman in me."

I silently scoffed. I was average. Average height. Average shoe size. Definitely average looks. That averageness was one of the things that made me so good at running events. I was there, yet invisible. "Thank you, Fynn. That's sweet of you."

He took my free hand in his. I hesitated. I was in charge. *No, I remembered, you've been fired.* "Since when do you dance?"

His smile teased. "It's a slow dance. How much damage can I do to your feet?"

I laughed, let him lead me to the dance floor. "Just one. Then I have to get back to the event."

The band played a slowed-down version of Taylor Swift's "The Dreamer's Waltz." The violin added a mournful cry that made my heart want to weep. *A last dance*, I thought and assumed a smile so I wouldn't cry.

His movements were so assured, so effortlessly at ease even

though he didn't like large crowds—or dancing. His hand at my waist was both a torture and a comfort. I tried to lose myself in the rhythm and sway of the dance. "When did you learn to dance?"

"In Europe."

Another reason for him to have gone there without me—to become who he was fully meant to be without an anchor.

"Is everything okay?" he asked, his voice a low rumble that echoed in my chest. His gaze searched mine, making my pulse quicken.

I widened my smile. "Of course. It's a beautiful night. And I'm dancing with the most handsome man in the room."

"Allie..."

"It's a big event." I half shrugged. "I have a lot riding on everything running perfectly."

He made a show of looking around at the other dancers, the guests enjoying conversation and food. "Looks like you've achieved your goal."

I tipped my head. "There's still time for a disaster to happen. After what happened with Senator Becker last June, I can't rest until everyone's left."

"Five minutes, Allie. For yourself. Nobody's going to begrudge you that."

"That's all it took last time."

He gave one nod. "You're here."

"I am." And I made myself savor the present moment. Fynn. This man with the tender heart and boundless talent. I didn't want to let him go. But I had to. I studied the rugged lines of his face. I memorized the feel of his arms. I inhaled his scent of a sunny summer day. "Let's just enjoy the moment."

"A song for the soul, a dance for the heart..." the singer sang.

I'd always been the outsider—at school, at work, at home. But now, for once, I was an insider. Apparently, this whole estate could have been mine. I had a hard time wrapping my head around the fact the earl, this stranger, was my great-great-grandfather. That he'd wanted me to be part of Brighton since I was a teen.

But without the Star, this unexpected legacy would poof away—just as my career had. Fynn wouldn't understand. And I couldn't explain.

The music swelled around us, violins wailing as if their sadness was unappeasable. Suddenly, my breath couldn't move my lungs, creating a throbbing knot. Keeping Fynn in the dark would hurt him all over again.

I spread a hand over my chest. Especially now that the earl had passed on the responsibility of finding the Star—and saving the village—to me.

"Are you sure you're okay?" His brow pleated. "You look like you're going to pass out. Do you need to sit?"

"A bit of heartburn from all the stress. That's all." I wanted to tell him everything, to have someone to share this burden with. But I had to hide this secret from him. I'd made a promise, and I always kept my promises.

And the earl was right. If I revealed the secret, panic would ensue. Whatever happened on Christmas Eve had to remain contained...that would be better for all concerned. I sighed.

And Fynn was an outsider—not part of Brighton.

But Fynn could always read through my false hostess front.

"Talk to me, Allie," he whispered in my ear, holding me closer.

I pressed my ear against his heart, listened to the bold and strong rhythm. He wasn't mine. I'd blown my chance to have him eight years ago. I would enjoy this dance, this evening with him, send him home, and protect him from whatever happened here in three days.

And if the worst happened, then he wouldn't even remember me.

He stopped moving, right there in the middle of the dance floor. Dancers flowed around us like water around rocks. "The night you disappeared eight years ago, I was going to propose to you."

I gaped like a fish on land. Propose? My heart beat too fast. He'd wanted to propose. To take me with him to Europe as his wife? What had I done?

"Fynn—"

I read hurt in his eyes. "And I really thought that this time would work out for us, that we'd both learned from our mistakes."

"Fynn..."

"But I can't do this again, Allie." He let go of my hands and they suddenly felt abandoned. "I can't have you shut me down with no explanation again. If you can't trust me, then what do we really have?"

"I trust you." *With my life, which is why I can't tell you.*

"Then let me in."

My throat worked around the knot climbing there from my chest. "It's complicated."

"It always is." He grazed a finger down the side of my face, a plea in his voice. "Talk to me, Allie."

I tried to blink back tears, but they slipped down my cheek anyway. "I'm sorry, Fynn."

His gaze clouded. "Me, too."

I reached out to him, but he was already turning away. I watched helplessly as he strode through the crowd and out the door, leaving me there alone in the middle of the dance floor, a crowd of people staring, whispering.

I'd just lost the most important person in my life.

No event, no career, no legacy was worth that.

As the last notes of the song faded away, I raced after him, the room swirling around me in a blur of lights and shadows.

But when I got to the front doors, he'd already disappeared.

The cold air hit me like a fist, reminding me that I had more than my own life at stake.

I crumpled on the granite step, letting the winter cold numb me.

I didn't go after him. What was the point? I was about to disappear along with most of the villagers.

But my heart didn't understand that. It wanted me to run after him, beg for forgiveness.

And when I couldn't, it broke into a thousand pieces all over again.

26

"I was always looking outside myself for strength and confidence but it comes from within. It is there all the time."

—ANNE FREUD

I don't know how I got through the rest of the evening, but somehow, I did. Somehow, I got through the gala clean up at the estate. Somehow, I ticked off the last item on my checklist. Everyone was gone. Everything was in order—just as it had been before the gala. I just wanted to go home, fall into bed and sleep for a week.

Of course, I didn't have a bed right now, because my mother —who I'd made a point of avoiding all evening because I didn't want to start a fight in the middle of an event—occupied it. And I didn't have a week. Only three days to find the Star and save Brighton.

Not that anything seemed to matter right now because, no matter what, my future wouldn't include Fynn. He wouldn't forgive me a second time.

I missed him. *Pathetic*, I thought, *moping over a man.*

I didn't want to miss him. And missing him hurt so much.

I saw him everywhere. In this foyer, looking so handsome in a tux, in the ballroom teasing Mom, in the basement snooping on my behalf. He'd made looking for the Star feel possible. Fun, even.

I stuffed my tablet and my heels into my bag, slipped on boots and my coat, then grabbed the handle of my rolling emergency kit. The lingering aroma of the guests' clashing perfumes and colognes still hung in the air, making my stomach wish I'd eaten something other than a protein bar throughout the endless day.

I'd almost reached the front door, when Robin's footsteps echoed down the hall and onto the marble floor of the foyer.

"There you are," Robin said, his voice like hot chocolate sauce over cold ice cream, overly sweet and cloying after a hard day. "I thought you might have gone home already."

I glanced at my watch. Almost 4 a.m. and sighed. "Still here."

"That was quite the event. Everyone seemed to enjoy the evening."

"Thanks for all your help." I buttoned my coat against the cold night outside. "Having someone who knows the estate inside out was a godsend."

He smiled, a smile that took on an oily edge in the stark light of the foyer's chandelier. "You are most welcome."

"It was nice to see the earl addressing the town." He'd spoken of all the villagers had accomplished in the past year, and I was amazed at how many people his foundation had managed to help. I hiked my messenger bag over my shoulder. "I hope he feels better soon."

"Yes, well, he did look especially frail tonight." Robin's voice softened as if he really cared for the old man. "I'm not sure how much longer he can hang on."

I pulled my messenger bag forward, tilting my head to try to read him. Had I misconstrued what he and Kay had said in the hallway? "I heard you talking to your lawyer friend earlier this evening."

"I'm sorry? Lawyer friend?" He frowned, the picture of innocence.

"Kay. The woman you introduced to me as your cousin."

His expression hardened. A shiver of danger went through me. *Don't, Allegra. Don't confront him. It's not your place.* I should let what I'd overheard go, but my overly tired mind wouldn't let me. I couldn't let him hurt an old man, an old man, who it turned out was my great-grandfather.

"I heard you tell Kay that you could run the business better than your great-uncle does."

He hiked a shoulder, unrepentant. "I'm good at what I do. I've created and sold a half dozen successful companies."

"So why do you need his?"

His smile flattened and he shook his head as if I was nothing but a naïve creature. "Why does anyone?"

"Is this why you're truly here? To take over what he's spent a lifetime building?"

"He's dying. I wanted him to understand he had family that cared, family that could take over for him and keep his legacy going."

"What you don't get is that this is more than a business to him, it's his mission. Profits are a side effect, not the main goal. The true aim is to foster community and cooperation so that *all* in Brighton benefit."

"That's a foolish way to run a business." His voice echoed in the cavernous foyer, reaching up to the chandelier, glowing with thousands of spiky snowflakes.

"It's a progressive way. It's the way of the future."

He snorted. "Without profit there's no incentive, no investment, no innovation."

"That's where you're wrong. Cooperation, community

allows all to thrive. That's why Brighton does so well year after year."

He scoffed. "I thought it was the 'magic' Star." He made finger quotes that managed to look disdainful.

"The Star is a symbol. You've had free run of the place for months now. Did you hide it, so you could take over from your great-uncle?"

"It's not nice to accuse someone of something nefarious when you have no evidence." His gaze went icy. "Besides, I believe in hard work. I believe in what I can see. Not some Star that brings good luck."

"So why bother hiding it?"

He lifted both his hands as if he had nothing to hide. "If I believed in this Star, do you think I'd have wasted so much time catering to every whim and whimper of a callous old man?"

No, I didn't. Robin would have taken the Star and left, thinking he could exploit its power.

Robin leaned forward, mouth twisted. "Did you know that he wouldn't even throw my mother a bone when she needed help? She raised me on her own. He could've made a difference in both our lives, but he refused."

That didn't sound like the earl. From what I'd heard and seen, he went out of his way to help the town of Brighton. And even so close to death and with his fear of spending eternity in purgatory, he still put their welfare above his.

The one thing I'd learned over and over again in the past three months I'd spent here was that the earl didn't give handouts. He expected people to help themselves. Villagers had to put in as much sweat equity as he gave out in financial aid. Which was fair, because people rarely appreciated unearned gain. And that equity fostered that sense of community and belonging. "Did she do anything to help herself?"

His answer was a scowl. The grandfather clock at the end of the hallway bonged four slow times like a warning.

"Why did Kay say I was the key?" I asked, redirecting the conversation.

"Because I've heard Uncle Harry and Regina talking about you."

I frowned. "About me?"

"How Brighton's future depends on you," he said, his tone mocking. As if little old me could not in any way be responsible for something so important.

"And on the magical Star you say you don't believe in." I played into his belief that I was a nobody—an easy role to act. "I don't see how. I'm just an event planner."

"That's what I've been telling Kay." He growled. "But she thinks there must be something to it, or they wouldn't stop talking about it whenever I enter the room."

"Well, I hate to disappoint you and Kay," I said, waving two hands down my simple ice-blue gown, "but I'm nothing special."

I stepped closer to him as if to tell him a secret, and sour sweat wafted off his tailored tuxedo. "You've underestimated one crucial thing about Brighton."

He scoffed and crossed his arms over his chest. "Enlighten me."

"The people don't need the Star to believe in miracles. They believe in helping and supporting each other. The earl understood that. He built this community on that value." A lesson he'd learned when he'd created the Christmas Village all those years ago. I'd seen families come together, businesses flourish, and the community grow stronger with every festival. "The village of Brighton won't follow your leadership because they won't trust you. You're an outsider."

"And you're not?"

"I belong in Brighton." I realized that was true. Even without the roots I didn't know I had, over the past three months, I'd created my own. I'd proven that I understood the town's values. And now with Fynn lost to me, belonging here meant more than ever. "They'll see right through your self-serving ambition."

He made a dismissive face. "You think any of that will matter once I have control of the estate?"

"The mutual support the earl and the town share aren't something you can manipulate."

"Who pulls the financial strings—" he mimicked pulling marionette strings "—controls."

I mimed scissors cutting his strings. "Not when those strings run in a circle rather than one way."

He dismissed me with a flick of his hand. "You have no idea what you're talking about. I spent my summers here, working my butt off for someone who didn't appreciate anything I did. I know what this estate means. I believe it can be even more."

I shrugged, acting more confident than I felt. "You can't just waltz in and take over. It's not that simple."

"I never said it would be simple. But sometimes change is necessary. Nothing should stand in the way of progress."

"Progress or profits? Try to bully the town, and you'll see just how strong this community is. They'll fight for what they believe in. They'll protect the legacy the earl built. With or without the Star, Brighton will go on." Maybe not in the way it had, but enough people, unrelated to the original one hundred and ten, influenced by the earl's values, would stay in Brighton and rebuild.

"Like I said, I'm not here to destroy anything," Robin said. "I want to build something better, more efficient." He pointed a finger at me. "But if you, or anyone else tries to stop me, I will tie up this town in so much probation red tape that the villagers won't be able to draw one cent from the estate for decades. And all their projects will fail."

He would rather plow under a whole village than admit he'd used the wrong tactic. "You'll regret that."

"I doubt it."

He opened the door and waved me out with an arm. "Don't come back."

I stumbled out into the cold night, shivering from both the chill and Robin's intent. And yet, a sense of hope took root, knowing I was right about Brighton, that its spirit of community and cooperation could win over greed.

In any case, I had to warn Regina, who would let the earl know that his great-nephew's intents weren't pure, that the earl might be in danger.

27

"The reward for conformity is that everyone likes you but yourself."

— RITA MAE BROWN

When I got home after the gala, I'd dropped my messenger bag and my coat on the floor with a plop and whoosh, then stepped out of my boots, leaving everything in a trail I couldn't be bothered to pick up. I'd changed into flannel pajamas and fallen onto the couch, needing the oblivion of sleep. But the sleep I craved hadn't come. I stared at the ceiling where the evening kept repeating on a loop like a bad movie—the earl, Fynn, Robin. And at the center of it all: the Christmas Star.

How had my life taken so many wrong turns?

I mourned the life I wanted but would never have. I mourned the Village disappearing on Christmas Eve. I mourned losing Fynn.

At six, I gave up the pretense of sleep and got up to make coffee. Sitting cross-legged on the couch, I sipped my mushroom-cocoa sludge, closed my eyes and tried to tune in to the Star like the earl had shown me. But with fatigue weighing my bones, I got not even a twinge.

Instead, Fynn's face kept popping up, pain filling his eyes. I wanted to cry, but if I started, I wouldn't be able to stop, so I kept busy, busy, busy—checking email, the task management program, making to-do lists for the next three days until the lighting ceremony.

By the time my mother got up at nine, I'd dressed, gone out to get scones for breakfast, bought ingredients to make sugar cookies and started a fresh pot of coffee. I'd also rechecked my email to make sure no gala-related problems had cropped up in the last few hours. All was well on that front. I'd had a gift and a thank-you note sent to Tessa for her help with the chairs.

When Mom came out of the bathroom, I poured her a mug and handed it to her. Murmuring her thanks, she accepted the red mug with the Christmas gnome with one hand. With the other, she tightened my plush blue robe against her chest. She sank onto a stool on the living room side of the counter.

"How did you enjoy the gala?" I asked, leaning my elbows on the counter and narrowing my gaze on her. What would she find to criticize?

She perked up, smiling all the way to her eyes. "You did an excellent job, Allegra."

"Do you really think so? No notes?"

She tilted her head, giving me a strange look. "Everything was superb, and everyone seemed to have a great time." She closed her eyes and drank in caffeine. "This is good coffee. I had the best time. I met the most interesting people."

Surprise, surprise. No criticism. That had to be a first. But while she was having a grand old time, my life had completely fallen apart. As usual, she'd been oblivious.

"Why didn't you tell me?" I asked, anger I hadn't realized had grown all morning turning each word into a bullet.

She jerked as if those word bullets had found their mark and frowned. "Tell you what?"

"That we're related to the earl?"

She set her mug down on the counter with slow, precise movements, as if it were filled with poison she couldn't spill.

"I didn't know." She gave a careless shrug. "Not for sure, anyway. Just a two-and-two-make-four thing. A conclusion I came to from the stories Granny told. Who told you?"

"The earl himself."

"Ah."

Ah, all I got was an ah?

"That's why you didn't want me to come to Brighton?" I tried to keep my voice calm, but it came out crisp with accusation. "You didn't want me to find out my true heritage?"

"Mostly because Granny was so afraid that we would die if we came here." Mom sighed loud enough for the whole town to hear.

"Mostly?"

"It's complicated."

"Then uncomplicate it for me."

One thumb stroked the side of the mug as if it were a magic lamp that would give her answers. "I know that, for some reason, you think I don't love you, but everything I did was *because* I love you."

"Right," I said, unable to hold back bitterness. "So, who are you, really? The earl called you Liz and said I should ask you about your history."

Her shoulders slumped. From the weight of her lies? From the weight of having been caught in those lies?

"I was born plain old Liz Knud," she said, her voice a monotone. "Not Elizabeth, definitely not Eliza. No middle name. Just Liz."

"Liz Knud?" That was news. I'd always assumed that the grandmother I'd never met was a Campbell.

Mom gave a small nod and steeled her spine. "I was the white trash a blue-blood college boy picked up and got pregnant."

The venom in her words stung. I may be angry with her, but I never thought of her as anything but refined, certainly not trash. "Mom, no—"

She waved away my denial. "His parents were tired of fixing his messes, so they told him he had to suffer the consequences of his actions this time." She gave a bitter laugh that seemed to come from a place of deep pain. "Not exactly the best foundation for a marriage."

No, more like resentment. And that's exactly what I'd felt between them growing up, so much resentment. It made me feel as if I had to hold my breath and tiptoe around them. "So, what happened?"

She clasped the mug of coffee as if her hands were cold. "When I refused to have an abortion, he asked me to marry him. And I said yes."

She shook her head, then stared at her coffee. "He belonged in a world that I never could, no matter how hard I tried." Tears glistened in her eyes. "He tried to mold me into the perfect wife, starting with changing my name. Knud sounded too ethnic somehow for him, even though it's a perfectly good Danish name. So, he went with Campbell. It means 'crooked mouth'—his little joke because one of the first things he did was get my teeth straightened."

She sipped her coffee and slipped off the stool. She found the half and half in the fridge and added a healthy slug to her mug. Was she no longer watching her figure?

"I was so eager to fit in that I let him." Her expression took on a mixture of regret and self-reproach. "I thought that if I could manage to mold myself into what he wanted, that I would be worthy. That he would love me. That his world would accept me." She snorted. "That I'd gain security."

Oh, that sounded so familiar. That same little voice in my head made me feel less-than on a daily basis, told me I wasn't good enough and I never would be. *If you dress this way, Allegra... If you do this for me, Allegra... If you plan my party, Allegra...*

"Money doesn't buy happiness," I said, shaking off my teenage angst.

"But it surely does make living much easier when you don't have to worry about the basic necessities."

She was right, of course. Struggling for the basics had to cause stress. I'd seen that in Fynn in college. I found it hard to believe that Mom had come from such an impoverished background. "How did you meet Dad, then? Because, obviously, the story you told me was fiction."

Her gaze unfocused as if she went back to that time and place. "No, that part was true. A friend dragged me to a fraternity party at UPenn. He smiled at me from across the room." A sad smile played on her lips, and she shook her head. "He was a handsome devil. We ended up talking all evening." She lifted her shoulders and let them drop. "The rest, as they say, is history."

"I don't understand," I said. "What does any of that have to do with you not telling me about your family?"

"I didn't want my past to taint you." She took her time sipping her coffee. "My mother was a drunk. She couldn't hold a job for longer than five minutes. I grew up hungry, Allegra. Scraping for food, for clothing, for a roof over my head. You have no idea what it's like to walk into a classroom and have the other children laugh at your charity hand-me-downs. Act as if you had cooties just because you got a free lunch. Hold their noses as they went by you because your clothes weren't pristinely pressed like theirs."

I snorted. "I might not have been hungry for food, and I might have had all the right clothes but that didn't mean that I fit in. I was still the odd girl out that everyone liked to pick on.

High school was hell, and you kept telling me to suck it up and sent me back there without any real way to deal with any of it." I remembered how glad I was on graduation day to flip my cap and leave it all behind, to start fresh in a new place where nobody knew me, even if they knew my father's name.

"I'm sorry," she whispered. "I wanted you to be strong, to claim your rightful place."

"Well, that's not what happened."

"All those parties you went to—"

"Parties I planned, so I could pretend I had friends, so that I could pretend I fit in, so that I could finally win your approval. I planned those parties, but I wasn't allowed to participate in them." Always on the edge, never on the inside.

"That can't be true. You were a Livingstone—"

My coffee had gone cold, so I abandoned my mug in the sink. I went to the grocery bags and unloaded the flour. "Those girls didn't want me in their circle any more than you did."

She flinched as if I'd slapped her. "How could you even think that! I wanted you. You are the most precious thing in my life."

"You have a strange way of showing it." I arranged the sugar, vanilla, butter and almond extract in a row. I folded the reusable bags for my next outing.

"Everything I did was for you." Her whole body shook with the intensity of her emotions. "I gave up *my* dreams so that *you'd* have a better life than I did, so that *you'd* fit into your father's world." Her fingers, white against the red of the mug, pressed the ceramic so hard, I thought the mug would shatter. "So that *you* would feel secure."

"I'm not sure how you thought ignoring me and criticizing me would make me feel secure." I reached beneath the counter for a bowl, rattling all of them until I found the right size. "All it did was make me feel as if I could never measure up."

"Oh, Allegra." Tears rolling down her cheeks, her gaze

pleaded with me, and her voice went strangely soft. "Do you know why I named you Allegra?"

I shook my head and jerked open a drawer.

"It means happy, lively. That's what I wanted for you right from the start."

"You and Dad constantly fought over who *wouldn't* have me for the holidays." The pain of sitting on the black walnut steps at the top of the stairway still fresh, listening to them bicker in the foyer about whose turn it wasn't to have me. Me ending up getting dragged to Grandmother and Grandfather Livingstone's house for a cold and silent Christmas where I was reminded at every turn that I was to be seen and not heard. Under the Christmas tree there'd be one box with my name. Inside, I'd find a bond or a stock or a mutual fund contribution.

"It's never too early to plan for your future, Allegra," Grandfather said, wearing a three-piece suit even on Christmas morning.

"Yes, you must make better financial choices than your parents did," Grandmother said, with a sneer in her voice, disappointed with her only grandchild.

I stirred around the mish-mash of culinary tools in the drawer until I found a spatula and a whisk. "And where was my father all those Christmases? Not around the tree on Christmas morning, that's for sure."

If he deigned to show himself at the dinner table—catered, not homemade—it was because my grandparents had invited someone he wanted to court to advance his business.

"I wanted you with me." Mom gestured wide, sending the gnome mug flying off the counter and crashing against the tile. "You have no idea how many holidays I spent alone and crying so you could bond with your father. I didn't want him to throw you away the way he's thrown away everyone else." She beat a fist against her chest, her face a mask of anguish. "I wanted you with me so we could do all the fun things I never got to do growing up—cookies, caroling, movies." Her throat bobbed. "I sacrificed, so I could ensure your future."

"Those fairy tale Christmases were what I'd wanted, too, Mom." I crouched to pick up the broken pottery pieces. They clinked as they fell to the bottom of the garbage can. Another mug I'd have to replace. "Baking cookies, singing carols, watching movies while trimming the tree. Now I feel cheated because those Christmases with Grandmother and Grandfather Livingstone were none of those things."

I got the sponge from the sink to wipe the counter. She reached for my hand, but I pulled it away, and went back to the floor.

"And what about all those stories about growing up in Philadelphia? You talked about the brick sidewalks and gas-lit lamps, Independence Hall, the Museum of Art, how everything was so close."

"I never actually said I lived there. You assumed." She shrugged, a sad smile twisting her lips. "And I let you."

I looked up from my crouch on the floor, the coffee-stained sponge dripping. "Why?"

"I didn't want you knowing I grew up homeless for the most part. I spent so many weekends walking the streets of Society Hill, dreaming I lived in one of those townhouses. I'd look into the homes, especially at night when people forgot to close their drapes, at how beautiful the rooms were, and I wanted to do that—create settings that would encourage people to relax and open up."

"You got your wish." Rinsing the sponge, I scoffed. "You had your Beacon Hill house to decorate."

She shook her head. "Not the way I wanted. The way I was expected to, so it would reflect the image your father wanted to project."

I did know how stubborn my father could be. He'd forced me to study business when I'd wanted to major in hospitality.

But I didn't want to feel sorry for my mother. Just because he made her suffer didn't mean she had to act coldly toward her only child. "You make it sounds as if I was too spoiled to understand what you went through."

She didn't say anything for a while. "I did things I'm not proud of to survive."

I turned my back to her and refilled my coffee mug. "I always felt like an outsider, especially around you and Dad."

"That was never my intent."

I glanced at her over my shoulder. "Maybe not, but it was the effect."

"I couldn't tell you any of it, Allegra."

"Why not?"

She hesitated, that unusual uncertainty pinching her face. "The thing is...your father...he threatened to leave us both with nothing if I ever revealed my past to anyone, including you."

Her gestures got expansive again. She would've made a terrific actress. "I couldn't have you growing up the way I did, always looking over your shoulder, always worried about where your next meal would come from. I had to keep my past a secret so he would keep supporting us. I couldn't risk losing everything, especially not you."

I banged the measuring cup against the counter. "He blackmailed you?"

She lifted a shoulder. "More like a bargain. He didn't want me to embarrass him, so I kept my past in the past. I also thought it would be best if you didn't know."

"Maybe we wouldn't be so distant if you had told me."

My mother came around the counter and pulled me into her arms. "My dearest daughter."

I took a shuddering breath, stiffening at the hug I'd wanted more than anything growing up. Knowing what I now know, what would I have done in her place? I'd probably have accepted the bargain, too. A child deserved a home and all the advantages their parents could give them.

I'd like to think, though, that I would have let my daughter know she was loved and not left her to wonder.

I wasn't quite ready to forgive Mom yet, but at least I had context for my childhood loneliness. So, I sank into her hug.

The anger that had sparked my confrontation with her, slowly evaporated into a fragile understanding. She'd done what she thought was best for her and for me.

Which, when you came right down to it, was what we all did. I'd done the same to Fynn eight years ago.

And look where that got me.

Don't think about Fynn. I blinked hard and fast. I didn't want to cry. I didn't want to have to explain what had happened between us last night. Better to focus on the other part of my dilemma.

"The Christmas Star," I said, reaching for my tablet. "What do you really know about it?"

28

"Don't waste your energy trying to change opinions... Do your thing, and don't care if they like it."

— *TINA FEY*

"I don't know anything more than what I've already told you," Mom said, squirming on the hard stool at the living room side of the counter. "Granny thought Brighton was cursed and warned me to stay away unless I wanted to die. And I'm quite partial to living."

"Still alive," I pointed out. I pulled the chain with the dodecagram charm and slipped it over my mother's head, giving her back her curse. "Both of us."

"Yes, well, it's not quite Christmas, is it?" She twirled the charm between her fingers.

"No, you're right." Christmas was the crux of the situation. "Did you know that if the Star doesn't shine on Christmas Eve, all the descendants of the original villagers will up and disappear?"

The little liar knew about the Star, so it wasn't as if I was breaking my promise.

"That doesn't sound plausible." She scrunched the robe tighter around her chest. "But it would explain Granny's unreasonable fears."

I placed both hands on the counter and focused my gaze on my mother. "I need to find it. And I need your help doing it."

"It's missing?"

I nodded.

"Of course." She perked up. "Anything."

Well, that went easier than expected. I thought she'd fight me, try to get me to leave again. I rummaged through the cupboards, looking for a mixer.

"What are you doing?" Mom asked, peering over the counter's edge.

"Making sugar cookies."

"Why?"

I pulled what looked like an antique mixer from the back of the cupboard. "You're the one who taught me that people are more apt to open up if you give them something first."

"True."

"Plus, you said you wanted to do this with me when I was little. Here's your chance to cross 'making cookies' with your kid off your list."

She swallowed hard. "There's no list, Allegra."

"There's always a list with you." I plopped the mixer on the counter. "If we turn on the TV and sing carols as we bake, we'll get through the whole trifecta."

Mom clucked her tongue. "You're in a mood."

"With good reason."

She nodded and looked down at the robe. "Let me get dressed. Can I borrow a sweatshirt?"

"It's not like you bothered asking all the other times you borrowed something from my closet."

"You weren't home."

I shoved the beaters into their slots on the mixer. "I wouldn't want you to get one of your designer shirts dirty."

With a long sigh, she went to the bedroom and shut the door.

I growled, leaning my elbows on the counter and holding my forehead. *Not helpful, Allegra.*

I needed to get over my anger, over my self-righteousness, and concentrate on the now, on finding the blasted Christmas Star. I ripped open the flour bag, sending a white cloud swirling around my head.

I wished I'd never heard of Brighton and the Star.

∼

In spite of the rocky start, Mom and I ended up having fun making the cookies. Needing to shift my mood, I'd put the TV on a marathon of Christmas movies. Mom had come out wearing her own clothes and donned an apron to protect her designer sweater.

She grabbed a measuring cup, smiled as widely as her Botox would let her and said, "Let's do this."

I pulled up the recipe on my tablet. She measured. I mixed. In no time, we had a ball of dough.

"Don't you need to chill the dough?" Mom asked when I attacked the ball with a knife and cut it into two.

"Not this recipe." I pointed my chin toward the back of the counter. "Grab the cookie cutters."

She lifted each one in turn, examining the details. "Oh, these are so cute."

"I found them at the Country Store." I'd picked out a star, a snowflake and a snow globe. They were plunger type cookie cutters. They would press a design into the dough that we could trace with the cookie icing I'd bought.

"They have everything there." She shook her head as if surprised such a treasure would exist in the back end of nowhere, as she called Brighton.

Soon, the kitchen filled with the aroma of baking cookies—sugar, butter and vanilla. Who could stay angry with sugar and vanilla molecules filling their nose?

As I slipped a cookie sheet into the oven, Mom rolled out another portion of dough. "Christmas was always so frantic. Your Dad hated the holidays but always felt as if he had to make a good impression on his investors then. He kept me so busy I hardly had a chance to breathe from September until January."

All the charity events, all the parties, all the never-ending lists she'd spent so much time planning. I cut out cookie shapes but didn't reply. "What about after the divorce?"

"He still needed a hostess." She jerked a shoulder. "I didn't want to risk him cutting us off, so I complied."

Just as I had once I'd been old enough to take over for my mother—once he'd seen how people enjoyed my events. I was making him sound like a monster. He really wasn't. Just focused on his business and on saving the world. Too bad he hadn't realized his family was part of that world.

"I should have taken time out for this with you." A wave of sadness flowed over Mom's face.

Water under the bridge and all that, but the fact she hadn't chosen to make the time for me still managed to hurt. "We're doing it now."

She gave me a watery smile. "So, what exactly do you hope to accomplish with these cookies?"

"First, promote the scavenger hunt." I placed the first batch of finished cookies into a red tin with a Christmas design on the cover.

"How do you know it's around?" Mom plucked a still-hot cookie off the cooling rack and dropped it on the counter where it broke in three pieces. "It could be anywhere in the world."

"The earl taught me how to feel it."

"Feel it?" She broke off an arm of the snowflake and blew on it.

"It has a vibration that kind of reverberates through the bones."

I wiped my floury hands on my apron, grabbed my phone and brought up the scavenger hunt app. "I figured that the more photos come in, the more apt we are to find some sort of clue."

"Like what? From what you've said, it's not like anyone would miss seeing it if it was around?"

I scrolled through the photos that had already come in. "But maybe something in the image will send out that vibration and help me locate it."

Even as I said it, the plan sounded lame. I could barely feel the vibration when I had the earl's help. How could I possibly tune in to it on my own through a photo, no less? I pressed too hard on a cutter's plunger, getting it stuck in the dough.

Mom picked off another piece of cookie snowflake and nibbled on the morsel. "These are really good. That bit of almond extract really elevates them."

"It's my secret ingredient. I learned the trick from a caterer."

"You're good at your job, Allegra."

Not good enough, though. But I kept the thought to myself.

I continued to look through the photos, each one bringing a sense of hope, quickly followed by disappointment. I mean, Mom was right, it wasn't as if something that big would just show up in the background. But I had really hoped some sort of clue would, that I would feel my supposed connection.

I closed my eyes and tried to tune in to the Star's vibration but felt nothing.

"Let's get out of here," I said, stuffing as many cookies as I could into the tin. "Maybe out there, it will be easier to tune in to the Star."

We bundled up and headed out, offering greetings and cookies, reminding everyone we saw to participate in the scavenger hunt, stopping now and then to try to feel for the Star.

The sky was a dull gray, a contrast to all the festive lights and the spirit of the season bursting from every decorated storefront window, every wreath, every ribboned light pole.

Fresh photos popped up every few seconds.

"Looks like people are really getting into the hunt," Mom said, perusing her own app.

"The more, the merrier."

We stopped by the bakery to warm up with large take-out cups of hot chocolate.

"I haven't seen Fynn around lately," Mom said, the statement sounding an awful lot like a prying question.

"He had to go back to Foster."

"Did something happen?" She asked the question as if she were tiptoeing through a mine field.

"Yep, something did."

"Talk to me, Allegra."

I stopped and turned toward her. "Fine, you want to know, here it is. Your secret cost me my second chance with Fynn."

She frowned. "How?"

"Because I couldn't tell him about the Star..." My throat worked hard. "Anyway, it doesn't matter."

"Of course it matters. You love him."

I blinked at her.

"Well, even a blind person could feel how you two are perfect for each other."

"So why did you put him on the spot that day at the pub?"

"Old habits die hard." Mom hooked her arm through mine and pulled me along.

"The church," Mom said, pointing her chin in the direction

of St. Maurice. "It all started there. Do you think it may have made its way back there?"

"That could explain why Father Lowe is so protective of the Church. He acts as if he's not a fan of the Star. But..."

"If he wanted to hide a secret..."

"The church would be the perfect place." Then I remembered the buzz of the rumor mill. "Except that he's left."

"We can still look around for evidence he did hide the Star."

We walked down the wide walkway toward the front of the church. The nativity scene stood under a protective barn-like box. A spotlight illuminated the scene, creating dark shadows on the concrete statues. The light from inside the church poured out the stained glass, making cheerful patterns on the snow. I pulled open the heavy wooden doors. The warmth and the silence of the sanctuary offering respite from the cold and calmed a bit of my frantic energy. Here, I could somehow still scrounge up a bit of hope that all would work out.

I groaned when I spotted someone kneeling in front of the altar. The man turned at the noise and strode down the middle aisle toward us. "Hello, ladies. How may I help you on this fine day?"

"We need to split up," I whispered to Mom. "You keep him busy, and I'll look."

As he strode toward us, I spotted his collar. Had the diocese found a replacement for Father Lowe?

"I'm showing off your beautiful church." I pasted on my hostess smile.

"You must be the woman who's using the church as a stop on the scavenger hunt." His gaze held a question.

"Given Father Lowe's objection, we changed the stop." I pulled Mom forward. "My mom is an art expert, and she wanted to admire the stations of the cross stained glass."

Mom gave me a look, then took the priest's arm and led him to the first station, asking questions. She may not technically be an expert, but she'd spent a lot of time curating art for my father. She knew her stuff. And she knew how to get people talking. I figured I had half an hour to snoop before the priest wondered where I'd gone.

I slipped away and headed toward the door off to the right of the altar. It led to a space no larger than a closet where priests changed into their garb for the service. No place to hide a Star here. I opened every door I found—a utility closet, a bathroom, a storage room. None were big enough to hide the Star. When the furnace kicked on, I followed the sound to the basement.

There, I closed my eyes and tried to tune in to the Star. I thought I made out a thin thread, but it came from far away, not here. I climbed back up to the main part of the church where Mom and the priest had arrived at the last station.

"This is fascinating," Mom said, spying me. I shook my head. Her mouth flattened. "Thank you so much for your time. You have a wonderful place here."

"Yes, well, I'm told that Brighton is less-than pious with all their concern for the commercial side of Christmas."

Mom ignored his Eeyore-like complaint. "I find one just complements the other. If the Star brings more people inside the church, what's the harm?"

He smiled at Mom—she had that effect of men. "I suppose that is a wise way to look at the situation."

"I'll make sure to come to your midnight mass on Christmas Eve."

Which, if the Star didn't shine, would never happen.

∼

"Thanks for taking care of the priest," I said once we reached the sidewalk. The wind had kicked up and seemed to blow right through my coat.

"You didn't find anything," Mom said.

"The Star's definitely not there."

"What now?" Mom asked, pausing at the end of the walkway.

I glanced up and down Main Street, at the cheerful people milling about, ignorant of the doom clock ticking away. "I don't know."

"We're running out of time," she said, a note of urgency creeping into her voice. "If we don't find it before the tree lighting on Tuesday…"

"I know."

"What are you going to do…if we don't?" Her hand gripped my arm and her fear soaked into me. "Do you have a plan?"

"Not really." I pointed toward the town green and the giant Christmas tree. "Let's go sit in the gazebo for a minute."

"We just can't give up."

"We're not. I just need to think."

We passed a stand of Christmas trees at the corner of Main and Maple.

"Oh, look! Christmas trees!" Mom said, pulling me toward the stand. "You don't have one. Let's get one."

"We don't really have time for that."

"You wanted time to think." She tilted her head toward her shoulder. "That will give us time to think."

"I don't have any ornaments." Decorating a tree felt frivolous when we could all disappear in just over a day.

"Your Country Store does."

"Fine." If nothing else, it would keep Mom busy.

A couple looking at a tree lifted their phone at me. "Hey, Allegra. What a great idea this was! We only have a couple more pics to take to complete the hunt."

"Fantastic!" I said with more enthusiasm than I felt.

Mom picked out a tree and somehow cajoled one of the attendants to deliver it to my apartment. She picked out enough ornaments to fill two trees and jabbered all the way home. By the time we got to the apartment, the four-footer leaned against the railing of my tiny stoop.

"It's looking less and less as if we'll find...*it*," I said, dragging the tree inside. "I feel like I'm failing."

"You're doing your best and that's all anybody can ask." She dumped the packages of decoration on the coffee table.

"Except that there's so much at stake."

She took off her coat, then gave me a one-armed hug. "We're not going to give up. We still have all of tomorrow and most of Tuesday."

"Yeah," I said, confidence waning, letting my coat drop to the floor.

"We'll find it." Mom turned back to the decorations, spreading them out on the coffee table. "We have to keep believing. I've found that keeping busy gives my mind a chance to work things out." She turned, holding a box of tiny lights. "By the time we're done, we'll have a plan."

"I hope so."

29

"Each time a woman stands up for herself, without knowing it possibly, without claiming it, she stands up for all women."

— *MAYA ANGELOU*

All evening, I kept refreshing the app, searching for clues. I lay awake all night, the weight of the ticking clock pressing down on me. The cheerful Christmas tree in the corner mocking me.

I had just one back-up plan. If we couldn't find the real Star, I would get Regina to light the fake one as if all was right. That way, people would gather on the town square for the lighting. As the earl had said, people needed to stand together. Especially if the worst happened.

On Monday morning, I strode into Regina's office as if all was normal and closed the door.

Regina barely spared me a glance before going back to her paperwork. "I thought I fired you."

"The job isn't done." I plopped into the chair facing her desk. "I'm rehiring myself."

Regina looked up, tilted her head appraising me, and laughed. "Now, there's the confidence I've been looking for since I hired you back in September."

"You didn't want me for the job."

"Your lack of confidence worried me. Brighton has so much on the line. But I never once wanted you to fail."

She had gone out of her way to make sure I succeeded. "You knew all along about my relationship to the earl."

"Of course. I was the one who found you."

"Back when I was in high school?"

Her lips curled in an I've-just-swallowed-lemon way. "Yes. I had a rather unpleasant encounter with your mother. It would have been so much easier to mold you into your role if you'd grown up with your legacy."

"Mold me?" Like my father had molded my mother into the perfect society wife? I was thankful my mother hadn't let that happen. I might never have met Fynn, and Fynn still made up the best times in my life. My hand went reflexively to my heart and pressed. I missed him so much that it made me wish I'd never found him again. *If I somehow survive this Star madness, then—*

Then what? You'll go beg for forgiveness? I'd already hurt him. Twice. I wouldn't blame him if he refused to even see me.

I'd once imagined that nothing could pull us apart. And now, we were nothing more than memories to each other.

"Being the earl's only rightful heir places a lot of responsibility on you," Regina said. "It would have been easier if you'd grown up understanding the earl's mission, what he was trying to build and how he was going about it."

I could see how more context would be helpful. "There's still time—"

"Did he not explain what would happen if the Star did shine?"

"That his sins would be absolved."

"He will die, Allegra. No matter what happens, this is the end of his life."

Somehow, I had expected him to live on, not this sudden end. Although, I supposed that for him, it wasn't so sudden. Not after one hundred and ten years of working toward redemption.

Regina closed the file on her desk and laid it on top of the pile to her left. "It's what he's been working toward since St. Maurice appeared to him all those years ago and gave him a second chance."

Just like the earl had given me a second chance by giving me the Town Administrator job. "How many people has he given a second chance to?"

"I stopped counting long ago." She got up from her desk, placing both hands flat on the top, gaze spearing me. "Let's go."

"Where?"

"We have a thorn to extract." She grabbed her fire-red coat and her soot-colored felt hat and gloves. She didn't pause, simply expected me to follow her. I trotted after her, catching up with her at the front door. She headed toward a shiny black Lincoln Continental parked at the curb. "Get in."

I got into the passenger's side and barely had time to buckle my seatbelt when she took off with single-minded focus, neglecting to look for traffic. I gripped the handle with both hands. Car horns sounded all around her.

"You're related to Amos Thannen," I said, once we were safely slotted into traffic.

"Our family is the protector of the Star."

"I thought Amos wanted it for himself."

"At first. He tried to take it apart to see how it worked. But as soon as he placed a chisel on one of the seams, the Star sent a ray of love so bright that he fell to his knees."

"What about the argument? Why did he leave?"

"The experience scared him."

"Love scared him?"

"I can't describe what it's like. It's so deep, so overwhelming, so..." She shook her head. "It's something you have to feel."

She drove around the curves of the earl's driveway so fast that I thought we'd end up in a snowbank. She jammed on the brakes by the front door, making me snap my arms forward to prevent banging my head on the dashboard.

"I don't know what the argument was about, but the end result was that Amos left and changed his name so that the earl couldn't find him." She turned off the ignition. "But later in life, he came to understand what the Star meant. He tasked his sons to become the Star's guardian, to help the earl protect it from people who might want to seize its power for themselves."

"Like Royce."

She nodded. "He doesn't get that a single person can never control the Star."

"Why are we here?" I asked as she pushed open her car door and bulldozed through the front door of the estate. I followed her in.

"To pluck out a thorn."

Robin intercepted us in the foyer. "What are you doing here? I thought I told you never go come back."

Regina looked at me and cocked an eyebrow. "Want to do the honors?"

"Yes, please." I faced Robin. "Apparently, this whole estate will be mine soon."

He snorted. "Over my dead body."

"Don't tempt me," Regina said.

"Let's be civilized about this," I said, wielding my own little bit of power. It felt strangely good to tell Robin where to go. "You're fired."

"You can't fire me."

I stood tall. "As the earl's only descendant, I can. He no longer needs your services."

Like a toddler about to have a tantrum, Robin crossed his arms over his chest. "I'm not leaving. I'll expose you as a fraud."

"We have DNA proof," Regina said.

"We do?" I asked.

Regina nodded, grabbed her phone from her purse and dialed. "Chief Hamlin, I have a situation at the Candlewick Estate. An uninvited guest refuses to leave."

Regina returned the phone to her pocket. "He'll be here in five minutes. I suggest you're gone by then."

"You'll regret this," Robin said, fire in his gaze and the taste of revenge tainting his voice. "I am also a relative. I also have a claim to the estate. I *will* have my rightful share."

"Not the way the estate was set up." Regina opened the door for him. "The estate and the business go to Allegra. Everything else is in trust for the village of Brighton."

"We'll see about that. Kay—"

"Will not be able to break the trust."

He sneered. "We'll see."

I swept an arm wide, inviting him out—just as he'd done on the night of the gala. "I'll have your things sent to you."

"What? You expect me to leave without a coat?"

Regina glanced at her watch. "Three minutes. Tick-tock."

He seemed to consider his odds, then headed for the door. "I'll be back."

We both stood watching him slip and slide toward his Tesla in the snow with his leather shoes.

"He sounds like a villain in a bad movie," I said. "Do you think he's a threat?"

"He's more bark than bite." She shrugged. "Tomorrow night, it won't matter either way."

I closed the front door. "Why are we here?"

"To plan for tomorrow night."

Tomorrow night. Without the Star. "If we're all going to

disappear," I said. "I suggest we make the lighting ceremony the event of all events."

∽

BY THE TIME I got back home after work, we had a plan in place for the best Christmas Eve party the town of Brighton had ever seen—hot chocolate and cider carts, cookies and candy canes, pretzels and donuts trucks. Lights, so many lights shone that a satellite passing by would pick up this dot on the map. And Santa on a red throne in the middle of the gazebo to hear children's secret wishes and hand out souvenir snow globes.

Gus and Lon would install the fake star on the tree in the morning.

I was exhausted and just wanted to fall into bed and sleep.

The scent of something wonderful hit me as soon as I opened the apartment door. Mom had made some mac 'n cheese—one of the few things she knew how to make. Not the box kind either, but the kind that required real cheese.

"Smells heavenly," I said, taking off my hat, gloves and scarf.

From the kitchen, Mom in her red apron, said, "I figured we both needed comfort food."

"You're right." What did calories matter at this point? *No*, I told myself. *Don't think about disappearing.* I had no time to mourn the life I wouldn't have, not if I wanted to make sure the earl's vision for tomorrow's lighting came to pass.

I changed into sweats and came back out just as Mom set out the food on the counter, along with a salad.

My phone rang as I sat on one of the stools, and I groaned. I didn't recognize the number, but the downside of my job was that I constantly got work calls from numbers I didn't know, so by the law of averages, I answered a lot of spam calls.

"Allegra Livingstone." I answered, unable to manage my

usual enthusiasm. Mom put a plate of food in front of me and silently urged me to eat.

"What did you do to Fynn?" a woman asked, acid lacing every word.

"Who is this?"

"Emilia. You know the person who used up her vacation and went out of her way to make the star ornament you needed so badly."

"Okay, thank you. You're very talented. You did a wonderful job. I'm still not sure what that has to do with Fynn."

"He's been an ogre since he brought you the star." She growled. "And that's just not like him. He's the nicest person I know. So, fix it."

I plopped an elbow on the counter and sighed. "It's a long story."

"I've got time."

"I don't." I still had a hundred things on my to-do list for tomorrow.

"Answer me this," she said, every word boring through the line like a spike. "Do you love him?"

I thought about saying no and ending the conversation. My feelings toward Fynn were none of her business. But I couldn't bring myself to deny my feelings. "I do. So much."

"Then why?"

I toyed with the cheese-laden pasta on my plate. "Sometimes love isn't enough." Or maybe it was too much. "He's better off without me."

"Not from where I'm standing. He did all that for you, Allie. He was all Allie this and Allie that. And it's got to work. And she needs this. And can't you work faster? I busted my butt getting this stupid star done." Her footsteps rang on concrete. Was she at the Glass Studio? "Because he loves you, and I owe him for all he's done for me." She growled again. "How could you hurt him like that?"

He loved me. My heart sank and my hand automatically covered the pain in my chest. "So that he can finally move on and be happy."

She blew out a raspberry. "I just don't get people."

I wasn't sure I did, either.

"After tomorrow," I said. "I can explain." Or disappear from his memory.

"What's tomorrow?" Emilia asked.

"Redemption day."

30

"If you don't like the road you're walking, start paving a new one."

— *DOLLY PARTON*

Tuesday. Christmas Eve. The Star was still missing. I had no choice but to get the alternate plan moving. I needed to find a way to gather as many people as I could at the town square for the lighting ceremony tonight.

Regina used her Dragon Lady fire to help, and we got through the arm's length to-do list just as the sun set. Lucy joined us as she could during the day, taking care of the logistics while I took care of the people. Even Mom lent a hand. By the time 7 p.m. rolled around, the scene was set—like the inside of a fantasy snow globe. People slowly gathered on the square, filling it to capacity.

Yesterday's cloudy sky had cleared. Tonight, the sky was clear and bright and twinkled with millions of stars. The red and green food carts, gleaming with fairy lights, scattered along the sidewalks added cheer to the night. The scent of hot chocolate and sugar cookies filled the air. Smiling faces milled around the square, choosing spots from which to watch the lighting ceremony. Children tugged on parents' hands, begging for one last chance to whisper wishes to Santa before his visit later that night.

Anticipation bubbled through the crowd.

Please, please, let this work. I didn't want the town to remember me as the one who ruined Brighton's most cherished tradition.

Almost time. Mom had promised to join me for the countdown, so we'd have each other to lean on. I stood by the massive Christmas tree, holding my breath. Regina held court on the small platform on which Gus had fashioned the giant button Regina would press to light the tree and star. I clutched my tablet, gaze racing down my to-do list. But really, there was nothing else I could do. I had done my best. I shoved one trembling hand into the pocket of my ice-blue knee-length wool coat. But even the more professional outfit than my usual comfy puffer jacket couldn't tame my nerves.

"Everything will be fine," I whispered to myself. The knot that hadn't left my chest all week somehow managed to grow even tighter. "Everything will be fine."

When the Town Hall clock struck eight, I searched the crowd for Mom, but couldn't find her. Then I leaned in toward Regina. "Ready?"

She nodded, put on her biggest smile and stepped forward to the golden button. "Welcome, everyone! Thank you for coming to Brighton's annual tree lighting ceremony!"

The crowd cheered.

"Please join me in a round of applause for Allegra Livingstone, our interim Town Administrator. All this magic around you is her vision. Make sure to enjoy all the treats she had prepared for you."

The crowd clapped and hooted, making me blush. I nodded and waved, then stepped back.

"First, let's start by naming the winner of the Christmas scavenger hunt and the basket of goodies provided by vendors all around Brighton, Stoneley and Granite Falls." She thanked all the sponsors one by one.

She glanced at Gus. "Drum roll, please."

Gus pressed a button on his phone and the sound of a snare drum rolled out.

Regina took her time opening the red envelope I'd prepared after the hunt closed at noon.

"And the winner is...Roslyn Shannon! Come on up, Roslyn."

The crowd clapped.

"Go Rosie!"

Roslyn, a grandma who was definitely not ready for a rocker, jogged to the platform to accept the huge basket brimming with gifts. "Thank you! I can't believe I won."

"You were the first to complete the race." Regina beamed.

Roslyn hugged the basket that was almost as big as she was to her chest and stepped off the platform.

"Hey, Ros, share, right?"

"In your dreams, Jeb."

"Had to try." The reporter for the *Tri-Town Times* shrugged, then lifted a camera. "Give me a smile then. For this week's edition."

Her family surrounded her and gawked at all the goodies in the basket.

Regina tapped the mic to bring the attention back to the platform.

"The Christmas Star is Brighton's symbol of unity and hope," Regina said. "It reminds us that light shines out of darkness, that darkness cannot overcome light."

Which, this year, took on a whole new meaning. Would this

upcoming disappearing feel like falling into a dark void or a welcoming into pure light? The knot in my chest vibrated. I tried to loosen it with my fingers to no avail.

"Come on, everyone!" Regina waved an arm about, urging the crowd. "Let there be light! Help me count down. Five! Four! Three! Two!" She paused, her smile widening. Regina's flair for the dramatic pause had me chuckling. "One!"

One hand pressed on top of the other, she mashed the button.

From the bottom of the tree, colored lights sparkled to life and raced up the layers of branches all the way to the star.

The crowd *oohed* and *aahed*. *Wows* and *fantastics* and *beautifuls* peppered the air.

But once the electric current reached the star, the light was nothing like the photos I'd seen. It barely shone through the thick glass.

Fudge, fudge, fudge. I scanned the crowd, gauging the town's reaction. Questions and murmurs rumbled like an earthquake.

"Oh, no!"

"What's wrong with the Star?"

I stepped up to Regina. "We have to tell them."

"We can't." The words came out like a hiss of fire.

"This isn't working," I said. "We can't let them leave. We have to keep the party going until midnight."

Three and a half more hours. The task seemed impossible.

Regina closed her eyes.

But I didn't give her a chance to answer. I took the mic from her. "As you can see, this is not the real Christmas Star. We had hoped that this star would shine as brightly as the original. But unfortunately, the original Star was stolen."

A gasp swept through the crowd.

"Stolen?"

"Who would steal our Star?"

"How could this happen?"

"What does this mean? Is our good luck gone?"

"Is the curse coming true?"

"What happens if the Star doesn't shine by midnight?"

Panic spread like a virus through the crowd. I had to contain it before they all scattered.

"I know this is upsetting," I said, keeping my voice steady. "But I've talked to the earl, and he told me the story of the year the Star didn't shine. In 1929, the Star barely flickered, and he feared he hadn't done enough for Brighton. The villagers wanted him to know how grateful they were for all he'd done during those difficult times, so they shared their stories of gratitude for all the good that happened in Brighton that year. The Star was finally able to shine.

"I firmly believe that it's not the Star but our community's spirit of generosity that lights the Star. We have nothing to lose. Who would like to start?"

A hush fell over the crowd. People stared at each other, but no one moved.

"I'll go first, then." I made eye contact with as many people as I could, so they could see the truth of my words. "I came to Brighton with a broken and beat spirit. All of you welcomed me with open arms and made doing this job of putting on a festival a month sheer joy. Because of your warmth and generosity, I found my confidence once again. I'm so grateful to all of you for welcoming me into your community."

Mom in her white coat and red hat and gloves lifted a hand toward me so I could help her onto the platform. "I'm a stranger, too. I came to Brighton because my daughter was here, and I'd come to take her back home. Instead, I found a new purpose. I have all of you to thank for that."

Mom glanced at me, tears shimmering in her eyes. I gave her a nod and a small smile. *Thank you*, I mouthed.

Lucy pushed forward and stepped up to the platform, Baby Autumn cocooned in her jacket. "I'll go next. I'm so grateful for my friendship with Allegra. She held me up when all I wanted to do was fall into a puddle of tears. I'm grateful for every person who dropped off crates of diapers and dinners after Autumn was born, allowing me to focus on her rather than making meals. I'm grateful I can stay at home with my baby for this extended maternity leave. Brighton truly is the best place on earth to live. And all that is thanks to the earl's generosity."

"Here, here!" someone in the crowd hooted.

One by one villagers stepped up to share their gratitude. An elderly man's voice cracked as he recounted the kindness of neighbors who cleared his driveway of snow and offered to mow his lawn, allowing him to stay in his own home. A woman spoke of a neighbor's kindness when she fell and broke her leg and couldn't drive. A teen thanked friends for seeing her through a difficult time.

The star flickered a little brighter with each story, giving me hope.

"It's working," I said, pointing up at the brighter light. "Thank you for sharing your stories. Let's keep this spirit of gratitude alive and make this Christmas unforgettable. Let's make the star shine as brightly as it ever has."

Men, women, children continued to step up to the microphone. Each story was greeted with cheers and appreciation.

"Psst!" Lon sidled up to me next to the platform.

I raised my eyebrows in question.

"There's something I gotta tell you." He inclined his head away from the crowd, asking me to follow him. He had to be cold without a hat and gloves and only that thin leather jacket to protect him for the frigid night.

"What is it, Lon?" I asked, once we got away from the crowd.

Hands deep in his jeans pockets, he took in a long breath and let it out. "I was paid to steal the Star."

My chest twisted, stealing my breath. "What? Why? By whom?"

His gaze dropped to the ground. "Who doesn't matter. He wanted me to destroy it. But I couldn't."

He had just confirmed my worst nightmare. "So, what did you do with it?"

He swallowed hard. "I'd rather not say."

"I promise I won't report you."

"That's not it. It's—"

I grabbed his jacket by both hands. "Brighton's future is at stake here, Lon. Tell me!"

He nodded like a bobblehead. "I, uh, dumped it in Brighton Lake."

"What?!" I followed his gaze to the dark expanse of water, covered by ice. "We have to get it back."

"The ice," he said, shaking his head. "That part of the lake is deep."

"We'll get a crane." I ran through my list of townsfolks. Regina's husband Eddie owned an earthworks business. Surely, he knew how to get ahold of a crane.

"The ice is thick," Lon said, raking fingers through his too-long hair. "But not thick enough to support that type of equipment."

"Show me," I said, jogging toward the lake. I wasn't going to give up. If the Star still existed, I would bring it home. "Show me exactly where you dumped the Star."

31

"At the core of self-confidence is unshakeable self-love. How you talk to yourself and perceive your abilities will manifest in every aspect of your daily life."

— *FROM "HOW TO BE A CONFIDENT WOMAN" BY VANESSA VAN EDWARDS*

I wove through town, Lon following behind me. We crossed Main Street and went down Birch to the parking lot between the dog park and the sports fields.

Breathing hard, I stopped at the edge of the lake. "Where, Lon, where did you dump the Star?"

Lon made a half circle in the snow with the toe of his boot and couldn't look at me. "Right in the middle."

I stepped onto the ice. He pulled me back, shaking his head. "It's not safe. The current's too fast under the ice, and the ice isn't even. You're gonna fall through."

Fudge, fudge, fudge. I stared at the lake, willing it to give me an answer. The Star was there. So close. And I couldn't get to it. "There has to be a way."

I turned toward him. "Why, Lon? Why would you wreck Brighton's treasure?"

He shrugged. "Why does anybody?"

Growl climbing up my throat, I said, "Enlighten me."

"I needed the money."

For a few bucks, he would jeopardize the town's future? Of course, nobody knew the full depth of the angel's prediction should the Star fail to shine. "What was worth ruining Christmas for the whole town?"

"My baby sister," he said, anger making hard planes on his face. "Gus couldn't work enough overtime to pay for all her rehab treatments. So, when the opportunity came up to help, I took it."

Well, fudge. I couldn't even hate him. "When did you take it?"

"On the way back to the vault last Christmas. I arranged for a flat tire. While I changed it, my buddies rolled it into their truck."

"How did you keep Regina and Gus from seeing what was happening?"

"Wasn't easy, for sure. But you know how Regina likes to show off her knowledge. I kept her on one side of the truck and blocked her view. Gus was busting a gut laughing at Regina trying to tell me how to change the tire."

A true comedy of errors. "Who hired you?"

"I don't want to say."

"I have to insist."

He puffed out a breath. "Frederick Hurst."

"Pauline's husband?"

Lon paced the edge of the lake, snow crunching beneath his boots. "He was sick of hearing her harp on about how unfair everything was. How Regina had an in over her because of the Star."

"So, he had it destroyed to get his wife off his back?"

Lon kicked at a wad of ice, sending shards flying in all directions. "That about sums it up."

"Unbelievable." All this chaos for selfish reasons. "So, if it was the middle of winter, how did you get the Star in the water?"

"Waited till spring. Hid it in a friend's barn."

"Why didn't you just keep it there safely?"

He looked at me as if I had no clue. "Because spring equals planting and it would've been discovered." He glanced back at the lake. "I thought the Star would be safe in the water. Hurst would never know, and I could always get it back."

"Just how are we going to retrieve the Star?"

Lon pondered my question. "We can use a winch and pulley system. The DPW has equipment. And a buddy of mine has a remote-controlled underwater drone. We can use it to pinpoint the location."

I shooed him with both hands. "Well, what are you waiting for? We have until midnight to get this Star shining. Go get your drone and start looking."

While Lon raced away, I called Regina and gave her the update.

"I'll have Eddie bring equipment. Once they've located the Star, he can help hoist it out."

I wasn't sure how he was going to do that if the Star was in the middle of the lake. Brighton Lake was twice the size of Candlewick Lake. "Have him come to the parking lot between the dog park and the sports field."

"Will do."

Lon and his buddy and the drone arrived in a squeal of truck tires.

Lon hopped out. The burly driver, dressed as inappropriately for the cold weather as Lon, pulled out a drone the size of a boogie board from the bed of his truck.

"Austin. Allegra," Lon said, waving from the burly guy to me and back. "Allegra. Austin Hines."

We nodded at each other. He went about setting up his underwater drone while Lon cut a hole in the ice with an auger.

Lon lowered the drone into the water. "Ready?"

"Let her rip," Austin said. The motor purred and the drone disappeared beneath the ice.

Austin worked the controls, guiding it toward the middle of the lake. Lon stared at the screen. "To the left. Yeah, right about there."

"Anything?" I asked, trying to get a look at the screen.

"Not yet," Lon said, frustration creeping into his voice.

I stood behind the men, squinting at the screen and trying to make out if any of the shapes in the murky water could be the Star.

I glanced at my watch. Ninety minutes until midnight.

"Anything?" I asked.

Austin rolled his shoulders. "Yeah, you know, this pressure isn't helping me."

"There's a lot at stake," I said.

"Me, I don't believe in curses."

Up until my talk with the earl, neither had I.

"I think I've got something." Austin adjusted the controls to circle a dark area. "Nah...just a rock."

I growled. "We're running out of time!"

"Yeah, I get that." Austin piloted the drone to the next area of interest.

"Are you sure you're having Austin look in the right place?"

Lon nodded. "That's where I dropped it. I made sure to notice which cottages were around so I could find it again. Between the one with the long pier and the one with all that red paint."

"You mentioned currents," I said. "Could it have moved?"

"Something that big?" He shook his head. "Kinda doubt it."

I stared at the water, the weight of failure pressing down on me.

"I'm sorry," Lon said, forehead pleating. "I really thought this would work."

I was about to say, *not your fault*, but it really was his fault the Star was in this predicament. "Keep looking."

32

"Always be a first-rate version of yourself, instead of a second-rate version of someone else."

— JUDY GARLAND

Wiping a tear away, I walked away. The sounds of singing from the town square broke my heart. At least Regina had managed to keep the villagers together. I couldn't give up. I had to think of something.

I found myself on the stone bridge over the narrow river between Brighton Lake and Candlewick Lake. Elbows leaning on the rocky parapet, I stared at the lake. Moonlight glinted off the snow and ice. From the parking lot, Lon and Austin still worked the underwater drone.

My breath came out in frosty puffs, my chest tightening at their lack of progress. They had to find it. They just had to.

I closed my eyes and tuned into the Star the way the earl had shown me. But I must have been too tense, because nothing came through, except the feeling of failure.

"Where are you?" I asked.

"I'm here."

I whipped around to find Fynn standing there, Chill at his side, tail wagging like a mad conductor's baton.

"Fynn!" My heart filled with joy. I never thought I'd see him again. "What are you doing here?"

"I've been looking for you."

Chill loosed a bark as if he was happy to see me, too.

"You've found me." A smile cracked my cold face.

Chill broke loose from Fynn's grasp and tap danced at my feet until I crouched down and petted his head, which brought out the tongue and the fish breath.

"Emilia yelled at me," Fynn said, one hand in his coat pocket, the other holding on to Chill's leash. "Told me I was an idiot. That only idiots gave up on love."

"She does seem rather opinionated." I rose, but Chill insisted I keep petting him. His crazy curls felt good through my gloved fingers. "She called me, too. Told me to fix it. So, here's me fixing it."

I took in a long breath and let it out. Then I told him about the Star, about the theft, about the curse, and how half the village was about to disappear. "I wanted to protect you."

"You thought having you disappear and me wondering where you'd gone this time was protection?"

"That's just it. According to the earl, you wouldn't even remember me. It would be as if I'd been erased from history." I glanced at my phone. "In just over an hour—"

Still holding the leash, he reached for my hand. "Then I'll hold on to your hand, and I'll go with you."

"That's sweet, but I'm not sure it works that way."

He pulled his other hand out of his pocket. A well-worn velvet box lay in his palm. "I let you go last time. This time, I won't let you go without a fight."

"Oh, Fynn."

He let go of my hand and slipped the sapphire surrounded

by diamonds—like a night sky and stars—onto my finger. It fit perfectly.

Sadness lapped like a wave around my heart. No time to enjoy this engagement. No time for a wedding. No time for a future. "It's beautiful."

"Like you." He stepped closer. "Marry me."

I wrapped my arms around his neck. "Letting you go a second time was the hardest thing I've ever done. I love you so much."

His very kissable lips met mine, and I got lost in the longing for a future, in the having of the present. Joy and sadness and anger and wanting, they all fought a fast battle with no winner. Everything I wanted was here. Brighton. The job I loved. Fynn. I didn't want to disappear into nothingness because of some ancestor's mistake.

The kiss spread warmth through my cold body, like warm honey, softening, softening, softening. Love, this was love, and I wanted it, wanted more. Now and forever.

Then the echo of loneliness came back. I'd found him once again, just in time to lose him. How could life be so unfair?

"I'll fight for you, Allie," he whispered in my ear.

"I'll fight to stay." And I reached for him again. If I was going to disappear, I wanted to do it in Fynn's arms.

Chill barked, slamming his body against our legs.

"What is wrong with you, Bud?" Fynn asked.

My gaze pulled toward a glow coming from under the bridge.

"Look!" I pointed at the ice over the river, glowing with light. My eyes widened. "The Star! We've found the Star!"

I rushed off the bridge to the side of the water, knelt on the bank to look in the direction of the glow. There, beneath a layer of ice, lay the Star.

"The current must have moved the Star, and it got stuck here." I took Fynn's hand. "We need help to set it free."

Fingers shaking, I pulled out my phone. "Eddie Buchanan? I need your help."

∽

REGINA'S HUSBAND, Eddie, arrived at the bridge with a truckload of equipment and two older men. He, George Fisher, Felix Rios, Lon and Austin talked over each other trying to come up with a plan to free the Star.

"The bank'll crumble under the weight of the truck," George said.

"Wasn't planning on driving it into the river," Eddie grumbled.

He drove the truck to the edge of the bank, shored the wheels with chocks, and anchored the winch. George and Lon drilled holes in the ice all around the Star. Felix and Austin placed pulleys over each hole to guide the cable.

"Can't use a hook," George said. "Or we'll break the glass."

"How about that cradle we used for the moose last fall?" Felix asked.

Eddie sifted through the equipment in the back of his truck and pulled out a leather cradle. "Got it!"

Lon and Austin waded into the water to attach a cradle.

"Careful, boys!" Eddie said.

They maneuvered the cradle around the Star.

Lon tugged at the cradle ropes. "Solid."

Eddie disappeared into the cab of the truck and started the winch motor.

Slowly, the Star rose. Lon and Austin had stayed in the water to help guide it out.

I held my breath, praying the Star wouldn't break into a million pieces. Water sloshed off its glass facets. Mud coated the bottom half and clogged the collar. But none of the debris could stop its brilliant light.

I reached for Fynn's hand. He intertwined his fingers with mine. "We did it."

He kissed me. The light coming from deep inside the Star shone brighter, emitting an eerie hum.

All six men maneuvered the Star onto the truck bed.

Eddie handed Lon and Austin a towel to dry off from their unexpected dip in the creek.

"Do you have more of those?" Fynn asked.

Eddie pulled out two towels more from the cab.

Fynn gently wiped the mud from the panels and unclogged the collar. "Not perfect," he said, staring at the angel aura glass that now shimmered with opaline fire. "But it's in great shape, considering what it's gone through. I can't believe none of the panels broke."

"Let's get this Star where it belongs," Eddie said.

George and Felix piled into the truck.

Lon, Austin, Fynn, Chill and I raced back to the town square.

News had spread of the find, and at the truck's appearance at the town square, the crowd cheered and parted. Eddie drove the truck right next to the Christmas tree, whose lights were turned off in preparation for the star switch. Using the crane Gus had set up, the replica came down and the Star took its rightful place.

"Let's try this again, folks," Regina said, smile wide and bright. "Help me count down! Five!"

The crowd roared, every single voice joining in.

"Four! Three! Two! One!" Regina paused, then mashed the button.

Lights raced up the tree and when the current reached the Star, the light was so bright, everyone gaped and grew quiet.

The angel aura glass shimmered in myriad colors that seemed out of this world.

My heart expanded. I'd never seen anything so beautiful.

The clock on Town Hall struck midnight, echoing like a herald through the village.

What looked like a hundred tiny sparkling eddies flew out of the Star, dropping onto the crowd like confetti.

I gasped, fumbled for the phone in my pocket and took photos.

I squeezed Fynn's arm. "I need to go see the earl."

"I'll take you."

33

"To be the best version of yourself, you have to start by figuring out *who* you want to be."

— FROM "22 HABITS OF A CONFIDENT WOMAN" BY LOGAN HAILEY

An eerie quiet had descended over Candlewick Estate. Not a single light shone in any window.

"I hope I'm not too late," I said, getting out of Fynn's truck.

I raced to the front door, Chill and Fynn following me.

In the foyer, I wasn't sure where to go. Then I thought that if I knew I was dying, I'd want to go to a place that brought me joy. That was the reason I'd arranged for the brightest event I'd ever planned to bring the town together on the town square.

Our footsteps echoing in the hallway, I led us to the solarium. Slowly, I opened the door. It hit me then that I had no idea what to call the earl. Grandpa seemed presumptive, considering I didn't really know the man. Earl sounded kind of strange.

"Harry? It's me, Allegra."

In the soft glow of a lantern, I spotted the earl sitting in his favorite club chair.

Fynn and Chill stayed by the door.

I sat in the chair across from the earl. I pulled out my phone to show him the photos I'd taken of the Star and the strange swirls of light. "We found it. We found the Star. And it's glowing like it's never glowed before."

His cold hand patted my cheek. "I knew you were the right person for the job."

The solarium filled with pure white light. In the middle of that light something like wings took form. Then a body took shape. My heart hammered hard. What in the world was happening?

"Allegra?" Fynn asked.

"It's okay." I hoped. I stayed at the earl's side, one hand holding his.

"You have kept your end of the bargain," the angel said. "For one hundred and ten years, the Star has shown because of your good deeds. The town and its villagers are thriving. And even knowing this was the end for you, you found a way to keep your legacy moving forward. I have also kept my part of the bargain. All one hundred and ten souls are now free from your curse."

St. Maurice offered the earl his hand. "It is time."

Smiling, the earl accepted the angel's hand. While his body remained in the chair, a body of light separated from the body of flesh and rose from the chair. Together they walked into the light's heart.

A voice echoed inside my head. "All the villagers are safe. They can all live a normal life. Keep the Star glowing, Allegra. As a reminder of all the good deeds done through the year."

The bright light receded in the earl and the angel's wake.

"This is what I have learned over this experience," the earl's voice said. "Choose love over fear."

With one last look over his shoulder, the earl said, "It is so beautiful here. Thank you. This is your home now, Allegra. Go live your best life."

With that, the light disappeared.

I let go of the earl's cold hand. He was gone, really gone. Tears streamed from my eyes. I wished I'd had the chance to get to know him better.

"What just happened?" Fynn asked, voice filled with wonder.

I rose from the chair and wrapped my arms around Fynn's neck. "We've just been handed a second chance to be together."

I kissed him. Chill barked, making us both laugh.

"Yes, Fynn," I said, looking deep into his eyes. "I'll marry you. Will you come live here with me and share my best life with me?"

"In a heartbeat."

EPILOGUE

"Your mind will always believe everything you tell it. Feed it hope. Feed it truth. Feed it love."

— UNKNOWN

The earl's funeral was both a sad and a joyous affair, celebrated by the whole town. The reading of the will soon after had officially made me the new owner of the Candlewick Estate and head of the Candlewick Foundation, which oversaw grants for new businesses.

The earl's death made the news when Robin and Kay tried to contest the will. Unfortunately for them, they could find no workaround the tight clauses.

Now, six months later, Lucy was back at work part-time, doing the portion of the Town Administrator job she loved—dealing with all the paperwork I hated. And I was back to doing the part of the job I loved—planning the festivals. Sharing the job worked for both of us, and for Brighton.

Mom decided to stay in Brighton and found a condo she was taking her time to decorate the way she wanted. It sat just off Main Street, right in the middle of all the action. Not as grand as her Beacon Hill home, but it suited her busy lifestyle. With my new access to resources, I had Mom's Romeo located and arrested. Too late to get her assets back. A lesson learned the hard way. At least he wouldn't swindle another woman out of her life's savings for a long time.

Shamed, the Hursts left town, and Mom took over most of Pauline's charity work, something that was right up her alley. With her knack for creating connections, I gave Mom a position on the foundation's board. She took that job seriously and helped many with her keen eye for innovation.

Our relationship was slowly healing.

Fynn had gone back to Foster after Christmas. He'd made a promise to finish out the school year and kept his promise. I missed him every day. But, as agreed, we took things slowly, getting to know and appreciate each other all over again. Building a solid foundation this time.

He was back in Brighton now, working on building his own glass studio. He'd bought a piece of land next to Aaron Carpenter's woodworking workshop. Their idea was to create a whole complex of workshops to share resources, teach and grow. I loved the idea for all the area craftspeople and for Brighton. It was yet another way to foster community and cooperation as well as to boost up the next generation.

My well-worn copy of *The Confident Woman* now resided on a shelf in my office at Town Hall. I no longer carried it around like a talisman.

If I'd learned anything this past year, it was that confidence didn't come from other people. My mother, my father, Regina couldn't make me feel confident. Another person's approval wasn't solid ground. No, confidence was an inside job. It came through the thoughts you fed yourself. I learned to feed mine with hope and with love and found a new trust in myself.

I would have had a good life without Fynn, but my life was

so much fuller and more vibrant with him and with Chill in it. I was thankful every day that our kiss on that stone bridge had allowed us to find the Star and save Brighton.

Fynn poked his head through the bedroom door. "Time to go."

"I'm ready."

Hand in hand, we headed out to watch over another Brighton festival.

There would always be people who didn't agree with what you did, who'd want to put you down to pull themselves up. You had to ignore all that and reach inside yourself. Find that best thought, that best feeling you could in that moment and keep the light flowing and expanding. Like the Star.

And every Christmas, the Star would be there to remind us that light shone out of darkness, that darkness couldn't overcome light.

Authors depend on word of mouth. So, if you have time, I'd be grateful if you would post a short review wherever you can.

All the best,
Sylvie

Want to keep up with what's going on in Brighton Village? Join my VIP Readers List today. The newsletter comes out once a month and contains book updates, behind the scenes tidbits, recipes, specials and extras that only my VIP readers receive. Go to https://sylviekurtz.com/newsletter and sign up now!

ALLEGRA'S SUGAR COOKIES

Yield: 3 dozen cookies, depending on the size of your cookie cutters
Prep Time: 30 minutes
Cook Time: 6-8 minutes
Total Time: 38 minutes

This sugar cookie dough keeps its shape without chilling, and bakes up perfectly every time.

Ingredients:

- 1 cup unsalted butter
- 1 cup granulated white sugar
- 1 teaspoon vanilla extract
- 1/2 teaspoon almond extract
- 1 egg
- 2 teaspoons baking powder
- 1/2 teaspoon salt
- 3 cups all-purpose flour

Directions:

1. Preheat oven to 350° F.
2. In the bowl of your mixer, cream butter and sugar until smooth, at least 3 minutes
3. Beat in extracts and egg.
4. In a separate bowl, combine baking powder and salt with flour and add a little at a time to the wet ingredients. The dough will be very stiff. If it becomes too stiff for your mixer, turn out the dough onto a countertop surface. Wet your hands and finish off kneading the dough by hand.
5. Do Not Chill the Dough. Divide into workable batches, roll out onto a floured surface and cut. You want these cookies to be on the thicker side (closer to 1/4 inch rather than 1/8 inch).
6. Bake at 350° F for 6-8 minutes, depending on the size of the cookie. Let cool on the cookie sheet until firm enough to transfer to a cooling rack.

ACKNOWLEDGMENTS

Sometimes, life throws you curveballs and the best of plans fall apart. Thank you to everyone who cheered me on as I went through a difficult time while writing this story. Somehow, I'm not sure how, this book will still come out in time for Christmas.

Thank you to Michelle Stewart for answering all of my many event planning questions with grace and patience. Any errors are, of course, mine.

As always, thank you, dear reader, for choosing to spend time in the fictional world of Brighton Village.

ALSO BY SYLVIE KURTZ

Love in Brighton Village Series
Christmas by Candlelight
Christmas in Brighton
Summer's Sweet Spot
The Christmas Star

Brighton Village Cozy Mystery
Of Books and Bones (novella)

Midnight Whispers Series
One Texas Night
Blackmailed Bride
Hidden Legacy
Alyssa Again
Under Lock and Key
A Rose at Midnight
Pull of the Moon
Remembering Red Thunder
Red Thunder Reckoning
Personal Enemy
Detour

The Seekers Series
Heart of a Hunter
Mask of a Hunter
Eye of a Hunter

Pride of a Hunter

Spirit of a Hunter

Honor of a Hunter

Action-Adventure Romance

Ms. Longshot

Paranormal Romance

Broken Wings

Silver Shadows

Holiday Romance

A Little Christmas Magic

ABOUT THE AUTHOR

Sylvie writes stories that celebrate family, friends and food. She believes organic dark chocolate is an essential nutrient, likes to knit with soft wool, and justifies watching movies that require a box of tissues by knitting baby blankets. She has written 25 novels in various genres.

Her first Harlequin Intrigue, *One Texas Night*, was a 1999 Romantic Times nominee for Best First Category Romance and a finalist for a Booksellers Best Award. Her Silhouette Special Edition, *A Little Christmas Magic* was a 2001 Readers' Choice Award Finalist and a Waldenbooks bestseller. *Remembering Red Thunder* was a 2002 Romantic Times Nominee for Best Intrigue. She was a 2005, 2007 and 2008 Romantic Times nominee for Lifetime Achievement for Series Romantic Adventure. Twin Star Entertainment optioned *Ms. Longshot* as a possible TV movie.

For more details, visit https://sylviekurtz.com.

facebook.com/sylviekurtzauthor
instagram.com/sylviekurtzauthor